MURDER IN
REAL TIME

Previously published Worldwide Mystery titles by
JULIE ANNE LINDSEY

MURDER BY THE SEASIDE

MURDER IN REAL TIME

JULIE ANNE LINDSEY

W💼RLDWIDE®

TORONTO • NEW YORK • LONDON
AMSTERDAM • PARIS • SYDNEY • HAMBURG
STOCKHOLM • ATHENS • TOKYO • MILAN
MADRID • WARSAW • BUDAPEST • AUCKLAND

To my readers, who do it with a smile ;)

Recycling programs
for this product may
not exist in your area.

Murder in Real Time

A Worldwide Mystery/September 2015

First published by Carina Press

ISBN-13: 978-0-373-26961-7

Copyright © 2014 by Julie Anne Lindsey

All rights reserved. No part of this book may be reproduced or transmitted
in any form or by any means, electronic or mechanical, including
photocopying, recording or by any information storage and retrieval system,
without permission in writing from the publisher. For information, contact:
Harlequin Enterprises Limited, 225 Duncan Mill Road, Don Mills, Ontario,
Canada M3B 3K9

This is a work of fiction. Names, characters, places and incidents are
either the product of the author's imagination or are used fictitiously,
and any resemblance to actual persons, living or dead, business
establishments, events or locales is entirely coincidental.

® and TM are trademarks of Harlequin Enterprises Limited.
Trademarks indicated with ® are registered in the United States
Patent and Trademark Office, the Canadian Intellectual Property Office
and in other countries.

Printed in U.S.A.

Acknowledgments

Huge, humbling thanks to Harlequin and Carin[ ]Press for their amazing, ongoing support in my que[ ]to make readers smile. Thank you, Elizabeth Bass, fo[r]pulling Patience from the slush and giving her life. You taught me so much and I am forever grateful. Thank you, Jennifer Anderson, for reading all my words. I couldn't do it without you. Thank you, Dawn Dowdle, for your unending encouragement in the pursuit of my dream. Thank you to my super bestie, Melinda Crown, for geeking out with me over shows and fandoms, coffee and books. Thank you, Mom and Dad, for making me believe I could change the world and giving me the confidence to try. Thank you, Darlene and Danny Lindsey, for the insane amount of child care and cheerleading you provide willingly and as needed. None of this would happen without you. It couldn't. I'm in awe of your tireless encouragement. Thank you, my poor children, for loving your crazy, harebrained mother, who leaves her coffee on the minivan roof and often wears mismatched shoes because she's deep in plot thought. You never complain when I accidentally get into the passenger side of the van and I'm the only adult in the car, or that I never know where we're going, only that we're late. You let me chase my dream. You eat unspeakable amounts of takeout. You endure my absences and you love me anyway. You are amazing young people. You will most definitely change the world. You've already enchanted mine. Finally, thank you, Bryan. It takes a special kind of patience to put up with all that you do. You drive me all around the state and fly with me all over the country, just because

m afraid to go alone. You make me smile. You let me
ve me. I am incredibly, undeniably blessed. It doesn't
hurt that you are the handsomest partner in crime a girl
could ask for and you have bail money. What do you
say? Let's do this another forty or fifty years, shall we?

ONE

My PHONE VIBRATED on the Tasty Cream table between a dish with four French fries and a bowl that once contained the world's greatest hot fudge brownie sundae. I glanced away from the bowl and placed a paper napkin over the chocolate carnage to cover my shame.

"Covering that bowl won't erase the fifty thousand calories you ate. You know that, right?" My best friend, Claire, smiled and sucked on the straw of her chocolate malt, unaffected by the damage we'd done to our waistlines by ordering half the Tasty Cream menu.

"It wasn't fifty thousand calories." My guilty gaze swept over the napkin barely concealing the enormous bowl. "It was maybe a day's worth of calories. I can skip eating tomorrow and it will be like this never happened." Lies. Skipping meals wasn't in my repertoire of practiced disciplines.

"Mmm-hmm." Claire shook her cup and poked the straw in and out of the lid. "Or," she smiled wider, "you could train with me. We can rock and run together."

I rolled my eyes and rubbed my tummy. "I can't run a marathon, even if there is live music." My phone buzzed again and I flicked it with my fingertips.

"The Virginia Beach Rock 'n' Roll Mini is a mini marathon. It's right there in the name. Only three-point-one miles. You could run that far without breaking a sweat." She made a sad face. "It's no fun alone. Please?"

"Stop making that face. I swear, when you're sad a little fairy dies somewhere. It's not natural."

This time I lifted my phone when it buzzed. Telling Claire no was tougher than keeping my internal promise to only eat half the sundae. I read the text display and scrolled through the few messages I'd ignored during dinner.

"Sebastian?" she asked.

"Adrian." I smiled, though I shouldn't have. Adrian had been my one true love, until he left me for college. I plotted my revenge for a decade and then moved home when the FBI downsized me in July. Guess who'd also moved home? Yep. Adrian. We sorted things out after I saved his well-toned heinie from a murder charge and again after he saved mine from a crazy lunatic. Somehow, the saving and the sorting left things...complicated. In some ways it had been easier when I wanted to shove an ice cream in his nose and be done with him. Now, I alternated between wanting to squeeze his middle or squeeze his neck.

I shifted in my seat. "He probably has another crazy plan to garner votes."

I needed to make peace with my waffling emotional attachment to my ex. The flip-flopping was exhausting, plus he was the town's homegrown golden boy and running for mayor. We were going to be sharing our little three-by-seven-mile island for the foreseeable future.

Most of the locals had watched Adrian and I grow up together and some still pined for us to reconcile.

"Adrian runs three-point-one miles before breakfast." Claire sighed. "I've seen him. It's nice to watch."

"So, ask Adrian to run with you." I sipped the tepid water in my glass, regretting my over-indulgence more by the minute. I blamed the Tasty Cream's inviting old-time soda shop ambience. The minute I treaded over black-and-white checkered tiles and pulled up a little red cushioned chair, anything was possible. Except eating only half my sundae.

"Uh-uh. Adrian's your man." She held a palm up between us. "I don't care what you say. You loved him once and that means I can say hi to him and we can have fun together, in your presence, but I'm not running a marathon with that man, mini or otherwise, if you aren't there. It's not cool."

I loved her so much.

"Besides, I need time to talk to you." Claire's long dark bangs fell over her eyes and she pushed them away without making eye contact.

"About what?" My phone buzzed in my hand.

"Answer the poor man. You know how excited he gets about things. What's going on now?" She crossed and uncrossed her legs, shifting in her chair.

"He says he has a surprise for me."

Claire clucked her tongue.

"It's not that."

"What?" Her large brown eyes widened in faux innocence. "I didn't say anything."

I pulled a few dollars from my purse and placed them on the table. "I know what you're thinking, and it's not that."

"You can't know what he has for sure. It wouldn't be a surprise if you knew."

I followed Claire to the register to pay the bill. Her sea-green pedal pushers were amazing with black platform heels and a black silk blouse. I'd break my neck in anything higher than a three-inch heel, but Claire could outrun me in stilettos. It had happened more than once in Macy's. With heels, she was average height.

Without them, she was stretching for five foot two. Her posture, confidence and general disposition screamed runway model. All those cotillions her parents forced her through gave her a taste for self-respect and fashion. The rest was lost in translation. Like the part where they thought she'd settle down and start a family. Claire had the crazy idea it wasn't 1955 anymore.

That reminded me. "Do you have plans to see the SWAT guy again next weekend?" She'd waited months for a member of the FBI's SWAT team to ask her out. They turned up at my birthday party together last weekend, but she hadn't mentioned him since.

She shook her head before I finished the question.

I handed the teen at the register my bill and some cash but fixed my attention on Claire. "Is that what you wanted to talk to me about?"

She shrugged. "That's part of it."

"I love talking about guys with you. Why on earth would you try to make me run three miles for that? Meanie."

Claire huffed while I stuffed the change from my bill into my wallet. "It's a *mini* marathon. Three miles, not thirty, and it's at the beach."

"I live on an island. I see the beach every day." Chincoteague, Virginia, was a delightful costal town adjoined to the mainland by a bridge, the harbor and the sky. The bridge seemed to attach us to the world but, in all honesty, Chincoteague was its own planet. We had a long history of traditions and customs. Some were quaint, and some were odd by mainland standards, but Chincoteague was the epitome of small-town living. Peaceful. Beautiful. Islanders were family. Granted, every family had its quirks, especially one with twelve hundred people.

"Come on. Virginia Beach." She threw her arms wide and held the door with one hip as I passed. "They play live music. There will be tons of people there. It'll be like college all over again."

"I'm too old for college."

"Speak for yourself." She stopped short and sighed. "You're right. Never mind. It was dumb."

I touched her elbow. "It's not dumb. I just ate a gallon of ice cream. I should be begging you to make me run a marathon. Look," I lifted my shirt. "I had to unbutton my pants."

She laughed. "Put your shirt down before someone takes a picture."

A flash illuminated the evening.

I blinked through the dots floating in my vision. A man speed walked away from us, wearing a navy-colored Windbreaker and khakis.

"Who was that?" Claire asked. "I think he really took our picture. Unless he was shooting the Tasty Cream."

I turned to examine the ice cream parlor behind us. Its cone-shaped roof interrupted the beautiful island sky. The sun set earlier since fall had arrived and though it was barely past dinnertime, deep hues of smoky gray and violet above us suggested the hour was much later. A few stars shone in the distance over the water. I rubbed my eyes and turned in a circle, seeking some other item of interest a tourist might photograph. A family pressed open the Tasty Cream door and a heavenly mixture of sweet and salty scents drifted on the air to meet me. Fries and ice cream rolled in my tummy. A tummy now captured on film, popped button and all.

"If I find him, I'm demanding he delete that picture." I stepped off the curb and crossed the street to my apartment, with Claire at my side.

"Tell me about the SWAT guy. Wyatt. What happened with him after you left my birthday party?"

Claire sighed but didn't answer.

I rented the only available space on the island when I moved home during the summer. Thanks to Adrian and a silly rumor about the house being haunted, no one ever wanted to live there. The owner hadn't rented the space in a decade. Not the upstairs apartment I now called home, and not the downstairs unit, which had housed numerous failed businesses over the years. Now I lived in the apartment for next-to-nothing rent and Adrian owned the building. He used the downstairs for his campaign studio. Lucky me, living upstairs from temptation.

Except, I wasn't tempted. Not really. Not normally. Possibilities for a future with Adrian had dissolved long before our reunion this summer. Destiny had already dropped six-foot-sexy, Special Agent Sebastian Clark into my life. Sebastian, my personal hero. When Adrian was accused of murder this summer, I'd called Sebastian for advice. These days, I also called Sebastian my boyfriend. I adored him. In fact, I expected to see him soon. He rented a room by the month at Island Comforts, the local bed-and-breakfast, but spent more nights at work or my place than at the B&B.

My tummy gurgled.

Claire looked at me. "You better hope that picture doesn't end up in the paper tomorrow."

I shook off her comment. Weirder things had happened to me since moving home. "You're dodging my question. What happened with the SWAT guy and what do you want to talk to me about?"

"I need your advice." She braced her palm on the exterior railing to my apartment and began climbing the wooden stairs. "Not as my best friend, but as, you know, the other thing."

Before the FBI downsized me from my human resources position, I'd finished my counseling degree and planned to work with agents under stress or those who had discharged their firearm or been injured in the line of duty, etc. It was a good plan. The FBI paid big money to contractors for those services. I thought hiring me would save the bureau a ton of money. They thought firing me would too. So, I moved home to chase my dream and open a private practice, which proved more complicated than one would think. Small towns. Nosy neighbors. Those sorts of things weren't always a counselor's friend.

"You want me to counsel you?" I worked to keep my voice flat. Any inflection on my part might be misinterpreted by her, and our friendship would take the hit. I slid my key into the lock, opened the door and motioned her inside.

"A little."

"Finally!" Adrian rushed from my kitchen to meet us at the door. "I texted you four times. I was ready to come and get you. What were you doing over there for two hours, anyway? Never mind. I don't care." His stormy blue eyes were wild with pleasure. "I have a surprise."

"You mentioned that." I normally complained when he let himself in through the secret staircase hidden in the wall of my bedroom closet, but clearly this wasn't the time. I hadn't seen him so excited since he won the state spelling bee in third grade and got a new Nintendo with all the games.

"Sit down." He motioned us to the couch.

"Is he okay?" Claire whispered. "He looks a little crazed."

Adrian stood before us, rubbing his palms together.

A sudden frown replaced his eager expression. "Where's Sebastian?"

"He had a deposition with internal affairs." Claire still worked with Sebastian at the FBI in Norfolk.

I envied that sometimes.

"What's going on?" A deep tenor sent tingles over my spine, and my cheeks ached with a sudden smile. Sebastian stood in my open doorway with flowers and a bottle of champagne.

Adrian's jaw fell an inch before he recovered some of his enthusiasm. "I have something to tell you guys."

"It's a surprise," Claire added.

Sebastian widened his stance. As a general rule, special agents didn't love surprises. "Go on."

Adrian cleared his throat, evidently thrown by Sebastian's entrance and gifts.

"Fine. I rented my home through Halloween night and it's all very hush-hush. I can't give you all the particulars yet, but details are coming, I promise."

"And?" Sebastian leveled his gaze on Adrian, who rolled his shoulders back.

"And I hoped I could stay here."

"With me?" My voice hitched on the second word.

"Yes."

"No." Sebastian moved inside and shut the door. He got a vase from under the sink and put the flowers in water.

Adrian gawked at me, waving his palms as if I could change Sebastian's mind. His panic compelled me to intervene, though I wasn't sure whose side I was on yet. I took a few deep breaths. Was the air thinner in the upstairs apartment? Getting in the middle of these two always made it hard to breathe.

I stood and faced the kitchen. "Um, well, let's think this through."

Sebastian turned narrowed eyes on me. I shook my head at Adrian. He motioned wildly again. I stood back up and stepped toward the kitchen. Sebastian glared from Adrian to me.

Claire giggled. The sound snapped me back to reality. This was *my* apartment. I decided who stayed here, not Sebastian. I anchored both palms over my hips and turned on Sebastian. Adrian took my seat on the couch and nudged Claire with his elbow.

"I don't see why he can't stay here. Is there a reason you have a problem with that?" I cocked a hip for good measure.

Sebastian looked past me to the couch, his expression blank.

I moved forward until the toes of my goddess sandals bumped Sebastian's shiny dress shoes. "Fine, then it's agreed. Adrian stays here. You can stay here, too."

The corner of Sebastian's mouth pulled down. "What if only I stay here with you and Adrian stays in my room at Island Comforts?"

Oh. Yeah. That was better. My moment's pause was enough to settle it. Sebastian tossed his key over my head.

"Sweet." Adrian jumped up and headed for the door.

"Hey," I turned to Adrian. "What was the secret you texted four times to tell me about?"

"I told you all I can."

"You didn't tell me anything."

He flashed his politician smile. "That's because it's a secret."

Adrian disappeared and Sebastian popped the cork

on his champagne. "I'm glad that's settled. Tonight we celebrate."

"What are we celebrating?"

Claire sashayed across the floor and leaned over the little island in my kitchen. "I take it the deposition went well?"

Sebastian slid a glass to Claire. "Internal affairs closed my case. I was cleared of all culpability. The board determined I'd followed every protocol on the operation and justice prevailed again."

"Congratulations." She lifted the glass in a toast motion and sipped.

Relief flooded through me. "What about Jimmy the Judge?"

Jimmy the Judge was the mob boss who wanted Sebastian dead. Sebastian had worked undercover for eight months in Jimmy's operation, infiltrating his crew and leading a bust that resulted in the death of five members of Jimmy's crime family. Jimmy somehow turned to vapor and slipped between Sebastian's fingers in the kerfuffle. Sebastian had moved onto the island to hide while he hunted Jimmy, and Jimmy hunted him. I got an ulcer.

"We have fresh intel suggesting Jimmy's in Vegas. I'm headed there in a few days to follow up on a couple decent leads."

I tipped my head and tossed back the alcohol. I didn't want to think of Sebastian chasing Jimmy, but I didn't want to open my mouth and ruin his good news either.

Claire set down her glass. "Well, congratulations, Sebastian. Thank you, Patience, for a lovely dinner. Now, I'm heading home. It's a long drive, and I have to get up early. I'll leave you two to celebrate." She winked.

"Hey, how'd it go with the marshmallow from SWAT?" Sebastian asked.

Claire screwed her mouth into a knot. "It's funny you call him that because he was kind of like talking to a marshmallow."

I scrunched my brows together. "I thought when you called people marshmallows it meant they were soft and weak."

"I don't know about that," Claire said. "He was all muscle. Unfortunately, his head was one big muscle too. Hard as a rock." She wrapped her knuckles against the side of her head.

I pushed my bottom lip into a pout. "Bummer."

"Yeah, but it's okay. Can we talk later?" She lifted a brow.

"Anytime."

Sebastian lifted my glass with his and followed us onto the stoop outside my door. He sat. I walked Claire to her car, enjoying the cool night air.

We reached the sidewalk as the Sheriff Fargas climbed out of his car. "Evening, Patience." He took off his hat when he saw Claire. "Miss Claire."

Claire blushed on cue, accentuating her flawless mocha latte complexion, and lowered her long curly lashes. "Sheriff Fargas."

Those two had started flirting a few weeks ago and it still confused me.

"I was on my way to the Tasty Cream for dinner," he said. "Would you like to join me?"

"I don't know." Claire looked at me. I wasn't sure what I was supposed to do. Make an excuse for her? Encourage her?

"Your phone's ringing," Sebastian called to me.

At the same moment, Sheriff Fargas pulled his phone

from his pocket. "Fargas." His eyes shut for two quick beats before turning to Sebastian. The set of his jaw and rigidity in his stance was grim when he returned the phone to his pocket.

Sebastian waved my phone in the air. "It's still buzzing."

"Mine?" I called up the steps.

"Yeah. Double-oh-seven." Sebastian read the display.

"That's Adrian," Claire interjected.

Sebastian answered my phone.

"I'm afraid I need a rain check." Fargas touched Claire's hand lightly and turned for his car.

Sebastian bounded down the steps two at a time, keys in hand.

"What's going on?" Claire demanded as Fargas tore away from the curb in his cruiser.

"Adrian found two dead bodies in my bed."

TWO

CLAIRE AND I walked to the B&B after strict instructions from Sebastián to "wait here." Nothing on the island was more than a few minutes away and parking at crimes scenes was terrible this year. Plus, the walk helped with digestion. It was a winning decision.

Mrs. Moore, the owner of Island Comforts, opened the front door of her home-turned-B&B and tarried on the wide wraparound porch. She wiped her cheeks and then rolled her shoulders forward, winding pale, thin arms around her torso. Three other couples, ranging in ages from twenties to geriatric, huddled together along the porch railing. Crickets and bullfrogs played the evening score.

I tugged on Claire's hand. "We should wait with her."

She nodded.

Claire and I moved along the sidewalk on quiet feet. Was there a proper way to approach Mrs. Moore without looking like busybodies? Maybe not saying anything was the answer. Sometimes just being present meant more than words. Mrs. Moore sniffled. My chest ached for her and the bodies Adrian had found.

A white van with the Chincoteague Community Hospital logo pulled up to the curb. Two men bustled past with a gurney and an old-fashioned doctor's bag. They would bring the bodies out soon. Another hospital van pulled up to the curb behind the first, and Claire squeezed my hand. Mrs. Moore whimpered as the men guided their gurneys into her home.

Claire looked past me. "So, what do we do now?"

I wrapped my arms around my middle. "I don't know. I had a glass of champagne and plans for a celebration. Now there are more dead bodies. I still dream of the last dead bodies."

She looped her arm around my waist and leaned her head against me. "I know, sweetie. How about I stay here until we know a little more."

One more reason I loved her.

Claire turned on me. "You okay?"

"Yeah." I took another step toward the porch. Mrs. Moore looked wretched. A murderer had been in her home today. A shudder ripped through my chest. I knew what that felt like, too.

Adrian joined her on the porch and Claire and I stopped short. He rubbed Mrs. Moore's back and tilted his head to hers. His whispers floated into the night, unintelligible to my ears, but clearly welcome to hers.

Claire sighed. "Look at him comforting her."

I nodded. Adrian smiled at the clearly terrified woman and guided her to a wicker chair against the porch wall. He was like that. Kind. Considerate. Real. I imagined Sebastian inside examining bodies and black lighting the room for prints and bodily fluids. That was his wheelhouse. Catching the bad guy. Finding answers. Bringing justice.

Sheriff Fargas strode onto the porch from inside the house, wearing a mask of concentration and carrying a notepad. Claire made a strange hiccup sound.

"What was that?" I asked.

"What?"

"That. That noise you just made."

She pursed her lips and waved to Adrian.

He darted down the steps and met us on the sidewalk. He hugged Claire. "Hey."

"Hey," Claire and I echoed.

"Can you believe it?" He pulled me close, squeezing both of us against his broad chest. I inhaled his familiar scents of shampoo and mint. Adrian smelled like home. Like safety. Like assurance.

He rested his chin on my head. "Someone shot them while they were in bed. What's wrong with this island? It used to be so sweet and crime free. Now it's like an episode of *The Twilight Zone* where everything looks warm and inviting, but then you realize it's not what it seems, and there's danger lurking in the pretty little package."

I pulled back for a better look at his face. "This island isn't like that. A few deeply disturbed people did some bad things in a short period of time. That doesn't equate to whatever you're describing."

He frowned from the eight-inch height difference between us. "Hey, I'm traumatized over here. You have no idea what it's like to find people like that."

I disentangled myself from his arm. "Don't be so theatrical."

Adrian grimaced. "Funny you should say that. Theatrical." He rubbed his chin.

"Why?"

"You haven't asked who was in the bed."

I hadn't. I wasn't ready to lose another islander. Putting names to the losses would make them real. Official.

"Who was in the bed?" Claire leaned back, angling her head for a better look at Adrian's face, a full foot above hers.

His blue eyes flashed. "Rick Fitzgerald and Anna Copeland."

Claire gasped. She covered her mouth with one tiny hand and pressed shiny green fingernails against her lips. "No," she dragged the word out several syllables. So much for no more theatrics.

Adrian nodded. He rubbed her back and shook his head.

"Who?" I was the only link between Claire and Adrian. Wasn't I? How could they both know someone I didn't?

Claire's hand dropped to her side. "You're kidding me. Right?"

I made a crazy face. Why would I joke?

She angled away from me, focusing completely on Adrian. "What were they doing in there?"

Adrian's pursed his lips and lifted both brows.

"No." Claire covered her mouth again. "They were *in bed* in bed." She pushed her fist back and forth between them.

"Yep."

She stomped her heels against the ground. "Oh. My. Glory. And you found them like that." Her eyes bulged.

"Yeah." He grimaced. "It was bad."

"When you say bad…"

I held my hands in a *T*, hoping that was still the sign for time-out. "Stop. You want to catch me up?"

Fargas whistled from the porch. "Davis. You're up." He waved to Adrian.

Mrs. Moore zombied down the steps to my side. She pressed a tissue to the corners of her eyes.

"How are you holding up?" I asked.

She groaned. "I feel absolutely horrid about this. Sebastian never stays in his room. I know it was wrong of me, but he rarely comes back at night, so when Rick Fitzgerald showed up and my other rooms were full, I had to do something. I couldn't let him leave when a perfectly empty room was waiting. I didn't think anyone would ever find out." She sniffled into the tissue.

"Wait. You knew him, too?" I ran through a mental list of islanders. I didn't know any Rick or Anna. Definitely no Fitzgeralds, but I was gone for ten years, so they might've moved in while I was away.

Mrs. Moore blinked her watery eyes. "Of course, dear. Who doesn't know him?"

Claire pointed to me. "Patience."

I shut my eyes and counted to ten slowly. What was I missing? How many ways could I ask the same question before someone answered?

"Uh oh, she's counting." Claire stroked my arm. "Rick Fitzgerald is a reality television show host. He hosts *Real Dates with Rick*, *Smart Girls Can Hunt* and *Cooking with Criminals*."

I recognized the last one. "The cooking show filmed inside American prisons?" I bit my lip. I hated that show. Anyone who glorified prison life was bottom-feeding. America needed healthy role models, not corn muffins made by convicts. "Wait. What was he doing here?" There wasn't a prison for a hundred miles.

"I invited him," Adrian called from the porch.

"Nothing wrong with his hearing," I muttered.

Adrian shot me a thumbs-up while Fargas made notes on his pad.

"Why'd you invite him here?" Claire hollered back. "Do you know him?"

Fargas turned to look at her and she blushed. That needed to be addressed soon. "Why don't you talk with the mayor while I finish up with Davis?"

I assumed he was talking to me. "Okay."

"Not you." Sebastian appeared behind me with a Maglite and a scowl.

I pressed a hand to my chest. "How do you do that? Good grief. Are you trying to give me a heart attack?"

His flat expression said no. "I'm checking the perimeter. Would you ladies mind moving off the walkway and onto the sidewalk until we finish up?"

Mrs. Moore, Claire and I went to lean on Sebastian's Range Rover.

Claire elbowed my ribs. "Here comes the mayor. What do you think he has to do with this?"

Mayor Hayes speed-walked up the road to us. "I came as soon as I heard."

A line of neighbors and spectators appeared across the street and down the block, keeping a respectful distance.

Sebastian shot warning looks to the bystanders and closed in on the mayor. "You've heard the preliminaries? Victims' names?"

The mayor nodded.

I interrupted. "Do you know why Rick Fitzthomas was here?"

"Fitzgerald." Four voices corrected me.

Right. Fitzgerald. I didn't get why Adrian invited him to the island. Was it some promo stunt for the election?

The flash of a camera blinded me.

"No pictures," Sebastian called.

The flash came two more times in quick succession.

Sebastian growled, "Reporters."

The mayor tugged at his collar. "Tourism took a big hit last month. The shark sightings hurt our commerce in a mighty way. The influx of birders helped, but we're a tourist town. We need every dollar. I thought I could boost winter tourism with a little something special, maybe put our town on the map before my term's up. I really wanted to think outside the box, as they say. When I ran into Davis on the golf course, he had some ideas."

I turned my attention on Adrian. If he was asked to think outside the box, who knew what might happen. "How far outside the box?"

"We arranged to have several episodes of *The Watchers* filmed on the island."

Claire stuffed half her fingertips in her mouth and jogged in place.

Sebastian crossed strong arms over his chest. "What's *The Watchers*?"

I raised my palms in the air. Finally, someone as lost as me.

"It's a show on the Educating America Channel," Claire explained. "A lucky group of people get to travel the world, learning about different customs, food and art. The producers give the contestants a new challenge in every city and one player wins. Someone else gets sent home. You know the drill."

I shook my head. Nope.

"Come on. You're a counselor. An observer of human behavior. You should love reality television."

I shrugged. "I never got into the whole reality television fad. I think it's all rigged."

She gasped. Again.

Sebastian chuckled.

"Agree to disagree then," I said. "So, what's the point? What do they get for doing this?"

I looked from face to face. Mayor Hayes shook his head in clear disappointment. Mrs. Moore's dazed expression said her thoughts were miles away. Sebastian squinted at Claire.

Claire huffed. "They get to travel the world. Live in

luxurious homes and eat the finest cuisine. Discover countries steeped in history and tradition."

"What do they win?" Sebastian asked.

"Two hundred fifty thousand dollars."

My jaw dropped. "Holy crab cakes. Where do I sign up? That's ridiculous. I bet I could win the Chincoteague challenge. What's the challenge they're doing here?"

The mayor shifted his weight. "They aren't doing a challenge here. Fargas and I arranged for them to film their big Halloween special on the island. Adrian let them rent his place. We're remote enough for the crew to have privacy. We're down to year-round islanders for the next six months. Once the show airs, we'll get a second wind of tourism and maybe some airtime on a national news show. It sounded like a win-win situation. I'd be remembered as the mayor who put this town on the map."

I groaned. I didn't want Chincoteague on the map any more than it already was. I liked it fine the way it always had been. "Oh no."

"What is it?" Sebastian wrapped his fingers around my elbow.

"The guy taking pictures. I bet he was the same guy who took a picture of me when I lifted my shirt earlier."

"Excuse me?"

Claire hummed. "Paparazzi."

"I bet he knew Rick was here. When his death hits the internet, this place will be flooded with people." I pressed my forehead to Sebastian's shoulder. "We just said goodbye to the birders last week."

The mayor shuffled his feet like a little tap show. "Commerce."

I lifted my eyes to his. "Did you leak the location?"

"What? No. Of course not." He patted his lapels and averted his eyes.

"Really? Because news like that would bring a lot of looky-loos and reality show stalkers." I cocked my head. "They'll all need a place to stay and food to eat. Mayor Hayes?"

The mayor fumbled for words, blowing the same syllable over his lips. His gaze bounced around the perimeter, now filled with onlookers. "I-I-I-I…"

Sebastian stepped forward. "Where were you around seven fifteen?"

The mayor's eyes fluttered. "I-I-I was at the office."

"Can anyone confirm that?"

Mayor Hayes stepped back. "Am I a suspect?"

Sebastian shook his head. "I'm just gathering facts. Only a handful of people knew Mr. Fitzgerald was here. I'd like to account for the whereabouts of those people."

"I see."

I moved to Sebastian's side. "Wife? Secretary? Were you on the phone or on the internet? Those logs can show where you were."

Sebastian dropped a stern look my way. I raised my eyebrows.

"Yes!" The mayor clapped his hands once. "I traded emails at my desk for more than an hour."

"Could one of your correspondents be a hit man?"

Sebastian snorted.

"No! I emailed a few select journalists and well-respected names in the media."

Here we go. I clucked my tongue. "How's Fargas supposed to solve a murder if the town is teeming with chaos and reporters snooping around?"

He guffawed. "I didn't know this would happen. How was I to know there was a murder going on?"

Fargas lumbered off the porch with Adrian at his side. Fargas stopped behind Claire and addressed Sebastian. "No prints. We dusted everything and found nada."

Sebastian nodded. "Light switch?"

"Just Adrian's and Rick's prints there."

Interesting. The killer wore gloves and worked in the dark. "It was premeditated."

Everyone looked at me. No one spoke for a long beat until Fargas placed a hand on Mrs. Moore's shoulder. "Do you have someplace else you can sleep tonight? We're bringing a team in from the mainland to comb over the grounds, but they won't get here for another hour and they'll be at it most of the night. We've moved the other couples to Miss Holly's Inn for the remainder of their visits."

She nodded without making eye contact. "I can stay with Mrs. Tucker, I think." Her eyes glossed with barely tamped emotion.

Mayor Hayes wrapped an arm around her shoulders and addressed Fargas. "I can drive her if I'm free to go."

The sheriff nodded. "We can talk tomorrow."

"So, this is why you don't have any place to stay?" I asked Adrian. "You rented your house to a reality show?" Who did that?

"Yep."

Sebastian pressed his palm against the small of my back and watched Adrian with appraising eyes. "You're the richest homeless guy I've ever met."

"I think you mean the coolest."

"Nope. I meant homeless. You can't stay in my room now and you loaned your house to a reality show."

Adrian looked at me for help. "I have to stay with you now. I've got no place to go."

Sebastian pressed his palm tighter to my skin. "Homeless."

"Okay," Adrian conceded. "We can talk about this later. You're in cop mode. I get it."

Claire whispered into my hair. "You sure you're okay? You look pale."

I pulled in a shaky breath. "Who was the woman? You called her Anna?"

Claire rubbed my arm. "Yeah. She was on the show."

"Oh." Was that allowed? Did Hollywood allow fraternization between hosts and contestants?

Sebastian set his mammoth hands over his trim athletic hips. "Claire and Adrian seem to know a lot about this guy and his show. They might be a resource to get you started."

Fargas's eyes lit up. "You're a fan of *The Watchers*?"

Claire's head bobbed. A cheesy smile spread over her face. "Yes."

"Me, too."

Adrian slapped Fargas's shoulder. "You want to order pizza and hash this out?"

"I've got to get to the station. Frankie's fielding calls until I get there." He looked at Claire. "Can I drop you somewhere on my way?"

"I'd love that. Patience?"

Fargas looked at me.

"Yeah, okay. Go with Fargas. Sebastian can drop me on his way to the station, too."

Adrian lifted his cell to one ear and ordered a pizza to be delivered to my apartment. "Let's meet at your place in thirty, roomie."

I smiled at Sebastian, who didn't return the sentiment.

Lucky for me, it wasn't the time to argue about where Adrian slept. Sebastian had slipped into special-agent mode the minute he heard the word "bodies." He'd spend the night with Fargas at the station or back here at the crime scene. This was what he did, and he was the best.

Fargas opened the passenger door on his cruiser, and Claire dropped inside.

I climbed into the Range Rover. Sebastian shut the door and leaned on the open window frame. "What's that about?" He slid his eyes toward the cruiser.

If I only knew.

Adrian squeezed his head in beside Sebastian's. "Pizza's on its way. I've got to run home."

Sebastian straightened to his full height. "Why?" He positioned his right hand over his sidearm. Men and their subtle threats. Freud would have a field day with these two.

Adrian smiled wide enough for his dimple to cave in. "I've got *The Watchers* seasons one through four on Blu-ray."

He jogged to his Jeep and climbed in. What a nut.

Sebastian rounded the hood and folded his long body behind the wheel. "Man, that guy's impossible not to like and it drives me crazy."

Amen to that.

THREE

When Sebastian and I climbed out of the Range Rover at my place, Claire and Fargas were lingering on the sidewalk.

Fargas's low tenor mingled with Claire's higher-pitched whispers. He shook his head. "I doubt the cast knew about Rick and Anna. They'd have written that into the script for sure."

Claire tapped her little green clutch against one palm. "I don't know. I mean, everyone on the internet message boards thought Rick was sleeping with one of the girls. I always assumed it was Elisa."

"Elisa has a boyfriend. He attends all the red carpet events with her."

My mind wrestled with the night's information. Maybe there was a bright side. These murders seemed pointed, intended for this man and woman. The job was done. The killer was probably already back on the mainland establishing his alibi and distancing himself from the scene of the crime forever.

Sebastian cleared his throat. "Fargas, reality television. Red carpet events. Really?"

Claire huffed. "Everyone watches some kind of reality television."

"I don't." Sebastian and I spoke in unison.

Fargas smiled. "You two must have a guilty viewing pleasure. Watching trash television is part of our culture. Like Taylor Swift music and online shopping."

Sebastian folded his arms. His lips twitched. "Taylor Swift?"

Fargas shuffled his feet on the loose gravel. His attention moved to Claire. "I better get to the station. Frankie's got her hands full, fielding calls and managing worried neighbors."

Claire nodded. "Good night."

Fargas turned to Sebastian with an expectant look and dawdled near his cruiser.

"Be there in a minute." Sebastian took my hands. He crouched to meet my eyes. "You going to be okay here?"

I forced a smile. "Yeah. Go. Fargas can use all the help he can get. If reporters are onto this already, the island will soon be a madhouse."

Sebastian laced his fingers with mine, trapping me. "Did you say you lifted your shirt earlier and someone took a picture?" His dark expression sent chills down both my arms. "Flashing is illegal here, you know. They have a name for it and everything. Indecent exposure. I have legal grounds to arrest you." His dark eyes traveled over my shirt. The corner of his mouth lifted one cheek.

"I wasn't flashing."

He squared his shoulders. "Is there or is there not a camera on this island in need of confiscation?"

"There is," Claire said.

Sebastian's jaw ticked. He'd had his share of run-ins with the press, following undercover busts. Reporters were on his short list of people to avoid. Paparazzi were equivalent to parasites in Sebastian's book. Now that one had a picture of my popped button and stuffed tummy, I didn't disagree.

I turned toward the little blue hatchback crawling down my street. "Oh, look! Pizza." The lighted pony on top wore a black Stetson hat and four matching boots.

Pony Pizza delivered anywhere on the island in twenty minutes or less.

Sebastian tipped the pizza kid and kissed my forehead. "I'll find that camera. Meanwhile, no more flashing…until I get back."

Claire followed me up the steps to my apartment and waited for Adrian to arrive before she headed home. He made up the couch, dug into the pizza and started season one of *The Watchers*. I skipped the pizza and went to bed. This sort of publicity would bring chaos to the island. Not the anticipated crowds of summer vacationers or the scheduled tour bus loads of birders in the fall, but an unprecedented, unregulated stream of people vying to get the scoop, land a hot story or take a selfie picture at the scene of the crime. I worked the blankets up to my chin and prayed I was wrong.

SUNLIGHT DRIFTED THROUGH my window and settled on my eyelids. I pulled a pillow over my head, but it was too late. Scents of fresh coffee coaxed me to my feet, despite my better judgment. Waking at six fifteen was for fishermen, joggers and yoga enthusiasts. A perk of undercover counseling was sleeping in. No one ever dropped by to talk about their problems before lunch.

The couch was empty. No sign of Adrian, except the fresh pot of coffee on my countertop. Scents of soap and shampoo mingled with rich coffee in the air, saturating every inch of the apartment. I inhaled. My lungs filled with brisk and comforting aromas. Adrian was never a lay-in-bed guy. He'd started his days with a jog and a shower since middle school. For two years, he'd been the shortest kid in our class, and he hated it so much he decided to get fit to compensate. Soon, the taller, skinny guys were overlooked. Adrian's solid frame drew every girl's eye. If that wasn't enough, he grew four inches one summer and already had the physique to go with it. It was a wonder every guy in school didn't hate him. Anyone else, maybe, but no one disliked Adrian.

I poured a second cup of coffee, wrenched my hair into a knot and went to my room. It didn't look as if Sebastian had come home during the night. I yanked on some soft jeans with an old shirt from our FBI softball league. I'd bring Tasty Cream coffee to the police station and score some girlfriend points with my overworked crime fighter. I finished cup number two and set it in the sink. My coffee was good, but nothing beat Tasty Cream coffee.

I poured a saucer of creamer and set it on the stoop outside my door. A little gray poof ball posing as a kitten lived there. I called him Freud. Freud wasn't waiting for me as expected. I tilted my nose to the sky and sucked in the air. No wonder he wasn't there. Something nearby smelled like heaven. Normally, island mornings smelled of stale coffee, salt and brine, but today, oh gracious… I drifted down the stairs like Fred Flintstone on a whiff of brontosaurus stew.

My feet planted on the bottom step and I gripped the railing. Throngs of people filed in and out of the Tasty Cream. Food trucks lined the crowded streets. Groups of people in *The Watchers* shirts, toting cameras and paper plates of food, wound past my apartment.

A woman with red-rimmed eyes headed my way. The hood on her jacket covered most of her face. She leaned forward, arms wrapped around her torso. She stopped a few feet away from me. From her expression and body language, she was either coming off a long crying jag or some sort of narcotic.

I formed my most encouraging smile. "Hey. Everything okay?"

She ran a wrist under her nose. "I don't know. I mean, no, something is really wrong on this island. Why do people keep dying?" Her voice dissolved to a whisper on the final word.

"Have we met?"

She turned her eyes to mine briefly. "I'm Dawn."

"Hi, I'm Patience."

Dawn turned away from me, watching the traffic back up. A soft sniffle drifted from her hood. "I know who you are. What do you think about the murders? Do you think the killer's still here?"

A very good question. One I hoped I was right about. "No. I think whoever did this left to create an alibi and won't ever come back."

Dawn wiped her cheeks. Her hood bobbed a fraction. "I worry. I have anxiety." A long gust of breath escaped her. "People scare me. I thought moving here would help, and it did for a while." She laughed. "No crime. The travel agent, real estate agent, mayor and the internet promised. No crime. I guess everything changes."

My heart ached for her. I understood fear more than I cared to admit. "Listen, those B&B murders weren't about the island. Considering the victims, it was more likely a crazed stalker than a hometown maniac. I don't think there's someone dangerous living among us. Most importantly, none of these crimes were about you. They weren't random. They were all pointed, and you're way outside their target. You're safe here. The last few months..." I stopped to gather my thoughts. The last few months had been a nightmare. How could I pretend they weren't? "I grew up here and I came to visit plenty while I lived on the mainland. These last few months of crime aren't normal for us. This will pass. We're safe. You're safe."

Dawn turned her gaze on me, a flicker of hope in her eyes.

She was at least five years younger than me, maybe closer to ten. I cringed internally at the realization a grown woman could be ten years younger than me. I shook it off. *Thirty is the new twenty.*

"Do you think I'm crazy for worrying so much I cried myself to sleep last night?"

I shook my head. "No. Fear is real and it'll trap you if you let it, but if you use it wisely, I think fear helps us make smart decisions. We should be anxious sometimes. We're designed that way. A healthy amount of fear keeps us safe." Not me, of course. I ran headlong into insane situations. Fear wasn't my problem. I had a much more dangerous affliction: curiosity.

Dawn tugged the strings of her hood. "Like when we avoid dark alleys and never park beside utility vans with no windows."

"Right." Always avoid creepy kidnaper vans.

A little smile formed on Dawn's lips. "Yeah." She nodded. "So, you're saying pick my nightmares and they can keep me safe."

"Well." I didn't say nightmares. "I think it's smart to be vigilant. Being aware is the best way to stay safe."

"No one's coming to kill me?"

"Nope." Probably not. Hopefully not. I pursed my lips.

Dawn dug into the messenger bag on her hip. "I have something for you." She handed me a small circle covered in string. "It's a dream catcher. I make them. They'll filter the bad things from your dreams."

The little object didn't seem to help her much, but I smiled anyway. "Thanks."

"Oh, and this." She handed me a gift card to download music to my phone or computer. "Everyone was right about you." She turned on her toes and headed away from me.

I dropped the dream catcher into my purse and tried not to think about what people were saying behind my back. Getting paid in American Indian talismans and digital music tokens was a new one. If only my landlord accepted those as payment. Then again, Adrian had better not ask for rent after I saved his behind last week. Maybe he could show me how to use the gift card. My tummy growled.

I counted to ten and shuffled to the Tasty Cream for a healthy, low-calorie, ice-cream-gut-busting breakfast and coffee to go. A horn honked as I pulled open the heavy glass door. *Honked.* At six-thirty in the morning.

"Good morning, Patience." Mrs. Tucker waved from behind the counter. Mrs. Tucker had run the Tasty Cream for as long as I could remember. Her skin was white and freckled, despite fifty years of island life, because she preferred serving ice cream indoors to the myriad of outdoor activities Chincoteague was known for.

I slid between two teenage girls in black shirts with large luminous eyes drawn across their chests. They propped signs against their legs with the same logo. Underneath the eyes, block letters proclaimed We Like to Watch.

Oh boy.

Forget the healthy breakfast. I needed sugar.

"Coffee?" Mrs. Tucker pushed a to-go cup across the counter. "We're out of clean mugs." She looked over my shoulder. "We're going to be out of disposable cups if the local police don't buy their own cappuccino machine soon."

I followed her gaze to a smiling Frankie.

I smiled back. "How'd you get away?"

Frankie was the receptionist at the police station. I scanned the area for Fargas or Sebastian. The only other face I recognized was Mr. Glazer, the town mailman, wheezing at a table in the back corner.

Frankie tapped one finger against a new star on her chest. "I passed the civil service exam. Fargas swore me in last night. I'm officially a Chincoteague police officer."

"Wow. Look at the uniform on you. Nice." I nodded in appreciation.

She beamed. "Melinda Crown and her little girl are manning the phones while I get more cappuccinos. She promised to stay until three when her boys get home from school, then Missy will come by for the afternoon shift until we hire a new receptionist."

"On the house." Mrs. Tucker waded through the crowd with a carrier full of lidded drinks. "You tell those two I can use more of their pastries. Those Sugar and Spice numbers went like hotcakes this morning. Literally. I was out of both by six."

My chest puffed with pride for Melinda and Missy. When they decided to start Sugar and Spice Catering I'd worried. Most new businesses around here failed or morphed into something utterly bizarre, like my counseling practice. If Mrs. Tucker was buying their pastries, and selling out of them at six in the morning, their business was off to a great start.

"Wait." I peered between tightly packed bodies at the counter, angling for a better view of the display case. "You still have fritters, right?"

Mrs. Tucker shook her head.

My shoulders drooped. "Crullers?"

"Sorry, sweetie. How about a muffin?"

"Chocolate chip?"

"Raisin and Bran."

My tongue stuck to the roof of my mouth.

Frankie pressed through the crowd, balancing the cappuccinos in one hand and tapping customers on the back with the other. "Excuse me. Coming through. I'm right behind you. Hot coffee. See ya, Patience."

I took my coffee and looked for an empty seat. Mr. Glazer's face went from crimson to white and his shoulders rolled forward.

"Mr. Glazer!" I dashed to his side, burning my fingers with sprays of coffee popping through the drink hole in my lid.

I set the coffee beside his glass on the speckled Formica tabletop and dropped to my knees. His cheeks scorched my palms as I gripped his face. "Mr. Glazer. You're having another panic attack."

His eyelids pinched into a tight series of wrinkles. His chest rose and fell in rapid little gasps.

"It's okay. Listen to my voice and shut everything else out." I grabbed a wad of napkins from the silver dispenser on the table and dunked them in his ice water. "I want you to pretend it's just the two of us here. We're having a nice cup of coffee and getting ready for a very boring day at work. Can you hear the geese honking at your mail truck to get out of the way?" I pressed the wet napkins to the back of his neck and he sucked air.

He cleared his throat. "The birders just left. The tourists were here before them. Now this."

I handed him his water and overlooked the bits of napkin lint floating on top. "I know."

"I don't understand," he whispered.

"Two people were murdered last night at Mrs. Moore's bed-and-breakfast." I flipped his wrist in my grip and counted his pulse.

His eyes sprung wide. "Murdered?"

I nodded, keeping count in my head. "Your pulse is flying. Have some more water. Sip it slowly and focus on one thing at a time."

"Who?" His voice was a whisper.

"Rick Fitzgerald and Anna Copeland. They were part of a television show planning to tape a special on the island. I think all these people are fans or reporters. They won't stay long now the show won't go on."

He pulled in a deeper breath and color returned to his face. "I hate the crowds. They're impossible. You can't get anywhere. All the mailboxes are blocked and it's so loud outside. I can't hear the tugboats anymore." A whimper escaped him.

"They won't stay long."

My words merited a smile. He straightened in his seat. A bead of sweat clung to his brow. He smoothed his navy striped uniform top over his round belly and took several more deep breaths. "You said focus on one thing?'

"Yes. My voice."

"Can I focus on her?"

I followed his gaze to a familiar head bobbing through the room. "Sure." I chuckled. Whatever prevents a panic attack. I patted his shoulder. Kind of ironic having more pretty faces to focus on would get him through his attack brought on by the crowds.

Claire's voice pierced the hubbub around us. "There you are! I hope you didn't start without me."

I popped up from my squat and stretched burning

thighs. Claire got every man's attention. It was her curse. I smiled at Mr. Glazer mopping sweat from his brow with paper napkins.

"What are you doing here?" I hugged her.

She squeezed me. "I took the day off. I'm sick."

"Liar."

"Hey. You didn't let me finish. I'm sick of missing all the excitement."

"Did you clarify your sickness to the FBI or did you lie to the government?"

She jutted her bottom lip forward. "All they let me do at the bureau is file papers, answer phones and deal with embezzlement cases and internet fraud. You know, last week I had to track down someone illegally copying movies. It was like arresting one blade of grass for being part of the field."

I frowned. "Is that some kind of southern expression?"

"It's poetic."

Mr. Glazer's head swung back and forth with the conversation. His water glass was empty, napkin lint and all.

Claire bumped my arm. "Look at Adrian."

I scanned the crowded room. Bingo. Adrian stood in the center of a circle of pretty women whose dresses, heels and two-hundred-dollar haircuts screamed mainland. The wide white press badges on their jackets and purses turned my stomach. He was surrounded by a school of piranhas in push-up bras. Those ladies would eat him alive for an inside scoop on the biggest celebrity story in Virginia's history.

Claire giggled. "Relax. He's a politician. He's in his element with all those reporters."

He pressed one hand to the shoulder of a little brunette and steered her away from the pack, winking over one shoulder to the others. He and the brunette exchanged phones for a moment then parted ways.

"Adrian," Claire called.

He wove through the tables and wrapped his arms around her. "Hello, princess." Adrian had seen her listed as Princess in my phone's contacts, where I gave everyone nicknames for privacy. I never used real names in case anyone got nosy with my phone history.

She shot eye daggers my way and I smiled.

"What was that about?" I inclined my head toward the women.

He sighed. "I love the media. Freedom of the press. Freedom of speech."

"Yeah, yeah." I circled a wrist between us. "What happened to Becky, the EMT?"

"Becky was lovely, but she didn't challenge me."

I rolled my eyes. "And the reporter you met five seconds ago does?"

He hugged me. "Don't be jealous."

"Stop." I swatted his ridiculous chest. "I'm immune to you. Too many years of exposure."

"Impossible. So, where's your secret agent man?"

"At the station."

Claire said, "At the bureau."

I shoved free of Adrian, forcing the smile off my face. He was too playful for his own good. "You can't go around grabbing women whenever you feel like it."

He lifted both palms and released a killer smile.

"Stop." I avoided eye contact.

Claire took my wrist and turned toward the door. "See you later, Adrian."

I waved to Mr. Glazer, who no longer looked in danger of collapse. He waved back and Adrian dropped into the seat in front of him.

When we reached the parking lot, Claire stopped.

A moment later, my thoughts caught up with me. "I didn't know Sebastian went to the office. I thought he was at the station with Fargas all night."

She shrugged. "He looked busy, so I didn't ask. Your turn. Tell me the latest news. What else have you heard?"

I squinted into the morning sun. An enormous orange globe rested on the harbor, shining on the water and reflecting into my eyes. Nothing was as beautiful as a sunrise on the harbor. "I just woke up. I haven't heard anything."

She pinched her bottom lip between her thumb and first finger. "Have you seen any of the other cast members?"

"No, but I wouldn't recognize them. I went to bed last night after you left. Adrian watched season one by himself."

Claire gasped and swatted me with her clutch. "How can you investigate this if you don't know what any of the suspects look like?"

I batted my eyes. "I'm not investigating anything. I don't want to know anything. I want life to get back to normal. This—" I lifted my arms wide, emphasizing the scene around us, "—is not normal."

Cars jammed intersections, with drivers honking and waving finger-messages at one another. Vendors had set up carts on corners with inflatable glasses and telescopes. Half the people in my line of sight wore black shirts with *The Watchers* logo or a press badge or both. Lines stretched from food trucks and blocked the traffic up and down Main Street.

"This is like a street fair or a celebration of some kind. Two people were killed."

She nodded, a somber expression over her pretty face.

"Hey, I know it's bad timing, but I wanted to talk with you, remember. It's hard to get you alone these days."

"Sure. Tell me what's on your mind."

"The other night after your birthday party, Wyatt and I weren't really connecting. I was disappointed, but there's someone else in the picture, too. I meant to talk to you about this when it started, but this island is non-stop chaos and murders. You're usually in the center of it, and you have your own problems."

I nodded, encouraging her to go on. Did I have problems? Half of me thought that was an understatement. The other half thought life was pretty great.

A man stopped in front of us. His crisp white shirt-sleeves were rolled to the elbows. The hem disappeared into the waistband of crumpled khaki pants. He looked like a younger version of Adrian.

"Anything good to eat in there?" he asked.

Claire batted her eyes. "Everything's good at the Tasty Cream."

"Thanks." He nodded appreciatively. "Are you two from around here?"

Claire pointed to my apartment across the street. "She lives right there, and I'm visiting from Norfolk."

I fought the urge to smack my forehead. She listened to nothing at the monthly FBI seminars on common sense and self-defense.

"Nice." He smiled at Claire and took a baby step closer to her. "Have you been visiting her long?"

"I come over a lot. This is Patience Price. She's my best friend and this place is much more fun than Norfolk."

"I bet." He winked. "I'm wondering what's fun to do here after dark."

Nightlife? Seriously. "I'm sorry. Are you a reporter?" The question earned me a little shove from Claire.

"What?" *Nightlife?* Come on.

The man extended a hand between us. "It's okay. She's right. I am a reporter."

I looked at Claire. She shook his hand first.

"I'm Todd Ramone. I write for Hollywood Watcher, and I'm looking into the rumors about Rick and Anna. Are they true?" He lifted a weasely eyebrow.

"Yes." The word was a whisper on Claire's lips.

"So they were sleeping together." He pulled out a notepad.

Good grief. They were dead, and he was looking for gossip to slander them. Awful.

"Goodbye, Todd Ramone." I tugged Claire with me into the street of motionless, honking cars.

"He was from Hollywood Watcher." Claire craned her neck for another look behind us. "Can you believe it?"

"No."

"You were a little rude. All he wanted was our perspective on this story."

"Yeah, well, all I wanted was some time to talk with my best friend and maybe a donut. Today isn't that day."

"Where are we going?"

"The only place to go in times of crisis. Let's visit the local holistic healers."

AKA: My parents.

FOUR

FOOD TRUCKS LINED Main Street. I'd never seen a food truck on the island before today. Suddenly, there were at least two dozen, maybe more. I slowed every few steps to watch workers with bright smiles deliver paper boats of fancy food over metal counters. A heady mixture of deliciousness hung in the air. Salt and grease from bacon and eggs drifted around the Gravy Train truck where fishermen in waders hovered coffee cups to their lips. A few steps later I bathed in the syrupy scents of blueberries, whipped cream and pancakes surrounding the Baby Cakes truck. On and on it went—new truck, new name, new smells.

The scene was surreal. Chincoteague existed on predictable routines and capitalized on gentle historic charm. Giant, multi-colored tour busses of food with little chalkboard menu easels and coordinating tables on the sidewalk didn't fit the bill. Sunlight glinted off their unspotted windshields and glass tabletops. Children sat at the tables, swinging booted feet and facing off with short stacks that smiled back through strawberry lips. Cups of chocolate milk waited in parental hands as dads examined *The Watchers* maps. There were maps? I was a tourist on my own island. I squeezed my eyelids shut and reopened them. Nope. Everyone was still there.

Chincoteague had lots of events. The Seafood Festival, Blueberry Festival and Pony Swim were all big tourist draws. The Pony Swim, held in July, was the biggest event of the year. Cowboys herded the wild ponies then swam them across the marsh and auctioned them off to the highest bidder. Monies raised went to support the local volunteer fire department. A few street vendors brought hotdog carts and little fair trucks from out of state for the swim and auction, but nothing like the chaos before me.

Near the mainland bridge, a crowd was gathered beside a news truck. A cameraman followed a pretty lady in a pantsuit from person to person, thrusting her microphone in random faces.

"I wonder what she's asking them." I squinted into the distance. The sun moved higher every minute, changing from orange to amber to blinding white on the water.

Claire shielded her eyes with one hand. "I don't know, but they won't end up on the news. That crowd looks good. The news only puts people on the air who look like they just woke up and can't operate a comb."

"Mean." I chuckled. Mean, but not wrong. I finger brushed my hair.

Claire pulled the door to my parents' shop open and braced it with one hip. The Purple Pony was packed. She let out a long, slow whistle. "I bet your dad's in heaven with all these people to talk to."

I worked my way into the store, picking a path through shoppers crouched at moccasin bins and knots of teens trying on sunglasses around a mirror. Claire followed, singing softly to new age music that danced from hidden speakers overhead. My parents had opened the store before I was born. They stocked an eclectic blend of ingredients for a holistic lifestyle, mixed with scads of Chincoteague-themed novelties. Island shopping at its finest. Halfway through the recycled sneakers portion of the store, we ran out of places to step.

Claire tapped on the shoulder of a woman wearing a blue muumuu and white crocks. "Is this a line?"

The lady turned on Claire. "Yes. No cutting."

Claire elbowed me and tapped the lady again. "What's the line for?"

"Palm readings. I heard this lady's the best this side of Vegas, so no chitchat when it's my turn. I want to hear every word she says. For what she's charging, I've earned it." She pointed at my mom then shot a warning look to Claire and me. "You got it?"

I edged around the lady and rose to my tiptoes. "Oh, it's okay. We don't want a palm reading." Been there, done that. I only wanted to reach my parents before lunchtime.

Mom sat at a table, visible behind a curtain of beads. Her long wavy hair hung down her back, neatly braided with a wildflower crown at her temples. Her skin was unnaturally healthy from a lifetime of eating right, proper hydration and avoidance of toxins, like cigarette smoke and Red Dye #40. I couldn't say the same for my skin. I enjoyed processed foods, soda and sunshine. We looked alike, despite my poor skin care routine and the fact I'd blown my hair into submission with a brush and a hair dryer then wrangled it into a ponytail.

I turned in a circle, confirming Claire wasn't beside me anymore. When did she get away? I wiggled through the line.

Several voices rose in protest. "No cutting."

Claire waved her hands in the air. Her fingertips were barely visible over the crowd. "Over here."

"Excuse me. I'm really sorry. Pardon me."

Whoa. When I reached Claire, I straightened my shirt and smoothed my hair. "Is it a thousand degrees in here?" I fanned my face with a book on tarot and inhaled the patchouli-scented air.

She stooped behind the half wall of books. "Yeah, and it smells like incense. Reminds me of freshman year at college. Now, shush." She moved her fingers into a *V*, pointed them at her eyes and then toward the hemp jewelry display.

"I don't know what you're doing. I'm so confused by this day." I sank into a beanbag chair beside the bookcase and dipped my head back. "Down is up. Left is right. I don't know how to process all this."

"Shh. I'm spying." Claire rearranged the books and stuck her head between them.

"What are you doing," I whispered.

"That's Elisa French."

I slid off the beanbag and knelt beside her. She pointed between the books to a girl wearing ginormous sunglasses, with a silk scarf wrapped around her head. "She's from the show."

"The Watchers?"

"Yep."

I stood for a better view. Elisa thumbed through a rack of hemp bracelets with crystal accents. If she was here, how many other cast members were on the island? A better question popped into mind. When did she arrive? Since she was shopping for non-essentials, I doubted she'd rushed here as she heard the news. It didn't look like she was mourning the loss of a loved one, either. Why come here with the show's host and one cast member dead? I made my way to the jewelry.

"Can I help you?" I sidled up to Elisa, pretending to straighten the rack as she browsed.

"Do you work here?" She slid the oversized glasses down her tan, ski-slope nose and peered over the top. Her big blue eyes were round, lined in matte charcoal pencil and accented with stage-length false lashes.

I needed to step up my game. I used to wear eyeliner. "Yep. I work here."

"Where's your name tag?" Her gaze dropped to my chest.

"I don't wear one. It's a small island. Everyone knows everyone."

"Yeah, but what about tourists?"

I looked over my shoulder for backup. Steam from the shirt press curled into the air around Dad's balding head and salt-and-pepper ponytail. He loved making quirky custom shirts as much as Mom loved her watercolors.

"Dad!" I waved a hand overhead. He smiled back.

"That's your dad?" Elisa's voice dropped to a scandalous tone. "He's hot."

I eyeballed Dad. Mmm-kay. "Yeah. This is my parents' store." A proud smile split my face.

"And you work here? How old are you, like thirty?"

My smile fell, and my eyebrows crowded together. Thirty wasn't old. Thirty was the new twenty.

"Peepee." Dad held a black shirt to his chest. Bold white letters declared Ghost Hunters Do It in the Dark.

I gave him a thumbs-up. Why would he make a ghost hunter shirt?

Elisa's mouth turned down on both corners. "Your name is Peepee?"

"It's a nickname." I waved her off and changed the subject. Explaining the goofy nickname came from Patience Peace Price, the hippie train wreck of a name my parents saddled me with, wouldn't make it less weird. "How long have you been visiting Chincoteague?"

"We got in this morning." She held a bracelet up between us. "Is this really a protection stone?"

"That's a crystal, but it works the same." *In your mind.* I bit my lip. Mom begged me to say *in your heart* if I couldn't confirm the power of things in their shop with a straight face. I stopped believing in the power of talismans in preschool, but Mom insisted they didn't work for me because I didn't believe, so there'd been a twenty-five year agree-to-disagree clause in our relationship.

"Oh." Elisa turned the crystal over in her fingertips. She pushed the glasses onto her head.

"You're on the show, aren't you? *The Watchers.*" I cut to the chase before someone else recognized Elisa and ruined my chance to get a few answers. "Did you hear about what happened to Rick and Anna?"

Her eyes brimmed with unshed tears at the mention of their names.

I shuffled my feet, weighing my options. If I pushed her, she could cry and draw attention to herself, which would be terrible, considering the number of reporters lurking around, but I had more questions. She blinked back the shine in her eyes and blew out a long breath.

I softened my voice to a more soothing tone and leaned toward her to imply a shared bond. "Making the trip so soon after such a tragedy must be very difficult for you."

"I guess I needed to see for myself if it was true. You can't believe anything you read online anymore." She sniffled. "Part of me hoped I'd get here and Anna would jump out and say 'Fooled you!'"

"That wouldn't be a very funny joke." I stopped pretending ours was a casual conversation and focused on

Elisa. She was clearly hurting and I ached for her loss, but I had one more tiny little question. "Were you and Anna close?"

She nodded, running a fingertip under each eye to catch tears. "We were like besties. She knew everything about me." A little gasp bubbled through her pursed lips and her face darkened.

The change in her expression worried me. I scanned the room in case anyone was trying to listen in. "I'm sorry. I didn't mean to upset you. You're having a terrible day already. Do you want to sit down? Maybe get some fresh air? Can I bring you a glass of water?"

"No. I'm fine." Elisa's face reddened. "I'm better than fine. That bitch knew I was with Rick, and she couldn't let me have him. She had to trick him into bed with her. Anna was always jealous of me. She wanted everything I had. Well, look where that got her."

"Um." I scanned the crowd for Claire. She stood frozen near the bookshelf, mouth half open. Eyes wide. Well, if that outburst didn't make Elisa a suspect, nothing would. My fingers twitched to text Fargas. His investigation might be wrapped up by dinnertime. "When you said 'we' got in this morning. Did you come with the rest of *The Watchers* cast?"

"No."

Thank goodness.

Elisa slid sunglasses back onto the bridge of her nose, extinguishing the fire in her eyes. A moment later, a lanky guy with surfer hair and sideburns wrapped his arms around her middle and kissed her hair. "Babe."

My mind rewound the last portion of our conversation. She said she was sleeping with Rick. "Who's this?"

"This is my boyfriend, Dan Dirk. Dan, this is Peepee."

Claire choked behind me.

"S'up." He flipped his bangs away from his face with one sharp jerk of the head.

And then there were two. The boyfriend of a cheater and woman scorned sounded like another logical suspect to me. Though this particular boyfriend looked a little awkward for a cold-blooded killer, looks were often deceiving.

Dan kissed Elisa's cheek and released her. "Did you see my shirt, babe? It's custom made." He dug into a little Purple Pony sack and pulled out the ghost hunter shirt my dad held up earlier.

"You hunt ghosts?" A smile tugged my lips. That was cute. It was also a colossal waste of time and money, but who was I to judge?

"Yeah. Everyone who's anyone in ghost hunting is here. Your island's website says this place is crawling with specters. This beautiful land is replete with lingering spirits and longing souls. We're here to document the specters." He opened his arms wide, palms up. A reverent look crossed his face.

"Our town website says that?" I asked. What was happening? Our town had plenty of ghost stories, but they weren't reasons to visit the island.

"Everything says that. Your website, all the online ghost hunter boards, blogs and forums, Hollywood-Watcher.com, *The Watchers* website and all their Halloween special ads. Anyone researching ghosts right now is reading about Chincoteague, Virginia, America's hidden haunted treasure."

Uh-huh. Well, I couldn't speak for any other souls, but mine longed to take down the island website and also let Fargas know I'd stumbled across two viable suspects for Rick and Anna's murders.

Elisa and Dan had better hope their alibis for last night held water.

FIVE

I TEXTED FARGAS about Elisa and her boyfriend the moment we left the Purple Pony. Five long minutes passed in silence as Claire and I walked back to my place.

Waiting for his response put me on edge.

"What if he wanted us to keep Elisa and Dan busy until he could come and haul them in for questioning?" I asked.

Claire pulled her lips to the side, distorting her pretty face in a comical way. "You think we should go back?"

"No. They're probably gone now." Why hadn't I thought it before we walked home? We stopped outside the century-old two-story with my apartment.

She looked up the steps to my stoop. "We're already home anyway."

Bummer. "I thought he'd text back. Maybe he didn't get my message."

I followed Claire up the steps to my apartment and looked down on the crowded street. The change in altitude provided much-needed perspective and a bonus view of sailboats on the causeway. My nerves settled. The boats were graceful, skating on still waters. The tranquil scene was a perfect representation of island life: beautiful, peaceful and unchanging. I sighed. No matter what happened on land, fisherman never stopped hauling up nets of crabs and shrimp. The gentle waves never ceased to flap against weathered wooden hulls, and shadows of soaring seagulls forever shaded the daily catch as the birds searched for forgotten morsels on slick, water-soaked decks. The hoopla in town wouldn't last. Fans would head home after the memorial services and whatever else the reality show might have planned to exploit the untimely deaths of two young semi-celebrities.

My phone buzzed in my palm.

Claire peeked around me as I checked the screen. "Is that Fargas? What does it say?"

I placed a hand on my chest and cursed my shoddy nerves.

"Well?" Claire pressed.

"It's Sebastian." I opened the message. "He says to stay out of this murder investigation. Fargas and Frankie are fully capable of handling it on their own and I…"

"What? What was the rest?"

I vibrated my lips together. "I owe him a flashing. What is his problem?"

She shrugged. "Sounds like you owe him a flashing."

I angled in front of her on the tiny stoop and shoved my key in the lock. "What did Fargas do? Forward my text to Sebastian? That sheriff's a tattletale."

My front door swung inward before I turned the key. I screamed, threw my phone inside, and opened my arms to shield Claire from danger.

Adrian grabbed his forehead and danced from foot to foot inside my place. "Ow! You hit me with something. Why'd you do that?"

"I thought you were an intruder." I retrieved my phone and checked for damage. My bejeweled phone case could protect an egg going over Niagara Falls. "It's okay. It didn't break."

"Great. I'm not so sure about my head." Adrian went to the freezer and pressed a frozen bean burger patty to his forehead.

I examined the disaster I once called my living room. "What is all this?" I balled my fists. "What is happening in here?"

The couch, countertops, coffee table and floor were covered in Team Adrian posters and Vote for Davis signs. His mayoral campaign paraphernalia ran from one room to the next, and it was all topped with paper bags and boats of food truck food.

Adrian repositioned the burger on his head and looked at me with one eye. "I'm working."

"On what? A bigger belt size?"

A pastry box near the coffeepot caught my eye. Sophisticakes. The most delicious gourmet cupcakes in the country. No, the world. I never indulged. I couldn't afford a twelve-dollar cupcake habit. I still had a balance on my credit card from the brown leather riding boots I ordered online. Those boots had cost a lot of cupcakes.

Claire pushed a pile of food aside and sat on the couch. "I understand all the campaign gear, but I need help understanding all the food."

Adrian beamed. "I was multi-tasking. I visited all the local businesses, reminding fellow citizens about the upcoming election."

I unwrapped a pink Sophisticake with sugar crystals and red polka-dot icing.

Adrian smiled. "While I was on the campaign trail, I hit up all the food trucks and started a dialogue with the workers. I figure if anyone hears good gossip, it's people vending food. Right?" He cleared his throat. "Also, this is my island, and I think I should open a personal investigation into Rick and Anna's murder."

Icing fell off my lip. "You can't open a personal investigation." Sweet strawberry cupcake filled my mouth. I worked it down and licked my fingers, trying to concentrate on Adrian's bad idea. My eyelids fluttered in a successful pastry-gasm. I licked my lips. One down. Eleven to go.

Adrian bristled. "Why not?"

Can't had never been his favorite word. I'd shamelessly used that knowledge for years to get him to do things for me. Now I truly wanted him to *not* do this thing.

"Because you aren't an investigator. You are a very messy politician." I gathered bags of food from every flat surface in sight and piled them on my kitchen counter.

Claire turned to Adrian. "We're looking into this, too. Elisa is on the island with her boyfriend, Dan. Before the boyfriend showed up, Elisa confessed to sleeping with Rick and accused Anna of knowing Rick was already with Elisa."

He folded himself onto the floor beside the couch. "That's good stuff. You should tell Fargas. Elisa and her boyfriend both had motive to kill Rick. Anna might've been in the wrong place, if it was Dan on the other side of that gun. He must be mad at the guy who slept with his girlfriend. Elisa probably wanted them both dead."

"We already texted Fargas," Claire said. "Then, he tattled on us. Sebastian texted Patience to tell her to leave this alone."

"No." Adrian looked at me for confirmation.

"Yep."

Claire crossed her arms. "I'm certain those two were murdered because Rick was cheating. Love is dangerous. People shouldn't mess around with other people's emotions."

Adrian shook his head in disagreement. "Did you know the show's website says this island is haunted?

Mayor Hayes used local legends and folklore to entice
The Watchers to film here. I think the murders are tied
to all those ghost hunters out there trying to prove the
legends. Think about it. Fargas said they couldn't find
any fingerprints."

Silly. I licked frosting off my fingertips. "You think
a ghost did this?"

"No. I think someone wants it to look that way." A
crease formed between his eyes. "They didn't even get
the story right. The Island Comforts bed-and-breakfast isn't haunted. Miss Molly's bed-and-breakfast is
haunted."

I scoffed. "Nothing is haunted. I hope you have another theory."

"I do." His eyes twinkled. "Maybe one of your patients snapped."

He stared me down, daring me to argue or perhaps
announce which of my homicidal clients I suspected in
the murders.

"My clients—" I emphasized the word *clients*, not
patients, "—are not homicidal. This has nothing to do
with them or local legends. Though, I am pretty peeved
the mayor conspired to advertise our island as haunted.
Someone should revoke his admin privileges on our
website. Elisa's boyfriend named a bunch of websites
touting Chincoteague as some kind of ghost hunting
treasure trove and the hype is sending boatloads of ghost
hunters here. He also said *The Watchers* are promoting
the idea, no doubt to fuel interest in their Halloween
special. The whole ghost angle is a mess, but this isn't
about ghosts. This is about money. How can either of you
overlook the two-hundred-fifty-thousand-dollar reward
so easily? This is definitely about money."

"Love," Claire corrected.

Adrian shook his head. "Nope. I say legends or insanity."

I ground my teeth. The hubbub outside my apartment was bad enough. Arguing in my living room made me twitchy. I lifted the pastry box lid and liberated another Sophisticake. I passed it under my nose and groaned. The soft scents of apples and cinnamon intoxicated me. My toes curled in my boots. "This is an apple pie cupcake." I sniffed again. "It's brilliant. The baker is a genius. It's like a fritter and a pie wrapped inside a cute pink-striped paper and topped with icing." I stuck my fingertip into the cinnamon sprinkled icing.

Claire pulled her feet onto the couch beside her, shuffling posters and campaign buttons as she moved. "If you eat another cupcake, you might need to reconsider the marathon."

I sucked icing off my finger and put the Sophisticake down.

Adrian rubbed his palms together. "Let's investigate together. I've got a head start on you two, but you're smart girls. You can catch up."

Claire bounced a Vote for Davis button off his chest. "Don't call us girls. We are women, and you're darn skippy we're smart. Who do you think you're talking to? Your overconfidence is unappealing, you know that? You're a hottie until you talk."

Adrian beamed.

I moved closer to my friends before anything else was thrown. "Sweetie, that was an insult."

Adrian kept his eyes on Claire. "She said I'm sexy and confident. That's two compliments."

Claire guffawed. "Fine. I'm in. I bet I can figure out what happened to Rick and Anna before you."

"Deal. I know you have an advantage with Fargas, but I like a challenge." He waved off the point in her favor.

"You're obnoxious." Claire stood, hands braced over her hips. "How does Fargas give me an advantage in that pinhead of yours?" Her coy smile said she had an idea.

I'd like those details, but this wasn't the time.

Adrian tipped his head back and laughed. He walked to her side and wrapped an arm over her shoulders. "How about we work this case together." He held a fist in front of her, waiting for a bump.

She bumped her tiny fist against his giant one and looked at me. "Get over here, Patience. We know *The Watchers*, and you know how people think. Let's find out what really happened last night."

I took a baby step back. "No thanks." I had a horrendous track record where my curiosity was concerned. In other words, I found dead bodies and got abducted and or shot at.

I posed an alternative. "What if you meet back here to exchange information and bounce ideas off one another after work?" A double win for me. I didn't want to be alone so soon after a double homicide, and Sebastian had a history of working all-nighters. Plus, I was a little curious what they'd uncover.

Claire dropped back onto the couch and patted the space beside her for Adrian. "I took the rest of the week off. I have until Monday to dig up the details. Let's make a plan."

Adrian swung his keys around a pointed finger. "I have a cot at my house. I'll go get it first. You can take the couch and I'll sleep on the cot in my office downstairs. You two want to come with me? We can set up our theories on the way."

"Sure." Claire and I agreed.

I opened the door. "You know a real investigator isn't supposed to have a theory. They're supposed to follow the clues. Theories can bias the investigation."

"No. You're supposed to make a hypothesis and try to prove it."

Claire grabbed her clutch and walked outside. "You're thinking of scientists, except they try to disprove the theory."

Adrian passed her on the steps. "Why would I want to prove myself wrong?"

I locked up behind them.

"Because you can't prove a theory. You can only support it." Claire crossed the short lawn at the bottom of my steps. "It's science."

Adrian caught up to her. "That's dumb. That's not what I'm doing."

"I know. That's what I said."

I paced my strides behind them, enjoying the beautiful fall day and the joy of amazing friends. The horn honking had died to a minimum. Most cars were parked, their owners probably having given up on using the streets. Why wait at the town's only stoplight when there were plenty of bicycles and feet for transportation. If I concentrated, I could still smell brine and salt in the air. Some things were unshakable.

The walk to Adrian's house was short, like the walk to anything in Chincoteague. He lived in an outrageously oversized house on the marsh, with seven bedrooms, two fireplaces and a fancy marble shower I dreamed about. His family owned and operated one of the largest frozen seafood operations in the country. Adrian was the only heir, but that didn't stop him from working hard and choosing a simple life on Chincoteague when he could easily live anywhere.

Before Adrian's big wraparound porch came into view, a cluster of men in shirts with *The Watchers* logo stopped us in the street. They were carrying boom mics and cameras.

A guy no taller than Claire, sporting a blue Mohawk, stopped us. "Sorry. We're filming. You can take the alley to the next main road and head back to Front Street that way."

Adrian pulled out his identification. "I'm Adrian Davis. This is my house. We won't be long. I just need to grab something from storage."

I leaned against Claire to whisper, "When did all these workers get here?"

The little guy radioed in our request to enter, and we waited in awkward silence for approval to disturb "the set" with our civilian presence. The walkie-talkie chirped on his hip a few minutes later.

A voice buzzed across the line. "All clear. Send him in, Noah."

I'd always liked the name Noah, but I'd never imagined meeting a Noah with a blue Mohawk.

We followed Adrian to his front door and slipped inside. A woman with a clipboard shushed us in the entranceway. In the next room, a pair of women in black cargo pants and matching shirts crept across the carpet with their backs to an enormous green screen. Their images projected onto several monitors behind the camera, where a man sat, rubbing his mustache, in a chair marked Short. On the monitors, the women weren't inching through Adrian's living room. They were in a dark cave with black glistening walls, where water dripped from the ceiling. I shivered and willed the cupcakes to stay put. My last visit to a cave hadn't gone well.

"I don't understand." Why were they taping? It was

as if no one cared about Rick and Anna. Not a single face showed concern for their deaths.

A round of hushes rose behind me.

One of the women on screen stopped to don a pair of night vision goggles and recount the island legend of the ghost pony. The ghost pony was a children's story meant to endear local children to the wild ponies roaming our island, but it had backfired on me. It terrified me. I was thirty and the ponies still scared the bejesus out of me.

I turned to the clipboard lady. "Why would the ghost pony be in a cave?"

"Shh."

"Isn't the point of being a wild pony that you can run free?"

Several people turned our way. "Shh."

On the monitors, a wavy image appeared behind the women. The waves morphed into a translucent white pony, and the hair on my arms stood on end.

I moved to Adrian's kitchen for a drink of water. That green screen was creepy. I wasn't waiting to see what other horrors it conjured. My throat thickened and heat rose up my neck. My phone rang and I jumped. Dumb ghost pony.

The screen announced the caller—Camo, my code name for Sebastian. "Hello?" I fanned my face. The bureau called him a chameleon because he could blend in anywhere. He'd closed more undercover cases than anyone else while I worked there.

"Hey, boss. Everything okay?" His familiar tenor sent goose bumps over my arms.

"Yeah. We're at Adrian's. Can you believe *The Watchers* are still here? The house is full, and they're taping a scene in the living room. It's disgusting. How can they just pretend those deaths never happened?"

"I don't know. Money, probably."

"Sick." Money motivated everything.

"Are you going to be okay if I'm out late? You sound upset. If Adrian tries to comfort you, don't let him. That's a politician move."

I smiled. "Don't worry. Claire took the rest of the week off work to stay with me. She's dying to know what happened." I cringed. *Terrible word choice.* "Adrian brought us here to get a cot. Claire's going to sleep on the couch. He's going to stay downstairs in his office."

"My day just got brighter."

"Were you having a bad day?"

He groaned. "I haven't slept. We can't get a finger on Jimmy the Judge's whereabouts. We receive rumors and anonymous tips, but nothing pans out." Fatigue saturated his words. "The longer he's out of our sight, the more likely he won't be back anytime soon. When he does come around again, it'll be on his terms and not in cuffs like he deserves. It's like trying to catch vapor."

"Come to my place tonight. Get some rest. Start again tomorrow with a fresh mind. He won't know you took the night off."

"I can't take that chance. Listen, I've got to go. Hang in there. Tell Claire I'm glad she chased the politician off your couch."

"Sebastian." I pulled in a breath to settle my thoughts. "Sebastian?" I turned the phone in my hand for a look at the screen. Disconnected. He was gone.

I stuffed the phone into my pocket and grabbed a glass from the cabinet. Adrian's sink was perfect, like the rest of the house. Shiny, new and cleaner than a real Hollywood set. I tested the water temperature with a finger and shoved my glass under the faucet. Outside the window, a line of people laughed and kicked a beanbag. They wore ghost hunter shirts and giant crucifixes. Most had a line of strange-looking apparatuses hooked to oversized tool belts.

A voice bellowed, "Cut," from the living room.

Cast and crew moved down the hall toward me. The rolling cloud of black shirts filled every inch of space around Adrian's kitchen island. They flipped open a stack of pizza boxes on the counter and hauled slices of leftovers to their lips. Claire and Adrian rode on the heels of the man from the chair marked Short.

"How many episodes will you tape? Claire asked. "Will you stay for Halloween?"

The man chuckled, basking in the attention. "Four or five episodes, I think, and two specials. The Halloween party will be the event of the century. We'll go out with a bang for the midseason break."

I set the glass in Adrian's sink and met the trio near the archway to the dining room.

"Patience Price." I extended a hand.

He wrapped his clammy fingers around mine and pumped gently. "Jesse Short. I'm the show's producer."

I frowned. "You're staying here after what happened? Why aren't you packing up and going home? What about the funerals? Doesn't the cast need time to mourn? Two of their friends died last night."

Jesse placed a palm over my shoulder and tilted his head like a puppy trying to understand humanspeak. "Honey, this is show business. The show always goes on. Besides, Rick would want it this way. He taped every aspect of his life. That man lived on camera. This is for him." He lifted one hand into the air. "Now, if you'll excuse me, I have to run lines with Elisa." He ducked through the archway and took the back stairs to the second floor.

Excitement rolled off Claire in waves. "I can't believe we're on set at *The Watchers*." She smacked Adrian's chest. "*The Watchers* live at your house."

Adrian watched me. "You don't look well. Was it the ghost pony?"

My gaze snapped to his. "No."

Claire edged closer. "Is it Sebastian? Everything okay with him?"

I leaned against the wall, processing. "He's trying to find Jimmy the Judge. He didn't sound like he planned on coming back tonight."

Claire rubbed my back. She worried about him too. Jimmy the Judge was notorious and landing on his hit list usually ended with a funeral.

Adrian snaked an arm around my waist. "I know what will cheer you up. Let's go see the Halloween decorations in the trailer outside."

"Okay." We moved through the rooms together, with Claire leading the way. I didn't care about Halloween decorations, but I needed a distraction. Whatever was in the trailer, it was nowhere near as scary as the thought of Jimmy the Judge finding Sebastian.

SIX

ADRIAN AND CLAIRE borrowed a black logoed golf cart from a line of *The Watchers* vehicles in his drive. Claire drove and Adrian did his best to keep the folded cot from bouncing off. Even folded, the cot was much too large for the little cart. Claire honked on her way past. I waved them off and walked home, taking side streets to avoid most of the food trucks and ghost hunters. From the corner of Colt Court, a banner became visible over Main Street, only a few blocks away. Another black canvas with *The Watchers* logo and a pair of giant creepy white eyes. The eyes were everywhere. Something moved in my periphery, and I looked over my shoulder. A man across the street turned his head away when our eyes met. As if on cue, cool wind whipped through my shirt and I picked up the pace. Living on an island had never seemed so much like living in a fishbowl.

I darted across the street, eager for anonymity in the crowd. Pretty fall displays adorned the storefronts on Main Street. Shop owners had anchored Vote for Davis and Vote for Thompson signs in scarecrow hands and hay bales outside their windows. Giant pumpkins and cornstalks gave our island a fun Midwestern touch, despite waves breaking in the distance. I examined the signs. The election was ten days away, and most islanders were keeping their votes a secret. No one dared display one sign without the other. No favoritism among family. Except me. I displayed my Vote for Davis poster in every window and wore my button anytime I suspected I might run into his competition, or the competition's fiancé, my high school nemesis, Karen Holsten. Karen and I were both planning big victory dinners for our candidates. Unfortunately, Karen's dinner would be a consolation dinner but, in case that made her sad, I had invitations to Adrian's dinner printed for her and her fiancé.

If Adrian somehow lost to Beau Thompson, Karen would gloat for eternity, so that couldn't happen. I rolled my shoulders and stretched my neck from side to side. I had campaign stress, too.

"Patience."

I turned in search of the voice.

"Patience Price."

Adrian's mom shoved her way through a cluster of people carrying shopping bags and food truck food. She waved her hands overhead and puffed clouds of steam into the chilled autumn air. Whoa. I squeezed my eyes shut and reopened them. Her hair had tripled in length since last week, and she'd pinned and sprayed the lot of it into a giant pageant-perfect bouffant. The wigs from *Hairspray* came to mind. Instead of her usual too-tight tops and skinny jeans, she'd squeezed her curvy woman-sized figure into a tiny junior-sized sequin minidress. Her ankles wobbled with every hurried step on four-inch heels.

"Hi, Mrs. Davis." I ran through a mental list of what she could possibly want. Historically, she only sought me out to yell at me, and she'd never looked so happy to see me. Also, why on earth was she blond?

"How are you, sweetie?"

Uh-oh. Sweetie?

"Good." I dragged the word out a few syllables, still calculating her angle.

"I'm so glad I found you. Did Adrian have a chance to talk with you?" Her eager eyes widened, shoving the tips of giant false eyelashes into her eyebrows.

"No. What's going on? Why are you dressed for prom?"

She swatted my arm. "Silly. I had an Extreme Island Makeover." She placed her hands on her waist and turned on her heels, giving me a three-sixty view.

"Pretty." I scanned the street for help. A hundred faces, and I didn't recognize a single one.

"It's my new business. Extreme Island Makeovers." She moved her palms from shoulders to hips, outlining her body. Her congenial smile vanished. "Well?"

"Um. Cool?" She wanted something from me. I just hadn't put my finger on it yet. I shifted my weight foot to foot.

She huffed. "Adrian was supposed to talk to you for me. I want you to be the face of my business. You're still young. Well, you look young and everyone loves you. If you get an Extreme Island Makeover, people will be lining up for theirs. You're a marketer's dream. With the island princess as the face of my business, I can't lose."

I took a big step sideways, clearing a path for my escape. "I don't know, Mrs. Davis. I'm not a princess, and I'm not sure I'm an Extreme Island Makeover kind of girl. I've got the whole girl-next-door thing working for me. I like cute shoes and casual wear. I can't..." I motioned to her dress, which reflected rainbows of sunlight onto the sidewalk. "I'm..." *Sweating.* I tugged my shirt collar. Did it get hot outside? "I'm not sure that look is something I can pull off."

"What if I offer packages? I could have a girl-next-door option."

I had a strong feeling all options would come with a spray tan, too much rouge and a Bumpit. "How about I promise to think about it, have that talk with Adrian and get back with you?" Never-ever.

"Yes! Thank you so much. You won't regret it." She put her arms in the air and shouted. "The new face of Extreme Island Makeovers!"

I shook my head behind her back and moved into the throngs of sidewalk shoppers. Good grief. I hid in the nook between the bay windows at Half Baked and texted Adrian a hate mail.

Knock! Knock! Knock!

"Gah!" I spun around, clutching the phone to my body. My friend and sometime client, Missy, waved cheerfully through the window. She shoved the door open and pulled me inside. "What're you doing out there? You look like you're hiding."

"I was."

She giggled and pulled out a chair at the nearest table. "Sit. Can I get you something?"

"Water." My throat was thick and dry from the scary sequined encounter. Her offer was generous, but also an Extreme Island Nightmare. She hated me already, so I shouldn't care if she finally had a reason to be unhappy with me, but I was torn. If I had a way to please her for the first time in my life, I kind of wanted it.

Missy went to the counter and I finished my text rant to Adrian. She returned with a tray, one bottle of water, two hot chocolates and two puffed pastries. "You said water, but I heard 'comfort foods.'"

"I love you." I dipped a spoon into the hot chocolate and scooped a bit of whipped cream off the top. "Mmm."

"Who were you hiding from?" Missy pressed the tines of a fork into one flaky pastry.

"Mrs. Davis."

She smiled.

My turn for questions. "Okay. I have two things I'm dying to say to you. First, how did the island's busiest caterer end up on phone duty at the police station every afternoon? Second, Sugar and Spice Catering is a total hit. Congratulations. This is so exciting."

"To answer your first question, Frankie's a policeman." She clapped her hands. "Can you believe it? When she told me they needed help covering the receptionist position because she's a new cop, I jumped in to help. When I told Melinda, she said she'd split the hours with me. Team work. And thank you. We're blown away with all the kind words and massive orders. I'm so glad you suggested this business for us."

I sipped the rich, buttery chocolate and relaxed. "How can you keep up with everything?"

"I get help." She winked and pointed a thumb in the direction of the Half Baked display case. "Half Baked splits some of the orders for baked goods with us when we get behind. We're supplying a ton of food to *The Watchers*, so that's fun. Who'd ever have thought a television show would come to our island?" She folded her hands and straightened her posture. "You think one of these young ghost hunters is single and loves big dogs?"

I laughed. "Definitely."

Missy lost her tiny teacup doggie, Mr. Tiptoes, in July. She'd overcompensated by replacing him last month with a hippopotamus posing as a puppy. No chance of misplacing that pooch.

Maple Shuster, the island gossip, and her crew poured in, forcing the line from the register to bend through the tables. A reporter wearing an oversized press badge took notes as they spoke.

"I grew up on tales of island wraiths and specters," Maple said, continuing her story in progress.

Her friends nodded, adding support phrases like, "Oh, my, yes." And "we certainly did."

The reporter scratched a pen over his notebook. "Have any of you ever seen a ghost or apparition?"

The line edged forward, and their group scooted along, filling in the new space between them and the register. Maple turned to keep pace with her friends. Her mouth stopped moving. She lifted a finger toward Missy and me. "Patience Price. That's the lady you need to interview. She lives in a building that's haunted. No one lived in her apartment for decades and things were quiet. Then she moved in a few months ago, and the whole town went crazy. Since she came home in July, people have been dying. Murders. Car bombs. Explosions. There was even a shark infestation last month."

Good grief. I didn't cause any of those things, especially not the sharks.

The reporter raised his eyebrows. "So, you're telling me this lady, Patience Price—" he scribbled on his paper, "—moved home and people started dying?"

Well, that sounded awful. "I think that's my cue," I whispered to Missy.

She moved her chair out of my way and I ducked out the front door.

"Hey," Missy called after me.

I motioned for her to follow, and we slipped inside Island Brew, the local coffee shop next door.

My heart hammered. "That was a close one. That reporter probably thinks I'm a psychopath."

Missy peeked through the window. "I don't think he

followed us. Hey, I wanted to ask about your costume for the secret Halloween party."

"What secret party?"

She rolled her eyes. "It's okay. I already know about it."

"Humor me."

"*The Watchers* are having this epic masquerade ball on Halloween. It's supposed to be a secret, but someone leaked it online. The website pulled it down a few minutes later, but it was too late. Word is out. I bet people will fly in from everywhere that day. I need a Watchers-worthy costume, but all my ideas are lame. Claire said she has the perfect thing in mind. Do you know what it is?"

"Claire's going?" Wait. Of course, Claire was going. "I don't think I'm going."

"You have to. You can't miss something this huge happening right here in town. Nothing happens here. This is a do-not-miss event."

"I'll think about it." I examined the giant chalkboard behind the counter. I'd left Half Baked without finishing my hot chocolate. "I'm going to get a latte. Can I get you one?"

"No. I have to get back. My popovers should be ready by now." Missy opened the door and Coach Peters walked in. She gave me a little wave and bustled onto the sidewalk, clutching her sweater around her waist.

A local teen behind the counter took orders while another worked the espresso machine and toppings buffet. Whipped cream and caramel sauce hung in the air. I inhaled scents of the heavenly aromas of vanilla and hazelnut. My mouth watered and my tummy groaned.

Coach Peters got in line behind me. "Can I buy you a coffee?"

"Sure." Buying me coffee was Coach's code for needing a few minutes to talk.

Ten years ago, he was my swim and track coach. I tried not to think about how many times he'd seen me kissing Adrian.

We collected our drinks from the massive mahogany counter and sat at a table in the corner farthest from the door.

I started the conversation. "How are you doing? Anything new?"

He rubbed his bald head. "I've got to be honest. I'm struggling. The election's coming fast and I've got a mint riding on Davis." He wrung his hands together. "My wife's ready to leave me. If I lose, I'm toast. I need help."

My heart crumbled. "What happened? You were doing so well."

"It's all the damn campaign signs. It's like Vegas out there right now. Pick your player. Bet on Thompson. Put your money on Davis. They're taking bets on every corner. How can I resist? I know Davis's going to win. He can't lose. He's the island golden boy."

Wow. "That's not the point. Beating this thing is about focus. Remember? We talked about this. You have to weigh the urge to bet with its importance in your life. Do you really care who wins the election? No. Do you care about your marriage, mental health and financial stability? Yes. You have to make the best choices for you and your family for the long-term. Betting lasts a second. The repercussions last a lifetime."

He slouched in his chair, defeated. "I know."

"Look." I laid my palm on his sleeve. "I had a really smart coach back in high school and he taught me to never give up. It's not over until you're dead, and I can still see you breathing."

"Yeah?"

"Yeah. I want you to think of your addiction in a new way. Consider yourself in the long distance marathon of recovery. When you think of yourself as an addict, you put on the attitude of defeat. Then what happens?"

He smiled, tugging his sleeves and adjusting the varsity football jacket on his shoulders. He'd encouraged me to keep going countless times with those same words, and I'd listened. I survived high school, miles of track and endless waves on those words. He looked hopeful. "You remember that speech?"

I locked my gaze on his. "I do. Do you?"

"Yeah. You put on the attitude of defeat and you get defeated. You think like a champion and you win."

"What about if you screw up?"

He chuckled. "You screw up. You get up. You dust off and get back in the game."

"What're you going to do, Coach?"

He slid his chair back and patted the tabletop. "I'm getting back in the game. I'm not an addict. I'm a champion running the marathon of recovery."

"Is it a sprint?"

He swallowed and nodded. "No. This one's forever." He reached into his pocket and retrieved a silver money clip. A pair of crisp fifties fell from the fold. He slid them under the edge of my cup.

I stood beside him. "It doesn't matter who wins the election. Whatever happens, keep your eye on the ball. Right now isn't important. Your goal is way down field." I hoped that was enough sports references to motivate a coach. Hopefully I didn't mess them up.

He slapped my back. "Thanks, Patience. Tell your boy to make sure he wins."

I flopped into my chair as he exited the building. My

head fell against the table. Longest day of my life, and it wasn't even noon.

The heavy wooden chair across from me scraped over the hard tile floor. "Patience Price. I hear you're a closet killer, an undercover psychopath and possibly possessed by the ghost haunting your apartment."

I moaned. "I'm an undercover psychologist. Not an undercover psychopath." I raised my gaze to the man before me.

It was the reporter from outside the Tasty Cream. Todd something. His lips lifted. "Really? That's the correction you want to make?" Beneath the smile was a bright blue shirt with white block letters: Reporters Do It on Camera.

"I see you've met my parents."

He brushed invisible lint off the shirt. "Yep. You like the shirt? I think it's quite clever."

"Very." My rebuttal was lost. The man I'd caught watching me on the street entered the shop and looked my way.

He snapped a picture of Todd and me then took a direct path to our table. "You're Patience Price?"

"Yes." I glanced at Todd. Todd looked entertained, but the men didn't seem to know one another.

I cleared my head of thoughts either man might be stalking me. "Have we met?"

"No. I've heard a lot about you, though." The guy's thick Boston accent sounded more out of place than anything I'd heard all day. "I hear you have quite an interesting history here."

Todd chuckled. "I heard she put an old lady in jail this summer."

My throat constricted. That happened a week ago and I wasn't ready to discuss it.

Todd tapped his thumbs against the tabletop, probably hoping for details about the old lady. I waited to hear whatever this new guy wanted. The man had a top-of-the-line camera on a strap around his shoulder. We bought the same ones for tactical teams at the FBI. Reporters didn't make that kind of money, so this guy must be paparazzi. Paparazzi made a year's salary off one picture of the right celebrity in the wrong position. They did despicable things to photograph private moments and ruin reputations. On further inspection, the differences between Todd's ten-dollar shirt and this guy's dress shirt and slacks was astounding.

I pointed to his shoes. "Are those John Lobb loafers? Who'd you shoot to get those?"

A grimace chased shock across his face, twisting his features in a knot. "What are you sayin'?"

"Just that you're a drain on humanity, but you've heard that before. You say paparazzi. I say go home." I clamped a hand over my mouth. Dang it. My big mouth was a curse I lived with. Most of the time I had control over what popped out. At the moment, I blamed my level of discomfort.

He snorted and pressed a twenty on the table. "Yeah. I'm a rich parasite. We can talk later. Until then, buy yourself a haircut."

I smoothed a hand over my windblown hair.

Todd turned in his seat to watch the guy leave. "Well, he was weird."

Frustration from a day made of suck bubbled in my chest. "I've got to go." I jumped to my feet and stuffed the coach's fifties in my pocket. I dropped the meanie's twenty into the tip jar on the counter. Emotion welled in my eyes. I had more on my mind than I could process in an overcrowded coffee shop.

"Wait." Todd followed me to the door. "I want to talk with you."

"Not today."

I hustled around the corner and down my street, praying Claire and Adrian were gone when I got to my apartment. I needed a few minutes alone. Some creep had insulted my hair for absolutely no reason. Sebastian was chasing a crazed mobster. *The Watchers* were staying through Halloween. At least one reporter thought I was a killer. Someone else said I was possessed and, at the moment, I couldn't argue because the next person to ambush me for random conversation was guaranteed an earful.

SEVEN

I FLOPPED ONTO my couch and stared at the ceiling. Something niggled in my mind without coming straight out where I could grab it. I peeled a brown banana and contemplated hypnosis as a way of wrenching the wiggly little thought free. The soft spotted fruit didn't appeal. I cracked the top portion off and examined it for bruising. Pass. I hoisted my body off the couch and went to the kitchen, wrapped the banana in plastic wrap and put it in the refrigerator for later. Maybe with yogurt at breakfast.

The steps to my apartment creaked and rattled as my friends returned with heavy laden arms. I unlocked the door. Adrian and Claire hauled in a box of food truck food and a bevy of new theories. I sampled kabobs while they carried all the campaign gear from my living room to Adrian's office downstairs and hashed out what they'd learned from *The Watchers* staff and miscellaneous fans outside Adrian's home on the marsh. In my opinion, all the new information fell into one of three categories: nonsense, hearsay or hooey. When they put in a DVD from season three, I took a nap.

I dreamed of running for my life in a darkened forest, only to have the scenery ripped away from me when the camera stopped rolling and a green screen reappeared behind me. What a mean trick to play on someone. Tiny cameras captured my response from every angle—wide eyes, pink cheeks, labored breaths. Adrian's house was wired to catch every whisper and secret moment. Rick liked it. I imagined lifting my phone to call Sebastian, but the world froze before me. I couldn't dial. Couldn't breathe. Jimmy the Judge's smile registered in a darkened corner of my mind. I broke free of his spell and dialed Sebastian, and heard a ringing nearby. Jimmy raised his palm to reveal Sebastian's phone. What had he done to Sebastian?

"Patience!" Thundering voices bore down on me.

"Ahh!" I shot upright, clutching the sheet to my chest.

Adrian wielded a baseball bat on one shoulder.

Claire pressed her palm to my cheek. "Shh." She stroked my hair.

Adrian kicked the closet door open and pushed his bat into my clothes. He turned and looked out my window.

I rubbed the haze from my eyes and focused on settling my wild breathing. "What are you doing?"

Adrian rested the bat on the floor like a cane. "You screamed."

Oh. I tried to remember. Something in my dream. My mind grappled with the memory as it turned to mist. "I had a bad dream."

Adrian exhaled audibly and hoisted the bat back onto his shoulder. "You want coffee?"

I nodded.

Claire gave me a weary look and stood. "You sure you're okay? You haven't been yourself lately." She shook her head. "You've been through a lot these last few months. Maybe you should try to get some more rest."

Too late. The dream plowed into me like a runaway train. I swung my legs over the bed's edge and grabbed my phone from the nightstand. "What time is it?" The room was darker than I'd expected. "How long was I in here?"

"All day."

I texted Sebastian a hurried message. We needed to talk right away.

Claire headed for the kitchen. "Come on. We've got every kind of food you can imagine out here. We finished season three of *The Watchers* and we've made a list of suspects on our theory board."

"Your what?" I shuffled behind her and stopped at the threshold to my living room. A giant white board on wheels stood along one wall. Colored Post-it notes and printed articles covered half the board, along with photographs of the cast members I recognized from Adrian's house.

Adrian hummed as the coffee percolated. "Hungry?"

I groaned.

He carried a mug of coffee to me and nodded at the board. He folded his arms over his chest. "I think we've got a strong start."

"Yep." I accepted the coffee. "Thanks."

My phone buzzed with a response text from Sebastian. He was already on his way back to the island. Thank goodness. I shoved the phone into my pocket.

Claire picked up the television remote and looked expectantly at me. "Are you ready for season four, or do you want us to start over with the pilot episode?"

Adrian handed me a notepad and pen. "You can take notes on anything you think needs exploring further. We're looking for clues that suggest how long the affairs were going on and if anyone else on the show was sleeping with Rick…or Anna."

I set the pad and pen on my coffee table and wrapped both hands around the mug. "I'm not quite awake. I think I'll enjoy this coffee and wait on Sebastian outside. You can catch me up on that later tonight." I tipped my head, indicating the rainbow-colored theory board.

By the time Sebastian's Range Rover appeared at the curb outside my place, I'd had three cups of coffee and an endless supply of adrenaline coursed through me. Freud, my little gray kitty, lolled on my lap, purring and cleaning his mittens. Something Jesse Short, the producer, had said worked its way into my thoughts. It was all I could do to stay seated. Curiosity tugged at every fiber in my body and my knee bounced wildly.

Sebastian beeped his doors locked and took the steps two at a time to greet me. "What's up, boss?" He turned and planted himself next to me on the stoop, scooping Freud onto his lap. "You're going to give him Shaken Kitty Syndrome with that bouncing leg of yours." He nuzzled Freud and scratched behind his ears.

I put my empty mug behind me and folded my fingers together. My lips were sore and dry from biting them. "Claire and Adrian have started investigating Rick and Anna's deaths. Their fandom for this show is crazy. Beatlemania crazy."

Sebastian huffed and twisted at the waist, squinting through my front window.

"Wait." I took his hands. "I had to tell you because they're making a crime scene board in the living room, but I want to talk with you before you go inside."

His focus snapped back to me. "Are you okay?"

I pulled in a long breath and swallowed. "I'm trying amazingly hard to listen to you this time and stay out of the investigation. I don't want to get involved and make trouble for you or incite another killer. I truly don't."

His expression darkened. "But."

I nodded. "But... I can't get something out of my head and it's making me so crazy I dreamed about it. I wanted to go and look on my own, but I didn't want to mess up the crime scene, and the last time I told Fargas anything about the case, he tattled on me and you told me to leave it alone."

Sebastian's eyes twinkled with emotion for a moment before he shut it down. His blank expression returned, extinguishing the tiny glimpse of boyfriend material behind dark, hooded, special agent eyes. "Tell me."

"When we were at Adrian's today, I met Jesse Short."

"The producer."

"Right. I asked him why they'd continue taping here after what had happened only twelve hours earlier. I mean, that's awful. Right?"

"Did you hit him?"

"What? No." I made my best crazy face. "Of course I didn't hit him."

"Did something blow up? Catch fire? Break in an explosive fashion? Was an ambulance necessary for anyone in the vicinity?"

Sure, I'd faced a few calamities in the past three months, but it wasn't like trouble followed me.

I glared at his handsome face. "Are you insinuating something, Agent Clark?"

"Just wondering how much cover-up work is required to keep you out of jail this time."

A smile cracked my expression. "Stop that. Will you please listen?"

He lowered Freud into his lap and curved his free arm around my shoulders. "Go on."

Freud rolled around a minute, looking for the sweet spot on Sebastian's legs, and resumed purring.

"Jesse said Rick lived on camera. He said Rick taped every aspect of his life, and he'd want the show to go on. Could he mean that? Did Rick literally tape every aspect of his life?"

Sebastian put Freud on the stoop and took my hand.

"You're a gorgeous genius. If Jesse's right, Rick Fitzgerald could have taped his own death." Sebastian kissed
my knuckles. "Let's go find out."

We took the Range Rover to the bed-and-breakfast.
Sebastian handed me a pair of medical gloves and told
me to limit what I touched in case the crime scene team
needed to come back. Mrs. Moore let us into Sebastian's room, though he still had a key. She smelled less
like Chantilly and more like blackberry brandy than I
remembered.

Sebastian went to work looking for a hidden video
camera. The crime scene crew had swept the room for
clues but hadn't looked for a hidden sex-camera. I lifted
a black light from Sebastian's duffle and moved it over
everything out of curiosity. Fingerprint dust was everywhere.

"Bingo." Sebastian reached toward the ceiling fan and
removed a little camera. He dropped it into a plastic evidence bag and winked. "You're brilliant and beautiful."

It was true. "He might've taped his own murder."

Sebastian stopped at the door and stared at the light
switch before tossing me a quizzical look. "Let's hope
this camera had night vision. The switches were off
when Adrian got here."

"Can I watch the video with you? How good is the
camera? Is it like a nanny cam from Radio Shack or
something sophisticated like we use at the bureau?" I
stumbled on the word "use." It'd been a few months
since the FBI downsized me, but I worked there for several years, and I'd expected to work there many more.

"This one's high end, but basic. It might be something
they use for his show."

Mrs. Moore was asleep in her recliner when we got
back downstairs. Sebastian covered her with an af-

ghan and whispered good-night. No sense in waking her. She'd looked half-tanked when we arrived. Self-medicating or not, I couldn't have stayed there alone at the B&B now. She was too stubborn to stay more than one night at Mrs. Tucker's, I guessed. Kudos to her. There wasn't enough booze on earth to convince me to stay in this place alone after what had happened upstairs.

We locked up when we left. I made a mental note to come visit Mrs. Moore soon and keep tabs on how she dealt with things in the coming weeks. Whoever killed Rick and Anna also hurt Mrs. Moore. I wasn't sure she'd recover anytime soon from the trauma, and her business might suffer, too. As far as I knew, renting rooms in her home was her only source of income. A vicious cycle of pain caused by someone she'd probably never met.

Sebastian held the passenger door of his Range Rover open for me.

He slid behind the wheel and started the engine. "Good job, boss."

I played with the corner of the evidence baggie. "Can I watch it?"

"No."

"What? Why?"

"I'm turning this over to Fargas and letting him handle it. He's a good cop, Patience. Trust him. I do." He squeezed my fingers and pulled my hand onto his thigh. "Be happy."

I tried to pull my hand free and failed. The corner of his mouth hitched up.

"I don't see why I can't know what's on the tape."

He kissed my knuckles and returned them to his lap. "Leave this alone now."

The view through his windshield was ominous but lovely. The sun had settled in for the night, but the moon had yet to make an appearance. As a result, the sky resembled an angry bruise. Sebastian passed the turn for the police station and drove into the national park. He hopped out and swiped his special card through the slot beside the guard gate. The striped lever rose. Sebastian had acquired the special law enforcement pass in July when he saved me from an arms dealer and pony killer. I didn't blame him for hanging on to the pass. Having a guard gate key for after-hours in the national forest was like having the key to Oz. No one passed the guard booth at night unless they were willing to leave their car to do it. No one except us.

I smiled. "Where are we going?"

"I wanted a few minutes alone before we head back for a slumber party with your buddies."

The Range Rover wound down the inky forest road. Headlights illuminated the road in a minimal-view, eighties-horror-movie way. Reflections of green eyes blinked in the trees around us. I kept a vigilant watch for ponies. Shades of lavender and gray ran together over the horizon, underscored by the occasional hooting owl and crashing waves as we neared the beach. Wind beat against the car, whistling through the air vents and sending shivers down my spine. Autumn storms were powerful on the island and one loomed over us, darkening the night.

Sebastian parked in the beach lot and shut down the engine. He rubbed his thumb in soft circles over my hand. His eyes widened as clouds race through the sky.

"Storm's coming," I said.

"Yeah." His voice was thick with emotion. He turned his sexy eyes on me. "I'm proud of you. I have no right to be. You're not mine to claim, but I'm proud anyway. I know how strong your curiosity is and I know how hard it must've been for you to wait on me when your friends would've loved to have this." He lifted the evidence bag between us and dropped it onto the backseat. "You trusted me to listen to you and follow through on your hunch. It means a lot to me." He turned in his seat, unhooked my seat belt and dragged me onto his lap. "You mean a lot to me."

Sebastian's lips met mine with fire. He cradled my head and deepened the kiss immediately. I melted into him, sliding my hands over his shoulders and knotting my fingers in his hair. I inhaled the spicy scents of cinnamon and cologne unique to him, memorizing the texture of his shirt and tracing the muscles in his arms, chest and abdomen. Sebastian wasn't perfect, and I loved that about him. He was guarded and distant, but those traits probably kept him alive more times than I could guess, so I appreciated them. I'd known he was different the moment I met him. That rare mix of scary and comforting, like the first time someone says they love you and you're overjoyed they feel the same but terrified of what it means. Being with Sebastian was like my first time on water skis, exhilarating and worth the pain from the inevitable fall. I let his words inflate my heart.

My head dropped back as he tossed my shirt into the passenger seat and ran soft lips over my throat and collarbone. A low growl rolled up from his chest and I was undone. The stress of my day fell away. The world shrunk until there was only the night, the ocean and us. Sebastian's shirt met mine on the passenger seat and it was my turn to growl.

EIGHT

I SLEPT TEN hours and woke with a smile. Sunlight streamed through my window, showcasing dust motes in flight. I stretched and twisted under the sheets. Everything smelled like Sebastian. I pressed my arm against my face. Even my skin smelled like him. I swung my legs over the bed's edge and reached for my phone. A tiny white pumpkin sat on the nightstand. I stroked its cool sides and tossed it between my palms. Tiny pumpkins were better than flowers. I took a selfie with the little fruit pressed to my cheek and texted it to Sebastian. Then I sent a follow-up text. Can I call you pumpkin?

I set the pumpkin aside and slipped into my favorite worn-out jeans. I tugged a white silk tank top over my bed head.

A click-clack of heels moved down the hall toward my door. "Knock knock. Patience? Are you up?" Claire inched the door open.

"Come in." I dug through my closet for something to wear over my tank top. I pressed my shoulder against the wall for leverage and pried the thousand hangers apart for a better look at my wardrobe. "I have nothing to wear."

Claire didn't argue.

I retrieved an emerald green sweater from the shelf and threaded my arms into the sleeves. "What do you think?"

"It's cute. How was your night?" She pressed a shiny red fingernail to her bottom lip like a pinup girl.

"My night was amazing."

She sat cross-legged on my bed and pulled a pillow into her lap. "How amazing?"

I wrangled the length of my hair free from the sweater collar and yanked a brush through the knots. How could I describe a night on the beach with Sebastian? We walked. We talked. We fooled around. He slept over until dawn. "Really amazing."

I twisted the untangled locks into a bun and secured it on my head with chop sticks. I couldn't use them to lift food, but they made an adorable updo.

Claire's shoulders dropped. "You have to give me something. I'm spending all my time talking to strangers and binge-watching a reality show with Adrian. Define amazing?"

I furrowed my brows. "It was rainbows and unicorns amazing."

"Rainbows and unicorns." She slid off my bed and headed for the door. "I think I just lost my lust for that man."

Adrian shoved my door open, half out of breath. "Are you talking about me in here? It's okay if you are. I heard someone say lust and I thought I'd check things out. Make sure you two don't need anything."

I laughed. Claire shot me a droll expression.

Adrian bounced onto my bed and propped his ear in his hand. "Is everyone ready for another day of investigation? I've already met with the breakfast crowd. It's almost time for my rounds again. The lunch crowd is different. Half the people on the island stay out all night chasing ghosts these days, so they miss breakfast." He scooped the little pumpkin off my nightstand.

"Hey." I pointed. "Put that down."

A Cheshire cat grin slid across his lips. The pumpkin rested on one of his palms. "I dug through a wheel barrow of gourds and pie pumpkins looking for one of these without any damage. It's perfect, right?"

My thoughts scrambled. "You left the pumpkin on my nightstand?"

He nodded and smiled at Claire. "We used to go crazy when the mainland farmers came in with pumpkins, remember?" He pulled me to the bed beside him and slung an arm over my shoulders. "Every year the farmers came to our school for the Fall Family Festival. The farmers set up a maze with hay bales and every student got to keep a pumpkin. Most kids went for the biggest one they could carry, but Patience always looked for a little white one." He laughed. "Like a tiny ghost pumpkin."

I leaned against his shoulder and he handed me my gift. "I loved it when they set up lanes for pumpkin bowling and served pumpkin pie with our lunches. On parent night, we had a big bonfire on the field by the track."

Adrian rubbed my arm. "Endless hay rides and cider."

Nostalgia hit me in the chest. Adrian had brought me a little white pumpkin freshman year with a face drawn on it. He presented it to me with a cup of hot apple cider at the festival. Both were slick with sweat from his palms, despite the chilly night air. That was the night he told me he liked me. He said he didn't want to be the kid I met in preschool. He wanted to be my boyfriend.

The pumpkin weighted my hand until I couldn't hold it up any longer. My shoulders stiffened. What was happening? I stood on wooden legs and marched to the kitchen. Claire and Adrian followed, lost in conversation. Adrian continued his stories of fall festivals past and she countered with the horrors of autumn in

Georgia. Apparently, for debutantes like Claire had been, fall was also known as cotillion season.

"My parents insisted." She rounded the corner behind me.

My parents would've protested a cotillion. I set the pumpkin on the countertop and poured coffee. Who cared if the pumpkin wasn't from Sebastian? He couldn't have known about my love for tiny white pumpkins.

I drummed my fingers on the counter. Sebastian would have gotten me a little pumpkin if he knew anything personal about me. Other than my bra size. My mom would ask me whose fault it was he didn't and remind me how guarded she thought I was.

Claire checked her phone and pumped a fist into the air. "He got her."

"Who?" Adrian and I asked together.

"Fargas texted me and said he's bringing Elisa in for questioning. When I ran into him last night, he apologized for tattling to Sebastian after we contacted him about her. He said Sebastian asked that he keep him in the loop because he worries about you."

I deflated. "Yeah?"

"Yes. Now Fargas will find out if Elisa had anything to do with the murders. When he proves this was about love, you both owe me your unending admiration."

Adrian inched closer to Claire. His face contorted with humor and mischief. "When you say you ran into Fargas last night—" Adrian made air quotes around the words *ran into*, "—what does that mean? Also, how'd you get him to change his mind about questioning Elisa? You texted him about her twenty-four hours ago and he ignored you."

"Yeah." I smiled. "What's the real deal with you and Fargas?"

She shrugged. "He said he looked into it. After you texted him, he sent Frankie to welcome Elisa to the island and they talked long enough for Fargas to confirm Elisa was in Virginia at the time of the deaths. Her plane landed on the mainland hours before the murders. She had plenty of time to get to Chincoteague and commit the murders."

Adrian made a little noise. "Oh! I know. Call Melinda. She's manning the phones until three. See if Fargas arrested Elisa."

I gave him a sour look.

"What?" He became still. "Woman-ing? She's woman-ing the phones?"

Claire snorted and patted him on the shoulder.

My eye twitched. "I don't want to get involved." I pressed the pad of my forefinger against my eyelid.

Adrian barked a laugh. "You're lying."

Claire raised her sculpted eyebrows. "You do want to get involved?"

"No."

Adrian laughed again. "Liar. You're lying or you're hiding something." He circled me like a shark.

I wrapped my arms around my middle.

"What do you know, Price?"

A traitorous smile spread. "Fine. Last night I waited on the stoop for Sebastian because I had a hunch. After Jesse Short said Rick recorded everything he did, I wondered if he meant everything-everything. You know? So, Sebastian and I went back to the crime scene."

Claire grimaced. "Ew. Everything?"

Adrian nodded approvingly. "Sweet."

Claire smacked him.

"Ow." He rubbed his shoulder where her fist bounced

off his shirt. "We've got the killer on tape now. That's sweet. So who was it?"

"I don't know. I didn't see the tape. Sebastian took it to Fargas. You think Elisa's on the tape?" Curiosity bubbled through me. "You think he saw the tape and confirmed our suspicions? That's why he brought her in. We tipped him off yesterday. I knew it."

I dialed the station.

"Chincoteague Police Department." Melinda answered on the first ring.

"Hey, it's Patience. How are you?"

"Good. The catering business is crazy right now and these phones never stop blinking. I keep answering them and sticking them on hold until they hang up. That's bad, I know. I'm overwhelmed. But I recognized your number and thought I'd better answer."

"Thanks." I put the phone on speaker. "Do you know if Fargas arrested Elisa French?" Melinda's voice dropped to a whisper. "No. She says she was on the mainland video chatting with her boyfriend all night."

Adrian said, "They can check that."

"They are. They're bringing the boyfriend in until they can confirm the video chat's timeline."

I took the phone off speaker. "Okay. Will you keep me posted? Maybe give me a call when you leave today if anything else comes up?"

The phones rang nonstop in the background.

"Sure, but for now, I better go."

"Right. Hey, you should try to answer all the calls. I know you're bombarded, but someone might actually need help."

"You're right. Talk to you later." Melinda disconnected.

I frowned at Adrian and Claire. "Do we know

anyone who can help with the phones over there until this passes?"

Claire pulled a lipstick from her clutch on the counter and ran it over her lips. "I'll ask around about the phones. Are there any more of those Sophisticakes left?"

I handed her the bakery box. "Wait." I lifted the lid and placed a black Sophisticake on the table. Chocolate chips and hunks of brownie topped the creamy spiral of frosting. "Okay."

"Give me half an hour." Claire slipped into her jacket and left.

I marveled. "Can you believe her? Where do you think she's going?"

"She's amazing." Adrian smacked his lips together. "Probably going to run into the sheriff again."

"Hey!" Half my cupcake was in his fingertips, the rest clung to his lips and tongue as he spoke.

"Delicious."

"You ate my cupcake!"

"Yeah, I did." He winked.

"Stop it."

He chuckled. "What'd you do this morning, Adrian?" he asked himself. "Not much. I had some coffee. Sampled Patience's cupcake."

I covered my mouth. "Stop. Just stop. Seriously. Don't do that."

He swallowed and smiled. The cupcake vanished behind straight white teeth and a dimple. He licked his lips. Adrian made me crazy, but I was definitely not in love with him. Any feelings that occasionally tugged on my heartstrings were residual. Eighteen years together on the island confused people. He was my first love, first kiss, first cupcake, but all the nonsense about how first loves never faded…didn't apply to us.

I pulled my sweater away from my chest a few times, circulating air against my skin. "I'm going to change. It's too warm for cashmere." I stripped the sweater off as I walked away.

Fifteen minutes later my phone rang. "It's Claire," I called. Adrian met me in my room. "I'm putting you on speaker, Claire."

"False alarm on Elisa. The boyfriend confirmed her story. They brought up the chat record and showed Fargas the time stamps. I heard every word from Frankie's desk. They recorded the whole thing, too. Can you believe that? They said they record all their sessions for posterity."

The alien concept confused and worried me. The younger generation recorded their lives and shared it thoughtlessly with the world. When I looked back on adolescence, there was very little I'd want made available for download. My life was almost normal at thirty, but I still wouldn't want it recorded. For instance, I could think of a few things from last night I absolutely wouldn't want to end up on the internet.

Adrian hovered his mouth over my phone. "Sounds like we're still on the case. You want to meet at my house so we can talk to more members of the cast and crew?"

"Definitely." Claire disconnected.

Adrian's stormy blue eyes scanned mine. "You coming?"

I shook my head no, but the word wouldn't form on my tongue.

He smiled a lazy, lopsided smile. "Yeah, you are. You're dying to know who else was on the island that night. Who had alibis? Who else was sleeping with Rick or Anna? You know that cast can't wait to dish the gossip on one another." He shoved his fingertips in his back pockets and leaned against my doorframe, looking simultaneously innocent and ornery. "Come on. Help me. You're excellent at reading people. You'll see everything I miss."

I folded my arms over my chest and rubbed them with my palms. "I don't want to get involved. I feel like meddling in this would be exploiting Rick and Anna's deaths. Let's let Fargas handle it."

Adrian chewed his lip a minute. "How about a counter offer? You come with me and don't get involved. Afterward, I'll buy you and Claire some lunch, and it'll be as if I'm taking you to lunch, but we're making a pit stop at my house on the way."

"Can I get ice cream?"

"Only if I can." He tossed his keys into the air and caught them. "Let's roll, pumpkin."

I puffed air into my bangs and followed. I texted Sebastian a recant of my previous text.

Never mind the pumpkin thing. I was confused. Be safe. Text me later—Patience.

THE DRIVE TO Adrian's was brisk. The dashboard inside *The Watchers* golf cart said sixty degrees. Adrian drove it back to his place, returning it after borrowing it to haul the cot. He parked behind a line of matching vehicles and met me on the passenger side. We mounted the sidewalk and Adrian waved to Noah, the guy who let us pass on our last visit. Noah nodded us through security. Half the trailer of Halloween decorations was gone, already set up on Adrian's lawn and wraparound porch. Faux spiderwebs clung to trees and bushes. A zombie torso in the grass appeared to climb out of the ground. Loud stomping and shouting permeated the house walls and met us on the lawn.

We slipped in through the garage door and mingled with the crowd in the kitchen.

I nudged a guy with no shirt and low-slung basketball shorts. "What's going on in there?"

He looked me over and lifted his chin in recognition. I lifted my chin.

"Taping. This is a fight scene."

Adrian scoffed. "You stage the fight scenes?"

"Not usually, but no one really feels like doing anything interesting right now. What if there's some crazed fan picking off the cast and crew one by one and keeping them as his puppets?"

I eyeballed the glass in his hand. "What's that you're drinking? No one kept anyone as a puppet."

"I drink water. Nectar of the gods. Sixty-four ounces a day for me and never an ounce of bloat you'll see."

I smiled at Adrian. "He rhymes."

The water drinker held his hand out to me. "I'm Vance Varner."

"Patience Price." I accepted his hand. "Are there usually a lot of fights on set?"

"Yeah. Everyone does what they have to do for face time."

I rolled the new term over a few times. "You mean you get more time on camera if you're making a scene."

"You got it."

Huh.

Adrian moved in behind me. "Vance gets lots of face time."

I put my hands on my hips. "You like to make a scene, Vance? Start a couple fights? Defile a few women? Commit a couple murders?"

He wrinkled his face. "I don't have to make a scene to get face time. I'm a model. People want to see this face. They send emails demanding it."

Uh-huh.

Adrian made bug eyes at me. I assumed he was urging me to question Vance further. I shook my head. Models probably had limits, and I wasn't getting involved. Adrian shoved me forward a step and I elbowed his ribs.

Vance squeezed my shirtsleeve and lowered his eyelids to half-mast. "You work out, Miss Price?"

Adrian bumped me.

I pulled in a long breath. "Sometimes I swim or run on the beach." Lies. When I swam alone the last few months it was usually because someone chased me, and when I swam with Sebastian, I mostly gawked. I didn't run.

Vance rolled his shoulders back. "I could get into a cougar who likes long walks on the beach."

I glared. "I'm only thirty, not a hundred. You've got to be close to thirty."

He looked horrified. "I'm twenty-six."

Adrian gave me bug eyes again. He nudged my arm and tipped his head repeatedly in Vance's direction, begging me to keep him talking.

I cleared my throat. "Well, you're right. I definitely like walking on the beach. Did you know Anna and Rick were sleeping together?"

Vance slouched. "Are you a reporter or a fan? Never mind. It's cool. I'll sign your boobs. Come here."

Adrian giggled. He tried to cover the girlie sound with a cough but he ended up choking. A woman in a Staff shirt handed him a bottle of water.

I counted to ten and tried Vance again. "Where were you the night of the murders?"

"In my trailer."

Had I heard him right? "You were already on the island? Are there cameras in the trailer or anyone who can confirm you were there?"

"No, but everyone was on the island that night. Staff, crew and most of the cast. I think Elisa was still on the mainland, though. We all thought Nick and Anna were flying in the next day."

Claire hustled into the kitchen wearing an oversized T-shirt and carrying a Sharpie. "Hello." She slid gracefully between Vance and me, and then curtsied. "I'm Claire. You're my favorite. May I have your autograph?"

I looked at Adrian. He saw that too, right? "Did you just curtsy?"

"Shh." She waved one palm behind her back at me.

I turned to face Adrian. This was confusing. "Am I supposed to go away? What's that wave mean? What's she wearing?"

Vance scrawled gibberish across the front of her shirt, making sure to dot illegible I's over each boob, and then he pointed the marker at my barely B's. "Offer stands."

"No."

Claire zipped out of the kitchen. Adrian took the Sharpie and my elbow. We followed Claire's path and met her on the porch. She stripped out of the ugly oversized shirt and shook like a wet dog. Her cute pink top reflected the heat in her cheeks.

"What was that?" I asked.

She dropped the shirt in my hands. "I took one for the team. I got handwriting samples from everyone on the cast." She wiggled her eyebrows, looking very proud.

Adrian patted her back. "Nice."

Were these two from Mars? "What do you need a

writing sample for? And seriously, this isn't handwriting. This was you getting to second base with that marker."

She shook again. "Well, everyone else signed their name. I also learned they had a bonfire on the beach the night of the murders. Everyone except Vance and Jesse Short has an alibi with witnesses."

Facts circulated through my brain. My friends were building a viable suspect list. They were smart, resourceful and determined. On my island, those attributes were a deadly combination these days.

Claire checked her phone and smiled. "What's next?"

Adrian rubbed his palms together. "It's time for me to hit up the lunch crowd. I'll get the latest scoop at the food trucks."

Claire looked at the shirt in my hands. She rubbed her sides and tugged her top. "I think I need a shower."

I wrapped an arm around her little waist. "Let's go."

She shuffled along beside me.

I bumped my hip into hers. "You just had a male model's hands all over you."

She hung her head and laughed.

I squeezed her to my side. "Don't worry about it. I'm still waiting for that picture of my ice cream belly to hit the front page."

NINE

CLAIRE AND I moved at a snail's pace toward Main Street. The sun was out in full force, raising the temperature higher than it had been in weeks. I shoved my sleeves over my elbows. The number of people on the streets had doubled since breakfast. Adrian's theory about ghost hunters staying awake all night and sleeping through the morning made sense and, by the looks of things, was accurate.

A group of young people in black beanies spoke loudly near a poison green muscle car. They planned to do some "serious hunting" after dark. I could only imagine what that meant.

I picked up the pace. "There're too many people in this town."

Claire looked skeptical. She didn't understand the fragile island dynamic like I did.

"They aren't here to relax, like tourists and birders," I said. "They're here to spot ghosts and stalk a reality show. This will end in massive hoopla and shenanigans at best. More crime at worst." The charge in the air tickled my neck. Crowds were mindless beasts. Ghost speculation, a pair of semi-celebrity murders and reality television shows were like chum to sharks.

Claire flapped the hem of her shirt as the sun beat down. "I still think this has to do with a broken heart. Frankly, I'm shocked it wasn't Dan or Elisa. Is there any chance the time stamp on their video chat was fudged?"

I grabbed her arms. "You're a genius."

She looked over both shoulders. "You've got a crazy look on your face. I don't like it."

I dialed Melinda at the police station.

"Who are you calling?"

I held up a finger while the phone rang. When Melinda answered, I bounced on my toes. "It's Patience. I have an idea about Elisa and Dan's video chat."

Hold music cut me off. I frowned at the phone. "She put me on hold."

Claire stared. "Who?"

"Melinda." I tapped the speaker button and held the phone between us.

The music stopped. "This is Sheriff Fargas."

My mouth opened. Claire laughed and pointed. Melinda had turned me in.

"Patience, I know it's you. I asked Melinda to send all your calls to me, and I told her not to warn you. Why are you still nosing around? I've got this covered."

What could I say to that? "I'm not looking into this. I promise. I was only thinking about what I already know." I dragged my finger in a crisscross over my heart.

Claire shook her head. "You know he can't see you."

Fargas cleared his throat. "Fair enough. What were you thinking?"

I explained my run-in with the green screen taping at Adrian's house. "So, Elisa had access to the screen while everyone else was on the beach for a bonfire thinking she was on the mainland. Isn't it possible Elisa was using the show's green screen to appear as if she was in a hotel room when in fact she was already here setting up her alibi?"

Papers shuffled on the end of the line. "They chatted for three hours. I don't think so."

What did people video chat about for three hours?

"What about potty breaks? She had to use the bathroom at some point."

He tapped something against his desk or the phone, but he didn't respond for several long beats. "I haven't had time to watch the whole chat, but getting over to the B&B and back under the guise of a potty break would be cutting herself pretty short. I'm not convinced, but I'll look into it."

"Really?"

"Yes. I'll check the tape for any times when Elisa was off screen and compare her absence with the amount of time she needed to move from Adrian's house to the B&B and back. I'll see how portable the screen is in case she took it with her somehow and I'll check the IP address to try to confirm her location. Sound good?"

My heart grew. "Thanks."

"Hey, listen. If you get the urge to look into a hunch on your own, don't. Call me instead."

He valued my input. "'Kay." I blinked back emotion and disconnected.

Claire wrinkled her nose. "Are you crying?"

I ran my wrist under both eyes. "This is a weird week for me emotionally."

"Uh-huh." She took my arm and moved us forward. "Elisa's alibi might be sunk, thanks to you. Nice work. I know killers are unstable, but can you imagine her making sexy talk from a murder scene? Sitting there waiting for Rick to get back so she could kill him?"

I stopped walking, put the call on speaker and dialed the station again. "I forgot to ask if he watched the hidden camera footage yet."

"Chincoteague Police Station." Melinda's voice wobbled.

"It's me. Don't transfer me to Fargas," I yelled before she could put me on hold.

A cluster of girls in Vance Varner shirts looked my way.

"I am so sorry, Patience. He made me do it."

"Hey, no. I don't care about that. I wanted to ask you if you know if Fargas watched the secret video yet?"

Hold music cut me off again.

Claire pursed her lips and blew a long whistle.

The music ended. "Fargas."

I rolled my eyes. "Um, hi. I was also wondering if you watched the footage from the hidden camera yet."

Silence.

Claire leaned closer to the phone. "We promise not to call again. Today."

Fargas exhaled loudly. "Yes. We watched the footage. It's inconclusive. The room was too dark to identify anyone."

"Thank you," Claire cooed.

I shoved the phone into my pocket. Well, that information would only fuel speculation about our haunted island. The sudden influx of ghost hunters would love that. My phone buzzed and I pulled it free from my jeans. "It's my parents." I let the call go to voice mail.

Claire clucked her tongue.

"I need to think. I'll call them later."

A moment later, Claire's phone rang.

I cocked an eyebrow. "Don't answer that. It's probably my parents."

She examined her phone and bit her lip. "Hello?"

I shook a finger at her. "You're a weak, weak woman."

She handed me the phone. "It's for you."

My mom was already talking when I hit speaker. "...two-for-one aura cleanses and the line's around the corner. I guess this crowd understands the value in a healthy aura."

"Mom. What?"

"We need you to come in and read palms until I get these auras under control."

Claire covered her mouth with one hand. Her eyes widened until her lashes brushed her brow bone. If she laughed, she was in trouble.

"Sorry, I can't do that. Maybe you can schedule appointments instead of making them stand in a line, or give them yoga mats and put them in child's pose while they wait or something. Listen, I have to go, but remember I'm a licensed therapist. Call me if anyone becomes emotionally distraught."

I disconnected and handed Claire her phone. I narrowed my eyes. "Traitor."

She made a sad face. "I want them to like me."

"What about me? Don't you want me to like you?"

"Yes. Forgive me?"

I shrugged.

Claire ran one hand over her middle. "I'm hungry. I thought Adrian promised to buy us lunch."

A line of food trucks dotted the street as we rounded the corner. Crowds dithered in front of each truck, examining the signs and menu boards. *The Watchers* logo graced everyone's ensemble.

I'd promised to stay out of Fargas's investigation, but something bothered me about our talk. Claire stopped walking at the first menu board. The truck was shaped like a big hotdog. She moved on.

We stopped at a truck with a giant fork painted on it and my mouth popped open. "If the lights were off and the tape was too dark to see clearly, then how did the murderer manage to shoot and kill two people with any accuracy?"

Claire frowned. "How long were you holding that in?"

I pursed my lips.

"We don't know if it was done with accuracy," she said.

True. "Okay, but we know it was dark. Was the killer sitting in there a long time, letting his eyes adjust? And if so, why didn't Rick and Anna see the killer sitting there?" I scanned the crowd. "Look at all those night vision goggles. I bet half the island has them."

A police siren barked behind me, and I squeaked. The door slammed and Fargas hopped onto the curb beside us. "Hello, ladies." He took off his hat and shook our hands. "This looks like my lucky day. Would you like to go with me to the memorial tonight?"

I scoffed. "The what?"

"Jesse Short is filming a special episode to honor Rick and Anna tonight. I'll be working, but I know how you love the show and I thought you might want to join me."

I blinked. Clearly he was only inviting one of us to this atrocity.

"Maybe you'll let me buy you dinner afterward."

I opened my mouth to ask about the gunshot wounds and to list the multitude of reasons a television memorial was in bad taste, but Claire's expression stopped me short. She dropped her gaze like a proper southern belle and smiled at his shoes. "Sure. You can pick me up at Patience's place."

Fargas tipped his head in agreement and returned to his cruiser. "See you tonight."

With his brake lights out of sight, Claire stomped

her feet a few times before sobering up. The dorky grin fell from her lips.

"Too late," I said. "I witnessed that, you know. I'm standing right here."

She ignored me. "I'll see what I can find out about the accuracy of the gunshots."

"Seriously. What is going on with you two?"

"I like him. That's all I'm saying right now." She turned her back on me and marched down the street toward my apartment, swinging her hips.

"How much do you like him and does that mean what I think it means?" The only man to hold Claire's attention since I met her was Louis Vuitton. If she admitted to liking him, there was more to the story.

"A lady never tells."

My smile stretched wider until both cheeks hurt. I matched her pace. "Oh, yes you do. You always tell."

"I told you I needed to talk. I think I'm going crazy. I'm obsessing over him, what I look like, everything I say… I hate it. I'm not this giggly school girl, so why am I having so much fun?"

"I think you're in love."

She paled. "I'm going to need a minute to process that accusation."

"Give me five minutes," I said. "I'll get lunch and meet you upstairs."

Claire hustled down the street to my apartment, and I got in line at the food truck with the big fork on it. Claire and Fargas. The idea baffled. I lifted my chin and peered into the sky. It didn't look like I'd fallen through a looking glass, but anything was possible.

A boisterous laugh echoed over the conversations around me. Adrian lazed against the side of another truck, tucking unruly curls behind his ear and showing his dimple off to a woman with a press badge. I focused my attention on the menu board. The Fork in the Road truck had salads of every variety. I played with my phone and avoided eye contact with Adrian until it was my turn.

"What can I get ya?" A woman in glasses and a ponytail smiled at me from across the shiny metal counter.

"I'll take two of your Mango Mama salads. Dressing on the side."

"Anything to drink?"

"Strawberry smoothies."

She tossed a load of fresh veggies on the chopping board beside her and went to work, creating a beautiful multi-colored salad. Adrian touched the reporter's badge with his fingertips. I texted him.

Get a haircut—Patience.

The woman's hands stilled over the veggies. "I follow *The Watchers* everywhere. Are you a fan?"

"No. I'm a local." I angled my back to Adrian and focused on the woman.

She wiped her hands on a towel and scooped strawberries into a blender. "I'm Marie. This is my truck. We follow *The Watchers* around America. They finally noticed us last spring and made Fork in the Road their official food truck." She pointed to a framed napkin with messy handwriting that read Official Food Truck.

"Nice."

She smiled. "I think I get the tracking impulse honestly. My folks followed the Grateful Dead for decades. I grew up on the road. The Dead aren't traveling anymore, so I thought I should follow *The Watchers*. I've been bringing fresh greens to host towns around the country for four years now. It's hard on us when the show leaves the country, though." She rubbed the counter with one palm, as if maybe the truck was the other party included in "we."

I was slightly concerned by her use of the phrase "tracking impulse."

My smile waned. "I don't know much about the show."

"Oh? You should watch. I'm addicted. Can I be addicted to a television show?"

"Um. I don't know. Is it the show or the travel that compels you? Lots of people prefer moving to staying in one place. It sounds like this is your lifestyle, one you learned growing up. Are you happy?"

She beamed. "Yes."

"Then go for it. Too many people are unhappy." My smile strengthened. "Official food truck sounds like a big deal to me."

"Oh, it is." She leaned over the counter. "Hollywood-Watcher.com featured us." She lidded the smoothies and salads. "Here you go. It's on the house, Miss Price."

My hands stopped midreach. "No. You don't have to do that. What do I owe you, really?" I leaned back for a better look at the menu board and prices.

She pushed the food closer to the edge. "I insist."

I loaded my arms with salads and dressing cups. I curled my fingers around the smoothies. "Did I tell you my name?"

"Nope." Marie wiggled her fingers. I followed her gaze to a group of women behind me. Maple Shuster waved back. "I told you. HollywoodWatcher.com featured us. Fork in the Road. And you, too. You're very photogenic."

"Thank you." I made a mental note to find out what the heck the Hollywood Watcher website said about me.

"Sure. Hey, if you need anything, just ask. I know everything about *The Watchers*."

Mrs. Davis joined Maple and her friends on the sidewalk. I ducked past the line at the next truck. How could I get home without Adrian's mom seeing me?

Maple's voice rose into the air. "She was there a minute ago."

I cut in front of a family debating the merits of waffle cones over sundae cups.

"What's your scoop?" A man with a caterpillar mustache and white apron leaned on his elbows over the counter.

I checked for signs of Mrs. Davis. "I'm not sure."

"We've got fifteen flavors on board, twenty-five toppings and seven syrups. You like nuts?"

My head snapped around. "What?"

"Nuts. We've got almonds, peanuts, pistachios and macadamias."

"Oh. No. I don't like nuts." Did I? Where was Mrs. Davis? I bent my knees to appear smaller.

"You like brownies?"

Mrs. Davis was gone. I peered between arms in the crowd. My legs burned from the semi-squat position.

Mustache leaned farther across the counter, speaking louder each time he addressed me. "Banana splits?"

I needed a new hiding place. "I'll take two ice cream cookie sandwiches."

"What?" he hollered. "You're going to have to speak up from way down there. I'm deaf in my left ear."

Oh no. I couldn't speak up. Sweat formed across my hairline. If I walked away now, I'd look like a crazy person. I lifted two fingers on one hand and pointed to the picture of ice cream pressed between two chocolate chip cookies. Salads, dressing cups and smoothies threatened to leap from my grip.

He nodded and slid the display case door open to retrieve the cookies.

I restacked my packages to make room for desserts. Mustache rang up the order.

Adrian's six-foot-two body popped up beside me. "Did you hear Karen and Beau eloped? They ran off and got married on a cruise. What a cheap way to earn votes. I bet he thinks he'll look like the more stable candidate if he's married. He's angling for the family-man votes. Shameless."

"What?" I nearly dropped my lunch load. "Karen would never agree to that." My childhood nemesis never missed a chance to be adored. She once threw a puppy into the marsh so she could "rescue" him, then reported on her heroism all day at school. That was fifth grade, but still. Totally Karen. "I expected the wedding of the century from her. I thought she'd hire paparazzi to follow her all weekend and requisition the entire island." This was not the world I knew.

Adrian's mom called his name and my tummy lurched.

Jeez. "Why do you have to be so tall?" I slid a ten-dollar bill across the counter to the ice cream man and turned to beg Adrian to hide me from his mother.

"There you are." Mrs. Davis hugged Adrian's waist and looked me over. "Did you have a chance to speak with Patience about this exciting new business opportunity yet?"

Adrian shot me an apologetic look. "I forgot about it. I'm sorry. Things are crazy right now, Mom." He kissed her head.

She patted his cheek. They looked at me.

I shrank under the weight of their stares. "Hi, Mrs. Davis. I'm sorry I can't stay and chat, but I bought Claire lunch and it's getting wilted and our ice cream's melting. I have to get going, but I'll talk to you later." The inflection in my voice made the whole excuse sound as if I wanted permission.

She glared at Adrian. I darted away before she turned her frustration on me.

"Watch it!" Water splashed over my chin and shirt. Karen Holsten stood before me, wiping water from her dress.

"I am so sorry." I bent to retrieve her spilled bottle, but my hands and arms were loaded to capacity.

Karen swiped the bottle off the ground and groaned. Without calling me any names, or making jokes at my expense, she left. I stood, dumbfounded. Maybe marriage was good for her. More likely she was on her best behavior in public with the election closing in. I jostled the containers in my arms and started up my steps. Well, Adrian might have lost the family-man vote, but I was happy. After ten long years, Karen's usual infant-sized waist looked more like mine. *Mental note: do not take a cruise anytime soon.*

TEN

CLAIRE'S HEAD POPPED up when I opened the door to my apartment. "What did you buy? I showered, dressed and painted my toes already."

I juggled the food bags, wresting the key from my lock. "That was a nightmare." I stumbled to the little island separating my kitchen and living room. My arms tingled from the release of their burdens. "It's a mine-field out there."

"Well, it looks like you were victorious." She wobbled stiff-legged on her heels. Toe dividers protected the fresh polish. "Wow. What is all this?"

"Salads and smoothies." I divided the packages among us. "I didn't mean to get ice cream. I was hiding from Mrs. Davis."

Claire stuffed a straw into her smoothie and took a seat at the island. "How'd that go?"

"She found me." I put my salad in the fridge and opened an ice cream cookie sandwich. "I left Adrian with her. He needs to get me out of that mess. I'm not going to be the face of her new business. If I tell her no, she'll hate me."

"It's not as if she likes you now."

"I know, but she's warming up, and I don't want to ruin it." I bit into the ice cream. "Which really isn't fair since she's asking me to do something unreasonable. She shouldn't get to be mad if I don't want to do it. Adrian better fix this. I'm not dressing like a slutty Miss Chincoteague for anyone."

She tipped her cup and nodded. "Agreed."

Adrian's silhouette ghosted up the steps outside my window.

"Speak of the devil."

I opened the door and he strode inside looking like a champion.

"Who has today's scoop?"

Claire sucked on her straw. I ate my dessert. No one answered.

Adrian huffed. "Me. The answer is me. Thanks to a reporter who liked my hair." He shot me a smug look.

I chomped off another bite of ice cream cookie sandwich and powered through a brain freeze.

Claire pulled the straw from her lips. "Are you going to tell us what you learned, or is this a guessing game?"

Adrian took the seat beside Claire and grabbed the second ice cream off my counter. "Is this yours?"

Claire shook her head. "No. I got a smoothie with my salad."

"Is it yours?" he asked me.

I teetered.

"Patience," Claire scolded. "You need to do the marathon with me. All this junk food is going to catch up with you. You won't look twenty-five forever."

"Aww. You think I look twenty-five? I love you so much."

Claire smiled. "Back at you, which is why you need to do the marathon with me."

I looked at my body and shoved the last bite of ice cream cookie between my lips. "Uh-uh."

Adrian unwrapped my spare treat and waved it in the air. "My new reporter friend says our sheriff has contacted the FBI about this case. I also learned Elisa French made a statement on her blog this morning about her innocence. She did a photo collage of pictures with her and Anna Copeland. She included a letter of eternal love for her fallen BFF and then mentioned the special memorial episode tonight at nine Eastern Standard Time."

Elisa was a piece of work. Nothing like gaining notoriety by capitalizing on her friendship with a murder victim. Her blog posting was almost as tasteless as the show airing a special to cover the memorial service. Of course, something interesting did come from the memorial. "Fargas is picking Claire up tonight."

Adrian reared back on his seat. "Really? Do tell."

Claire opened her salad and drizzled dressing over the top. "It's not a date. He's working. I'm spectating. If I wind up on camera as an extra, what can I do?"

I guffawed. "I'm going to pretend not to see the wicked gleam in your eye."

"Sometimes I miss the spotlight." She turned shamefaced to her salad.

My jaw dropped. Claire never referenced her stint as a Disney princess and she complained whenever I brought it up.

Adrian looked at Claire. "Fargas asked you to go with him, and he's picking you up. That's a date." He pushed the ice cream cookie into his mouth.

Her smile twisted. "No wonder you couldn't keep Becky the EMT for long. Driving me to a memorial service where he's working is not a date. He's a nice guy who knows how much I love the show. We're getting to know each other. It's not a date."

Adrian made a childish face. "Becky will be back.

I'm an acquired taste. Fargas wants a bite of a Georgia peach, if you ask me."

Claire balled a napkin in her fist and threw it at his nose. "Oh my goodness. No one asked you."

"Right." I glared at Adrian as I peeled the wrapper off and jammed my straw through the lid on my smoothie.

Fargas could keep his murder case. I had my own mystery to solve, and its name was what-are-your-intentions-with-my-best-friend, sheriff?

I SLIPPED MY fingers between curtain panels and spied on Claire and Fargas. He opened the passenger door for her and closed it when she swung her black patent leather pumps inside. He smoothed his shirt and hair on his way to the driver's side door. She'd spent an hour on her makeup after Adrian left, complete with smoky eyes and lip plumping gloss, but she insisted it wasn't about Fargas. Looked like a date to me.

I walked around the quiet room, squeezing shag carpet between my toes. I'd originally planned to move into a nicer place as soon as possible, but I'd grown too fond of the worn-out orange carpet and dark seventies paneling to leave. People told me I was brave for living in the old haunted building, but the only ghost at my place was the ghost of boyfriend past. Back in high school, Adrian had worked at an art studio downstairs. He discovered an interior staircase leading from the studio to the space I now called home. In true prankster fashion, he'd staged ghost sightings and convinced the locals the place was haunted. Dumb, but I couldn't complain. Fast forward a decade and no one wanted to live here, so rent was in my price range. Unfortunately, Adrian still haunted the place.

Before he went to spectate with Claire and half the

island, Adrian had promised to talk to his mom for me. First, I'd had to drudge through an argument wherein he wondered why I was so stubborn and what was so bad about a makeover? Finally, he left.

For the first time in days, I had the apartment to myself. I turned the television on and switched the channel to Rick and Anna's memorial. Claire made me promise to record it in case she was caught on camera. I muted the sound and flopped onto the couch. Having my life and death recorded sounded awful to me. People like Elisa took it a step further and blogged their feelings.

I sat up. Sebastian's laptop stared at me from the coffee table.

I dragged his laptop onto my legs and opened a browser. Marie and Todd both mentioned Hollywood-Watcher.com. I typed the address in the search bar and hit Enter. Bright green-and-black print scrolled beneath the header. HollywoodWatcher.com was an online magazine touting the latest *The Watchers* news and updates. A line of tabs across the top divided the site into seasons, characters and specials. I did a search for my name. Marie from Fork in the Road said she'd read about me on the site, but that was silliness. I didn't know the show existed until this week.

"How is this possible?" I asked the computer. My name appeared seven times. I scrolled and skimmed the articles. "You've got to be kidding me."

Patience Price, a homegrown island princess and former government-agent-turned-rogue investigator, has tilted the sleepy Virginia town of Chincoteague on its head. Her official business is family therapy, but her claim to fame is crime solving, served with multiple attempted murders and a side dish of exploding buildings. Destruction has never been so sexy.

A snapshot of Todd Ramone, the reporter I kept bumping into, nestled in the bottom corner of the article. The byline identified him as Lou Pole. Very funny. Apparently online reporters considered their form of media one giant *loophole* because the only fact in his article was my name.

I shut the browser to settle my thoughts before I stormed out in search of Lou Pole to set him straight. He was probably at the memorial service. *Unwise.* I tapped my fingers on the edge of Sebastian's laptop. Laptops said a lot about their owners, and Sebastian's desktop was navy with white letters commanding, Never Quit, the portion of the Navy SEALs' motto that Sebastian lived by. I traced the letters with my fingertips. Standing in a line of icons on the screen's edge was a little disc symbol dated earlier this week. The night of Rick and Anna's murder. I bit the insides of my cheeks. On the one hand, I had no business peeking at Sebastian's files. On the other hand, he never told me he'd kept a copy of the video, and I was technically the one who had found it. At least, I'd suggested its existence was possible, which totally counted toward finding it. I double-clicked the icon.

Keys jingled in my front door lock, and I put the laptop down. Sebastian walked in and froze with one hand on the door. "What's going on? You look like you saw a ghost." He smirked. "I guess living here, that's possible."

"How was your day? What are you doing back?" I sidestepped in front of his laptop.

Sebastian shut the door and invaded my personal

space. "You're up to something, but before we fight…"
He leaned forward and pressed his lips to mine.

Frustration burned my chest. I pulled back. "Why do you assume we're going to fight?"

"Because you're going through the files on my laptop?"

"No, I'm not."

He sighed. His huge hands wrapped around my hips and moved me a few steps to the side.

"I can explain," I said.

Several moments passed. He didn't speak.

Okay. "One of the food truck ladies said there's an article about me on HollywoodWatchers.com, so I used your laptop to check it out. Mine's all the way in my room and shut down."

"What'd the article say?"

I rolled my eyes. "That I'm a sexy disaster."

The side of Sebastian's mouth twitched. "What about that?" He motioned to the video footage playing silently on his laptop.

"Gee. I'm not really sure what that is…"

He crossed broad arms over his chest. His trademark blank expression warned me there was no lying to him. He probably read half my thoughts based on my heart rate and body language alone. I relaxed my posture. "Fine. I saw the file when I shut the internet, and I wanted to see what was on it. Besides, what are you doing with it? You said you were giving it to Fargas."

"I did give it to Fargas. I kept a copy for myself. Habit. It's been my experience that hanging on to things comes in handy."

I turned my attention to the laptop as murky shadows moved on screen. "Wow. This really is dark. I can't tell who's who."

Sebastian pointed as long hair swung through the dim green light from a digital clock on the nightstand. "Anna's on top."

Anna fell over. The figure beneath her sat up and then fell back. Both their bodies appeared to bounce twice and were still. A lump clogged my throat. I swallowed and forced my mind to concentrate. We needed to find whoever did this.

"Did you see that? Did the bodies move again or did the video jump?"

Sebastian crouched beside the coffee table and touched the screen with one finger. "There's the time of death. We can confirm the coroner's estimation with the alarm clock."

Something else bugged me. "It's really dark in the room for seven in the evening."

"Blackout shades. I put them up with Mrs. Moore's blessing. I worked nights and slept days a lot in August when the sun was up till ten. Hey, play this again from the beginning."

I restarted the video. The image appeared and ended quickly, but there was no one in the shot and the bed was made. Then the video began again with the door open. The light snapped on. Rick and Anna walked inside, holding hands. Clothes came off quickly, and Rick hit the light switch again. Shadowy figures moved through the darkness to the bed. We'd seen the rest.

Sebastian touched my shoulder. "We see Rick and Anna come in, but no one else. I'm still wondering when the killer got there."

I bit my lip. My foot tapped. I sat on the couch and crossed my legs, but my knee bounced. I restarted the video. When did the killer get there? "Could he have been there waiting? Maybe in the closet or under the bed?"

Sebastian rolled his shoulders back and stretched his neck side to side. "One way to find out."

I grabbed my purse and keys. "I'll come with you. I'm smaller. If you can't fit under the bed, I can try. The killer might be smaller than you. The victims weren't overpowered, they were shot. With shootings you should keep an open mind. I could have easily killed them."

"Please never repeat that statement."

"Right. I meant to say that even someone little could have pulled the trigger."

SEBASTIAN LED THE way into Mrs. Moore's bed-and-breakfast. The home was replete with Victorian charms, from the gentle color palette to the scent of rosemary in the air.

"Mrs. Moore? It's Sebastian Clark. Are you home?" He moved silently down the hall from kitchen to dining room to parlor. Wide wooden beams shined beneath a line of throw rugs.

"Come in, dear. I'm watching my favorite cooking show."

I peeked around Sebastian in the narrow hallway. "Hi, Mrs. Moore."

"Oh, hello, Patience."

Mrs. Moore sat on a mauve wingback chair with knitting needles and yarn in her lap. An empty teacup stood on the table beside her. She emptied her tools into a white basket, pushed onto her feet and swayed. "Can I get you two something to drink? Tea or perhaps a hot toddy?"

Heavy burgundy drapes split the floral wallpaper from floor to ceiling, inviting limited light into her space. Gilded mirrors and picture frames adorned the busy walls. Clusters of dried flower arrangements and needlepoint creations worked as accents.

Sebastian motioned for her to sit. "No. We're going to take one more look around upstairs. We won't be long. Is there anything you need? Can I do something for you?"

"No. No. No." She shuffled to the table beside her television and searched through a stack of papers. "I'm fine. Here you are. Your friend stopped by and asked me to give you this." She handed Sebastian a note. He shoved it into his pocket without reading it.

We climbed the creaky steps to Sebastian's room in single file.

"Which friend stopped by to see you?"

"I don't know. I didn't look at the note."

I followed close on his heels. "Why not take a look and see then?"

"I'm working." He handed me a set of medical gloves before turning the doorknob.

Shivers rode up and down my spine upon entering the room. Rick and Anna's deaths no longer seemed abstract, like tragedies you heard about on the news. My feet rooted at the foot of the bed and a lifetime of island legends rushed through me like icy apparitions. Thirty minutes ago I watched two shadows die on that bed.

Sebastian dropped to his knees and lifted the bed skirt. "The bed's tall enough to hide under, but there's a half inch of dust under here."

I scowled. "Mrs. Moore is old. You think she should clean under the beds?"

He dropped the material and gave me the same crazy face I made. "I didn't say that. I said it's dirty under here. Therefore, it's evident no one lay under there in wait. If someone had been under there, there would be a break in the dust." He reached under the bed and held his fingers up. Gray fuzz as thick as dryer lint clung to his gloves.

"Ew."

He brushed his palms together and stood. "No one's hid under there in the last ten years."

I opened the closet and gasped. "Claire would have a stroke if she saw this." I pressed my palm to the wall inside the closet. "This closet isn't even deep enough for shelves." I shut the door. "How did people live like that?"

"Maybe they didn't have as many clothes."

I disagreed. "I watch movies. Those turn-of-the-century dresses were enormous. They practically stood on their own. Where'd they store them with closets like that?"

"Armoires."

"Oh." My parents had an armoire, but it had shelves and a flat screen television inside.

Sebastian examined the window, slid his fingers around the frame and looked outside.

Mrs. Moore knocked on the wall just beyond the door. "Find everything you need?"

I met her in the hallway. "Are you sure you didn't see anyone else come in that evening? You didn't hear anything?"

Her eyes glistened. "Nothing."

We said our goodbyes and left her to her hot toddy. Sebastian gunned the Range Rover to life and angled away from the curb. The memorial was in full gear at Adrian's house and people filled the streets. The food trucks had relocated closer to the action, too, slowing our progress.

I pointed to a small alley with fewer people. "Try that one." Traffic was jammed. We needed to move three car lengths before we had a chance at turning into the alley. He shifted into park on the street.

"This must make you bananas." He drummed his thumbs against the wheel.

"Nah." I silently cursed Adrian and the mayor for inviting this chaos to our town and for exploiting our legends and stories for profit. What were they thinking? "Maybe a little."

A group of guys on the lawn across the street called each other names and waved beer cans at one another in belligerence. Sebastian rubbed the back of his neck and turned to watch the argument escalate from name calling to shoving and swearing. A big guy in a red shirt plowed into a short guy in black and they tumbled onto the sidewalk. Fists flew. Sebastian muttered an expletive and released his seat belt.

On the opposite side of the street, somber music floated from speakers apparently hidden in trees and mounted on telephone poles. Women in black dresses sobbed into tissues. Pictures of Anna and Rick appeared on a billboard-sized screen erected in Adrian's yard.

Sebastian powered down his window and whistled loudly beside me. He waved his hand at Adrian.

"Ah!" I covered my left ear. "What are you doing? Calling your horse?"

Adrian jogged across the street toward us.

Sebastian opened his door and hopped out. "I'm getting you a new driver."

Adrian slowed. He faced the brawl, which now included approximately five guys rolling on the ground.

Sebastian clapped him on the shoulder. "Can you take her home? I'll handle this before it gets out of hand." He left before Adrian answered.

"What's that about?" Adrian slid into Sebastian's seat. "Why were you sitting here?"

"Traffic." Did he not see every car parked in the street?

Adrian shifted into drive and forced the nose of

Sebastian's Range Rover into oncoming traffic, which luckily wasn't moving either.

"What are you doing?" I gripped the dashboard.

"I don't want to sit here. I want to drop you off and come back before I miss everything." He pulled the gear-shift into reverse and hit the gas.

People honked.

He waved at the angry drivers. "Sorry. Excuse me." A few more back-and-forths and Adrian crossed the street, cut through a side yard and the beauty shop's parking lot. Sebastian's face was pale as we cruised past him where he knelt on the red shirt guy. Red Shirt's hands were pinned to his back and he sported shiny silver bracelets, courtesy of public intoxication and Sebastian's lack of patience for street fighting.

I slouched against the seat. "I could've driven myself."

Adrian smiled and pushed buttons on the dash. "You have bad luck with cars. How many Priuses did you re-place this summer?"

Three. One was shot, one was car bombed and one was T-boned.

I crossed my arms and looked out the window. "I get my new one tomorrow." Thanks to a mainland dealer-ship with zero percent down and generous financing plans, I'd have some wheels again soon.

We passed a colony of tents in the park and turned onto Mrs. Moore's street again, back where we started. "We just left here."

He craned his neck out the window frowning at traf-fic. "Why? Did you get a new lead?"

"No. Sebastian and I were testing a theory. We tried to see if someone might've hidden in the room and waited for Rick and Anna to come in."

Adrian looked surprised. "That's a good idea. Did you find any evidence?"

"No." We slowed at the stop sign on the corner. A flash caught my eye. Several tourists with cameras snapped photos of one another and a line of ghost watchers waved video cameras in the air. One stepped through the line and struck a pose.

My eyes widened and my throat thickened. "Gun!"

"What?"

Pop! Pop! Pop!

My window shattered and someone screamed. Probably me. My heart hammered painfully against my ribs. I turned to Adrian in a fog of fear and confusion.

"Holy hell!" Adrian punched the gas pedal and the Range Rover rocketed through the intersection. "Are you hurt?"

I patted my chest and torso. "No. No. No." I stammered. "No blood. No holes." Pain ripped through my chest. My throat thickened and my periphery shimmered. "You. You. You?"

"I'm mad as hell. Does that count?" He mashed the horn a few times and jumped out from behind the wheel. "Call nine-one-one!"

"Where are you going?" I leapt out and chased him a few steps in the direction of the shooter before running back to the Range Rover and climbing into the driver's side. People honked and screamed at me for leaving the car in the road, where traffic still had a chance.

Knots of bystanders stared silently, holding cell phones in my direction. I ran shaky hands over my body again in case I'd missed something. Adrenaline and shock blurred my vision and apparently impeded my speech. Someone shot at me! I dialed Sebastian.

Eventually, a few cars made room for me to pull the

Range Rover to the curb and park. Sebastian arrived two minutes later.

Adrian lagged behind him, looking anguished. "I'm sorry, man."

Sebastian didn't look back. "You had one job. One."

"I chased him," Adrian said.

Sebastian stopped. "Did you catch him? Did you get a good look at him? See which way he went? Could you identify him in a line-up of two people?"

"Hey." I met them on the sidewalk. "Don't blame Adrian. He was shot at, too. We're the victims."

Sebastian hugged me to his chest and leaned one cheek on my head. Ten seconds later he released me and circled his truck. He stopped at the passenger door and dragged fingers roughly through his hair.

I reached for his hand. "Say something."

He looked at Adrian. "Who were they shooting at?" He touched a bullet hole in the passenger door then pointed through the broken window to another hole inside. The second hole was in the doorframe on the driver's side near the sun visor.

I sat down and put my head between my knees on the ground. Someone wanted to kill Adrian or me. My tummy flopped, threatening to expel my dinner. The other possibility was worse. It was Sebastian's Range Rover and a mob boss was looking for him. Black dots danced in my vision. Or maybe Jimmy the Judge would start with everyone Sebastian cared about and remove a few members of his circle, the way Sebastian did to Jimmy.

It didn't matter who the intended target had been. I hated every possibility equally.

ELEVEN

MY APARTMENT SEEMED smaller than when I'd left to visit Island Comforts with Sebastian. Five adults filled the limited space in my living room-kitchen combo area. I pulled a blanket around my shoulders and curled in on my cup of tea, both feet tucked beneath me on the couch. Adrian and Sebastian rehashed the moments prior to the shooting with quiet vigor. Adrian hadn't seen the shooter. He'd chased a man dressed in all black, who had a sixty-second lead on him. The guy vanished into a crowd of others dressed in black. Sebastian was increasingly dissatisfied with this explanation.

Fargas crouched before me with a notepad. "Anything at all you can remember about the man's face, or perhaps his size compared to others near him?"

I shook my head. The right thing to think about would be identifying the shooter. As usual, my brain ran in another direction. "Someone shot Rick and Anna this week. Someone shot at Adrian and me tonight. That's not a coincidence."

Claire eased onto the couch beside me with a fresh cup of tea. "Maybe the shooter saw the article about you on HollywoodWatchers.com. The piece said you solve local crimes. What if the killer noticed you going back to the scene of his crime and wanted to squash that possibility?"

Maybe. I ran my thumb over beads of condensation

on the rim of my cup. "What if Rick and Anna were accidental murders?"

The room stilled. Tea, honey and anxiety scented the air. I inhaled steam from my cup, trying to warm my fear-chilled heart. I peeked at Sebastian. "It was your room and it was dark."

Fargas dropped his notepad on the coffee table and rubbed his face with both palms. "She's got a point. You could've been the intended target as easily as Rick or Anna."

Sebastian's naturally olive skin turned a sick shade of green. His brows crowded together and his jaw twitched.

Adrian glared at him.

Sebastian paced the silent room. He widened his stance and clenched his teeth.

Claire cleared her throat. "I think there are lots of interesting possibilities for this, but a wise woman told me not to make up theories. She said follow the evidence. So, before we start pointing fingers, let's stay focused on what we know." She rubbed my knee.

Fargas smiled. "Well said. We also don't know it was the same shooter. We'll compare the bullets in the truck to the bullets from the B&B. Forensics should have that information back tonight. With this many people on the island, two separate culprits isn't unthinkable. Until we know otherwise, these are still two unrelated shootings."

Adrian piped up, rubbing the scruff on his cheeks. "The ghost hunters are hyping our local legends to boost validity for their work, and *The Watchers* are capitalizing on the folklore for their Halloween special. Think about it. No prints in the room. No killer in the video." He paused. "Maybe there's something to our legends."

Fargas stood and stretched his legs. "I'd like to know

where the shots came from. The room is small and no one else is on camera."

Adrian's voice dropped half an octave. "Our Island Comforts is really haunted?"

"Oh." I sloughed the blanket from my shoulders and set the cup on the table. Adrenaline spiked in my system. "I know what happened."

Claire tugged my wrist. "Honey, you've had an awful night."

I wiggled free of her grip and took Adrian by the hand. Sebastian's mouth dropped open and snapped into a firm line. I looked pointedly at Adrian, willing him to understand and give me a sign of his approval somehow. I needed to share our secret. "I know why the killer didn't show up on camera. I think Adrian's right. Island Comforts might be haunted. Like my place." I emphasized the final three words.

Adrian's stormy blue eyes widened a fraction. He looked over my head, presumably to Sebastian and back to me. "He doesn't know?"

I shook my head. "No."

"You didn't show him?"

I averted my gaze. "It never came up."

Sebastian took a step toward me. "What never came up? What's he talking about?"

Adrian smiled. "Come on, big guy." He motioned to Sebastian and turned for my room.

Fargas and Claire followed Sebastian. I brought up the rear.

Once we were all crammed in my too-small room, Adrian opened my closet, ducked under the clothes and slid the panel away.

Sebastian pressed his hands over his hips and scowled. "You have a secret passage to her bedroom?"

"Yes." Adrian's wide smile revealed his dimple.

Sebastian held a palm out to Claire and Fargas. He swung his hand toward the closet and Adrian, then to me. His expression darkened. I could only imagine the thoughts running through his head.

Fargas was motionless. Claire's smirk was priceless.

I took Sebastian's hand, but he didn't grip mine back. "I'm sorry I didn't tell you. It's not what it seems, but it is the reason so many people think my place is haunted. This house was probably built around the same time as Mrs. Moore's. Maybe she had a second staircase, too, and it was covered over."

Fargas pressed his sheriff hat onto his head. "I'll go look." He took a few steps before turning back. "Good work, Patience."

I bit my lip. If there was a covered staircase, hope of finding the killer multiplied. The likelihood of finding evidence in an old staircase where the killer had hidden was much better than in a room he never entered. Detectives and forensics could wrap up a murder investigation with a single print or a few lost fibers.

Sebastian followed Fargas into my living room. "I'll ride along."

Fargas stilled at the front door. "You've got shotgun. Your Range Rover's being towed in as an official crime scene."

Sebastian swore under his breath and crossed the room to me in three long strides. I braced for something bad. A scolding? Dirty looks? A lecture? He backed me against the wall and stared down the ten inches of distance between us. Heat radiated off his body. His dark eyes burned with emotion.

"You could've been killed," he whispered into my

hair. "I left you alone for five minutes and someone nearly killed you."

I stretched onto my toes and kissed his chin. "You had nothing to do with that."

"What if I had everything to do with that? You said what I've been thinking. That was my room. My truck. You could be in danger because of me." His jaw ticked.

I rested shaky fingertips on his chest and squared my shoulders. "I'm fine. You can't follow me everywhere, worrying about Jimmy the Judge's vendetta. If you start that crap, I'll kill you myself."

His lips twitched, but the smile didn't stick. "Tell your marshmallow I forgive him. Protecting you is a big job. I should've started him smaller."

"It wasn't his fault. He chased the gunman, for crying out loud."

Adrian and Claire wandered past us, looking uncomfortable.

Sebastian pressed a kiss against my forehead and straightened to his full height. "Next time, Claire's in charge of you."

Claire held up her hand for a high five. "That's right. Finally some recognition. Nothing gets past this girl."

Sebastian tapped her hand and followed Fargas out the door.

I went after him but stopped on my stoop. Heat scorched my face. "I don't need a babysitter," I called down the steps. "I'm the only one in charge of me. I'm a grown, educated woman who does not need to be looked after."

Sebastian smiled as they drove away.

I locked the front door and went to the kitchen. I'd been shot at an hour ago. Tea didn't cover that. "Where are the comfort foods?" I opened bags and boxes of whole grain rolls and wheat flatbread. My refrigerator was stocked with Greek yogurt, low-fat string cheese and produce.

Claire turned on the television. "If you won't run the marathon with me, I thought you could still get healthy by eating better."

I pressed a finger against my eyelid to stop the twitch. "What happened to the Sophisticakes and fried butter?"

She pretended to gag. "They're where they belong."

I flipped the lid on my trash. Empty.

"Did you just look in the trash for your junk food? What if you'd found some? Was there a plan in place or were you just curious?"

I blinked and pressed my eyelid hard enough to form fresh spots in my vision.

Adrian opened his laptop bag and pulled out a three-pack of cookies. "Mrs. Freeman gave me these when I visited her yesterday."

I accepted the cookies and snuggled on the couch under my blanket. "Thanks."

Claire flipped the television channel to coverage of the memorial and our shooting. "They always interview the wild-looking ones."

The man on camera had a tall green Mohawk and better smoky eyes than Maybelline and I had ever managed. His big blues were slightly alien, probably from contacts. He had a gadget belt around his waist and pointed into the air. "I saw the whole thing from that tree. The gunman appeared out of nowhere, struck a shooter's pose and bang, bang, bang!" The witness posed for the camera.

I tugged the blanket lower on my shoulders. I didn't see the shooter's face, but I'd never forget his emergence through a line of identically dressed people and then the pose.

Adrian wiggled his fingers in a gimme sign. "You think I could pull off a Mohawk?"

I broke one cookie in half for him. "No."

He shoved the cookie in his mouth. "I think I'll advertise my final election rally as a costume party in honor of *The Watchers'* filming and all the ghost hunters around here. I need a high turnout to catch voters' attention. Plus, who doesn't like to dress up?"

"I'll go." Claire kicked her shoes off and rotated her ankles. "I'm here all week. Where are you having it?"

"Outside Patience's new office building. There's a nice open area there by Misty Park."

I would support Adrian's campaign no matter what level of crazy happened on the island. "Me, too, but no costume."

Adrian frowned. "What I heard was that you're both coming and you'll be in amazing costumes I'll never forget."

I looked at Claire. "How did he hear that?"

She shrugged. "I don't know, but he's right about me."

My phone vibrated on the table and I grabbed it. "Hello?"

Sebastian's voice rang through the speaker. "We're here. You were right. There's a covered staircase to this room. Good work, boss."

I disconnected and looked at my smiling friends. Now we just needed to figure out who else knew those stairs existed.

TWELVE

I RUBBED SLEEP from my eyes and peered at the clock on my nightstand. Six-thirty was a terrible time to wake up. Claire's voice mingled with two others in the next room. I knew the other voices well. I grabbed my phone from under the pillow and shuffled toward my door. I stubbed my toe in the dark. Jeez.

I squinted at my parents in the kitchen, working over a little bowl, and Claire doing calf raises in her cross trainers. "Why do you people hate sleep?"

Claire stretched her arms overhead. "Good morning, sunshine."

"There's no sunshine. It's too early for sunshine. Is there coffee?"

Dad poured contents from his thermos into my favorite mug and passed it over the little island to me. "I'll make a pot. We didn't mean to wake you."

Mom carried the bowl and a tiny roll of dried herbs into the living room. She lit the little bundle, puffed it out and waved the stream of smoke in the air.

"Mom." I sank onto the couch. "Stop cleansing my apartment. It's not haunted."

Claire sniffed the air and wrinkled her nose. "That stuff scares ghosts?"

"No," Mom and I answered.

Mom's reassuring smile irritated me. I sipped coffee and kept quiet. She could explain. If I tried, I would rant.

Mom streamed tendrils of smoke around the room,

concentrating on corners and windows. "The burning sage cleanses negativity. It's a wonderful, holistic way to reinstate calm in our environment and bring positive energy into the home."

I gulped hot coffee to busy my mouth, but it didn't work. "She burned sage in my room by the bale during high school. Everyone thought I was a pothead because the stink lingered in my clothes."

Mom kept moving in her methodical pattern. "We did it while you were at school so it wouldn't bother you."

"You closed the door and trapped the stink. My room still smells like burnt sage. It permeated the walls."

Dad chuckled.

Claire smiled. "But it worked so well."

I stuck out my tongue and Claire laughed.

Dad refilled my cup from his thermos as the coffee-pot chugged to life on the counter. "We brought breakfast. Are you hungry?"

"Yes, please." I turned my focus on Claire. "Did Sebastian come back last night? Is there any new news?"

Mom snuffed out her sage. "He's busy today. We saw him on our way in and he borrowed the love bus. He's worried about you. That reminds me. I can't believe we had to hear about our only daughter getting shot from Maple Shuster."

"I wasn't shot, and you hear everything from Maple Shuster. She's omniscient."

"It'd be nice to get a call." Mom lifted her flowing cotton skirt and walked into the hall to start her sage routine again on the other half of my apartment.

Sebastian took my parents' forty-year-old hippie bus to work? They'd bought it new before I was born and re-fused to let it go. The bus blew smoke at forty-five miles an hour and threatened to shake apart at fifty. Neither mattered on an island with maximum posted speeds of thirty-five, but Sebastian probably had business on the mainland, which meant highway travel.

"That was dumb. He could've taken my new Prius after we pick it up today."

Dad carried a tray of fruit and yogurt to me. "Bon appétit."

Mom responded to me through the wall. "He wanted you to have the Prius. It's no bother for us. We'll drive the pony cart." The pony cart was what we called my parents' other mode of transportation. The pony cart was a lavender golf cart with plum leather seats and the insignia of their store, The Purple Pony, painted across the hood and down both sides. Shockingly, it was more appealing than the blue-and-white love bus with over-sized hippie flowers.

I positioned the breakfast tray on my lap. "Thanks, Dad." I examined the healthy fare and resigned myself to enjoy it. I'd make a trip to Tasty Cream once I was dressed.

The thump of my morning paper hitting the steps jolted me, jostling my tiny pile of grapes into the yogurt.

My phone buzzed and I check my messages. Be safe. I'll be late. Call if you need me. Don't wait up.—Sebastian.

Dad opened the front door with a saucer of milk. "Kitty, kitty, kitty." He called for Freud, set the saucer on the stoop, and then returned with the daily newspaper tucked under one arm. "Let's see what's going on around town today." Dad shook the paper open. "Hey, you made the front page, Peepee!"

I dropped my fork.

He sat beside me, and Claire crowded in behind him. "Ohhh."

Patience Price, an island local and the rumored face of Extreme Island Makeovers, was involved in a shooting last night at approximately nine o'clock. Price was the passenger in FBI Special Agent Sebastian Clark's vehicle, with ex-boyfriend and current mayoral candidate Adrian Davis at the wheel. The former lovers came under fire by an unidentified shooter. The suspect was not apprehended. Last night's shooting was the most recent in a series of unrelated crimes directed at Price. No one was harmed in the shooting. No statements were made available. An investigation is underway.

"Unbelievable." I was not the face of Extreme Island Makeovers. Reporters were my nemesis. They frequently goofed up stories, to my detriment. If Sebastian wasn't ready to burst after driving two hours to work at fifty miles an hour, he'd be agent confetti when he saw me referred to as Adrian's former lover on the front page of the *Island Gazette*. The *Gazette* was admittedly more island tabloid than the official *Chincoteague Chronicle*, but that was why everyone read it.

Mom motioned from the hallway. Her hands fluttered, urging me to meet with her.

"Excuse me." I set breakfast aside and went to the hall.

Claire took my seat and Dad spread the paper between them.

Mom pulled me into my bathroom and shut the door. Panic strained her face. My heart rate sped at the sight. Mom was always the picture of calm. It was her thing. Even when locked in a jail cell for murder, she'd been all yoga and meditation.

On my best day, I was still a tightly wound type A. Seeing her this way set off a dozen red flags.

"Take this." She pressed a weird cell phone into my palm. It was pink and too chunky for current technology. "It's a stun gun."

"What?" I squeaked.

She pressed soft fingers to my lips. "It's a decoy. It looks like a cell phone so you have the advantage of surprise. Your dad bought it on eBay. It works." She grimaced and shut her eyes. "Don't ask."

"Mmm-kay." I turned the little weapon over in my palm. "I don't know what to say."

She shook her hands at the wrists and inhaled. "I don't condone violence, but I support protecting my daughter who refuses to get a nice safe lifestyle. When you came home from the FBI, I thought my heart would spill over from joy. When you decided to open a counseling practice for islanders, I knew you'd be safe, plant roots and thrive."

She leaned against the door, deflated. Her weary eyes drooped and my heart broke. Through all my shenanigans in high school, she never looked so distraught. She was too kind to be so sad. If karma was real, why would this gentle woman have had a wreck of a daughter like me?

I wrapped my arms around her neck and held her close. "I'm sorry I worry you."

She sniffled and my eyes stung. "It's your way. You're brave and curious. All the things I've never been."

"Sorry." I pushed her long hair away from my cheeks, inhaling the natural lavender of her shampoo.

Mom pulled her face back and gripped my cheeks into a pucker. "Don't be sorry for who you are. Be proud. I admire all those things about you."

My lips trembled. "You do?"

"Yes, you silly girl. Of course I do!"

We were so different. Our disconnect normally rivaled the ocean for depth and size, but for a moment, in my tiny bathroom, love bridged the gap.

WHEN CLAIRE AND I got back to the island after picking up my newly leased Prius, I met Missy and her giant white sheepdog, Thor, on the beach for some fresh air. Wind whipped my hair into my eyes, and I wrangled it into a tighter knot on my head. I inhaled the familiar salt and brine with a smile. Nothing on earth compared to the beach. Thor chased sandpipers along the surf on his retractable leash. Missy and I settled into the sand on a deserted strip where trees from the national forest intruded on the beach. The two habitats collided in a postcard-perfect picture.

I buried my feet in cold sand and wiggled my toes. Missy pulled her knees to her chest and wrapped her arms around them. She kept Thor's leash in a white-knuckled grip as he pounced randomly at birds and shells. Waves crested and broke in the distance, creating the soothing white noise and scenery. I doodled a flower in the sand with my fingers.

Missy watched for a moment. "Did you see the paper?"

"Yep." I dusted sand from my palms and dodged the conversation. "Is the catering business going any more smoothly? You mentioned you're spread thin with all the election parties coming up and a television show vying for your goods. I hope Half Baked is giving you a fair price for their assistance."

"They are, and Fargas hired some ladies from the book club to help with the phones so Melinda and I can concentrate on catering." She bit into the thick of her lip. "Guess who applied for the full-time receptionist position."

"Who?"

She covered her eyes. "I don't mean to gossip, but it's so ironic."

"Who?" I ran through a list of possibilities.

"Maple Shuster." Missy burst into giggles.

I joined her. Maple relayed information faster than the local internet connection. "Oh my gosh, that's fabulous." I laughed. "Well, her information will be direct from the phone lines soon." When she answered the phone, she could tell the caller everything she already knew about their complaint and close all the little cases herself.

I settled my breathing and eased back onto my elbows in the sand. I lifted my chin to the sun, soaking in the weaker rays of fall. "Have you found a nice man to court you in this crowd of fanners and ghost hunters?"

"No, but I'm into the whole ghost hunter thing."

My eyes popped open. *"Et tu, Brute?"*

She laughed. "I can't help it. I love the mysterious vibe they all have. The dark colors and piercings." She fanned her face. "The tattoos."

I liked those, too. "Yeah?"

"Yeah. Melinda and I recognize a few of them by their ink now. She'll elbow me and say, 'Don't look now, but Sprocket's on your right.' Sprocket is the one with giant green eyes and short blond hair. He has a sleeve of tattoos in the shapes of gears and sprockets. It's so cool. He's so handsome."

I could appreciate a nice tattoo and a handsome face. Sebastian's dangerous eyes and armband came into mind. I sighed.

Missy shifted onto her side. "Have I thanked you

lately for introducing me to Melinda? It's so much fun having a girlfriend and a surrogate family. Her kids call me Aunt Missy."

"That's great. I know she loves having a close friend, too. Who doesn't? Her daughter, Gigi, still calls me Ear." Gigi had found a human ear while taking a walk on the beach with me last month and the name stuck. With any luck, she'd forget that day before she grew old enough to have nightmares about it.

Missy piled handfuls of sand in little dunes between us. "How's Claire? I saw her jogging near the harbor today."

I smiled. "She's good. She's in love with *The Watchers*. The producer offered her a role as an extra in the Halloween episode. Now she's going crazy. She got the call after breakfast, and I thought she'd won the lottery."

Missy squealed. "I'm so jealous. Do you think you can get on the show, too?"

"No thanks. Claire and Adrian swear the show is normally about global culture and customs, but the whole town's black with gothic garb and all I see is Halloween preparations, based on old island legends meant to scare children. From where I'm sitting, I don't see the draw."

The trees rustled behind us and Thor trampled over Missy to take his place as sentinel. His tail whipped up a sandstorm as he flew past us. *Woof! Woof! Woof!* He yanked and pulled his leash, dragging Missy an inch or two in his direction with each powerful tug. I wiped sand from my eyes and tongue, then grabbed Thor's leash and helped Missy get a footing to reel him in.

"Sit!" She fell into the sand beside Thor, who gave up his pursuit in favor of a seated rant. *Woof! Woof! Woof!*

A trio of men in dirty jeans and black canvas coats marched out of the trees and onto the sand. They stopped to take in the enormosaurus barking and paw-ing in their direction.

"Can I pet him?" the guy carrying a tent asked.

"Really?" Missy's eyes twinkled as the one with blond hair met her on his knees in the sand. Thor fell onto his side and rocked his belly into the man's legs.

I scanned the pair waiting at a safe distance from Thor. "Were you camping in the woods?"

They bristled. The barrel-chested one tapped the gad-gets on his belt. "We were hunting. I'm Rex. This is Fetch."

Thor flipped onto his tummy, ears at attention.

I stifled a laugh. Rex would be wise not to repeat that name. "Catch any ghosts?"

Rex scoffed. "We don't catch ghosts. We monitor them, and yes, we found plenty of spiritual residue in these woods. The electromagnetic fields are off the chart. We witnessed a mist following the spotlight's path around the lighthouse at midnight."

I dropped my chin to my chest and counted to ten. They believed. I didn't have to.

Beside me, Missy and her new friend laughed. Thor climbed into the man's lap and toppled him over. The guy dusted himself off, removed his jacket and shook out a pound of sand. Up one of his arms was a beautiful tattoo made of gears in varied shades of gray and blue. I caught Missy's attention and widened my eyes in ques-tion. She nodded. So, this was Sprocket.

I shoved my hand Sprocket's way. Thor licked it. "I'm Patience Price. Nice to meet you…"

"Chance Huntley."

"Hi, Chance. This is Missy, and—" I motioned to the sand-caked dog between us, "—you've met Thor."

Chance knelt beside Thor and rubbed his head. "Thor, huh? I think you're more of a Loki."

Missy wrinkled her forehead in confusion.

Chance could explain mythology. I needed to think. "I'm going to go check out those EMPs. I'll catch up with you later, Missy. Nice to meet you Chance, Rex and Fetch."

Rex grumbled, "EMFs." The others called out good-bye.

I stuffed sandy feet back into well-worn sneakers and followed the forest trail toward the lighthouse. The Assateague Lighthouse stood watch on the highest point in the forest. I kept a careful eye out for wild ponies and forced my thoughts away from the last time I'd seen a pony in the forest. It hadn't ended well for the pony, thanks to the arms dealer who'd been chasing me. Images of that night blurred my vision and I sucked air. I didn't have time for panic attacks. So far I'd kept them at bay on sheer willpower and hardheadedness.

A twig snapped nearby, and I nearly swallowed my tongue. I put my head down and moved more quickly toward the lighthouse steps. Horses couldn't climb stairs. I hoped. Behind me, branches cracked and feet thundered. Not horse hooves. Feet. Panic took over, igniting my fight-or-flight response. In other words, compelling me to flee. Fighting was for tough guys. I was one hundred forty pounds of fear and curiosity. I sprinted through the forest, ducking under low hanging bushes and pulling spindly branches with me. I released one as the footfalls drew nearer.

Crack!

"Ow!" A slew of curses echoed through the forest.

"You!" I marched back the way I'd come, burning with indignation.

Todd Ramone rubbed his throat and gasped for air.

"You big creep! What are you doing out here? Why are you following me? Why'd you chase me like a freaking mob boss?" I swallowed mouthfuls of air.

"A what?" His voice was froggy. He leaned against a tree, panting and scowling.

"You heard me." I wrapped my fingers around the stun gun masquerading as a cell phone in my purse. "Why are you stalking me?"

Todd braced his hands on his knees and pulled in shallow breaths. "That limb hit me in the throat. It seems like you're the one trying to kill me, not the other way around."

"Why'd you chase me?"

He face crumbled in confusion. "You ran."

"Because you were chasing me!"

"I was observing you, not stalking you. I would've caught up if you didn't take off like a gazelle. I'm a reporter, not a sprinter. By the way, you're fast."

Too bad Claire didn't hear that. I knew I didn't need a marathon. I eyeballed Todd. "You didn't tell me why you're following me."

His blue eyes sparkled. "I've been on the island long enough to see that you're where the story is."

I moved closer. "I'm not your story, and Todd's not even your name. What's that about, Lou?" I mocked.

He beamed. "You read my stuff. You looked me up."

"No." Yes, obviously. "Not the point. At all. You lied about your name. Probably everything that comes out of your mouth is a lie."

"I use a pen name—" he elongated the words, "—for anonymity. I have to protect myself."

"You mean you have to cover your rear."

"No. I mean anonymity. I can't have every woman on

the planet after me, can I? Writing about *The Watchers* is a sticky job. Fans will do anything to get at this cast."

"Sure. What else do you lie about?"

He straightened and shoved both hands in his back pockets. A tuft of sandy hair fell over his forehead. "I don't lie. I report what I see."

"Right." I turned my back on him and finished my walk to the lighthouse steps. He followed on clumsy feet, alerting every living creature in a ten-mile radius of our approach. No risk of running into a pack of ponies with him around.

I climbed a few steps and sat while my heart settled. The leaves were a painter's pallet, from amber to crimson and every shade in between. Evergreens anchored the colors together, with their wide brown trunks and knotted roots poking free from the ground before disappearing again over the forest floor. Occasional shafts of light illuminated patterns over fallen leaves. I inhaled the cool earthy scents of soil and sand. If only the streets in town were half as peaceful.

"What are you doing?" Todd obstructed my view of the trees.

I peered up at him. "I'm thinking. I come here to think, and I like to watch the trees and look for birds."

"Birds," he deadpanned.

"Yes. I met some birders who taught me about the birds living in the forest and sometimes I come and look for them. It's peaceful. If you hold still, you can see things you can't see when you're giving me an inquisition." I held a finger to my lips and he eased onto the step below me without another word.

Wind tickled the leaves, jostling the stubborn ones and sending flurries of their weaker brethren to the ground. Something caught my eye as the nearby limbs danced in the steady breeze. "Sonofa…"

I inched past Todd on the steps and stopped at the foot of a large oak tree.

"What do you see?"

I kicked the leaves at my feet. "I need a long stick. Help me find something I can reach into this tree with."

Todd jumped into action, offering a steady stream of branches until one suited my goal. I hefted it into the air and knocked it against the tree. Something snapped over our heads and a black plastic apparatus careened off branches, cracking and busting at my feet.

"What's this?" He picked up the camera and stared open-mouthed. He inspected it with a look of intense intrigue and concentration before turning his wide-eyed expression on me. "Someone bugged the forest."

"No. Someone's *watching* the forest."

THIRTEEN

I WANDERED THE paths through the trees with my face tilted skyward, searching for more cameras. Todd followed. He asked more questions than I'd ever heard from one person. I ignored as many as possible and concentrated on knocking cameras from trees. An occasional blinding shaft of sunlight sent me stumbling backward and blinking away spots. I made a mental tally of possible laws broken by setting up cameras in a national forest.

Todd grabbed my elbow when I stumbled. "I can't see how one gal can cause so much trouble. I've done my research. Did you know before you returned home this summer there was a crime rate of zero here? I dug up a couple property line squabbles between neighbors and a high school kid shoplifting condoms, but aside from that, nothing. Then you move home and…"

I spun on him. "I know perfectly well what has transpired since I moved home. None of it has had anything to do with me." Mostly. "Reporters like to make drama where none exists and beef up their stories so they seem more interesting. You should know that." I stretched my neck side to side and winced.

"Are you okay?"

"My neck hurts." I kneaded the muscles across my shoulders. "Owie."

Todd touched my neck lightly. "May I?"

I slapped his hands away. "No. You may not."

He huffed and moved closer, as if I was the one both-
ering him. "Come here and don't be so stubborn. You've
been looking into the trees for twenty minutes." He
pressed the tender muscles with the pad of his thumb.
"There?"

I bit my lip. "Yeah."

He applied pressure across both shoulders. "Is that too
much?" Heat from his body burned through my jacket.

I fought to keep my eyes open and my chin up. "Nope.
That's perfect."

Todd massaged my neck while I fought an inex-
plicable blush heating my cheeks. Was it cheating on
Sebastian if I really liked this shoulder rub? What if I
definitely did not like the liar giving it to me?

He cleared his throat. "I think you should stop camera hunting for today. You've found four. I'd say that's
enough evidence to get a few forest rangers worked up.
They can take it from here. You're hurting and besides,
they probably posted cameras all over town to capture
the best crowd shots. You can start collecting them in
town after you go soak in a tub or ice your neck. I'm not
sure which is the better move."

I wiped my mouth in case of drool and rolled my
shoulders. "Who do you think posted the cameras?" My
first inclination was the moronic ghost hunters who had
left the woods carrying a tent, but Todd sent my thoughts
in a sickening direction. A couple of kids with some gad-
gets and a web cam didn't worry me nearly as much as
a television show capable of airing my late night romp
with Sebastian during prime time.

Todd frowned as though I'd lost IQ points. "*The
Watchers* crew. If they want candid shots and conversations, they have to be prepared. This show isn't about the
contestants living in the house. *The Watchers* is about

the contestants participating in a culture or community. They came here for ghosts, so they probably plan to stage some strange happenings and tape the reactions."

Like a mist circling the lighthouse. The ghost hunters did see something. Hollywood special effects.

We reached the forest's edge and I headed for my Prius. "Where's your car?"

The beach lot was desolate. The few campers and pickups parked with mine when I'd arrived were replaced with seagulls picking the ground. Missy and Thor were gone, hopefully to visit with Sprocket a little more.

"I walked."

I beeped my door open and scanned the area. "Why?"

Todd shrugged. "I see more when I move slower."

True, but nuts. It took forever to walk to the beach from town. "Get in." I waved my hands over the Prius' roof. "It's getting cold and looks like rain." I shook from my mind images of him walking alone down the road back to town. Herds of frustrated ponies probably waited to punish the morons who kept them up at night searching for ghosts and pinning cameras to trees.

Todd opened the passenger door and slid inside. I tossed my bag and the busted cameras into the backseat. I hit the gas and didn't stop until I reached the police station. Todd climbed out and walked away.

"Where are you going?" I asked.

His wide, cocky smile reminded me of another blue-eyed pain I had. "Will you miss me?"

"No."

"See you around, Patience Price."

"See ya, Lou."

I marched into the station and waited for Melinda to finish her call. The room was quiet. I peeked out the window. No cruiser in the side lot. I'd parked alone on the curb. At least the hubbub had died down since *The Watchers* had first arrived. The call volume seemed more reasonable than the last time I called.

Melinda had the phone to her ear as she scratched notes on a slip of paper. No other lines blinked in wait for her attention. Still, a bead of sweat clung to her brow. She hung up and pressed her forehead to the desk. "This job is misery."

I laughed. "I'm sorry you're stuck answering phones in the middle of all this. At least it's calmer here today."

She lifted her head and peeled a Post-it off her eyebrow. "It is. I know it is, but I'm exhausted. Everything's so dramatic here. I thought having four kids was crazy. My family has nothing on this place."

I folded my hands and leaned forward in an encouraging pose. "Other things are going well. I saw Missy earlier. Your catering business is booming. Sugar and Spice is the talk of the town right now."

Melinda's eyes misted over. She wiped shaky fingers under each eye. "I can't do it. I can't keep up. What was I thinking? I have four kids! I didn't need to start a business. I didn't even have time for a hobby. I was temporarily insane. I claim insanity. Is that a good reason to drop out?"

"You can't drop out. It's your business." I moved to her side and crouched to eye level. "You can do this. I hear Fargas has the ladies' book club covering some of your hours and someone's interested in the position full-time. You can focus on catering and mommy things soon. Don't give up yet. The light is shining right around the corner."

Air whooshed from her lips. "Do you really think so?" She wadded tissues from the box on her desk and dotted her nose.

"Yes."

"Okay." She sat taller and opened her desk drawer. "Are you here to see Sebastian or do you need some kind of form? I have complaints, petitions and permits right here. Frankie showed me how to fill most of them out, if you want help. If you'd rather wait on her, she'll be back anytime."

I looked over her shoulder. "Is Sebastian here? I thought he went to work today."

She shook her head. "I saw him in the love bus earlier. I assumed he was sticking around here in that thing."

I pinched my bottom lip between my thumb and first finger. "Where did you see him?"

"On Blueberry Lane."

Blueberry Lane was a newer residential section. The two-story houses had vinyl siding and picket fences instead of clapboard and stilts. "That's weird."

"So, no form?"

I lifted my hands to take a complaint form but couldn't. Filing a complaint wouldn't help. Fargas and Frankie already had their hands full with physical crimes against innocent people and Range Rovers. *The Watchers* would film their Halloween special and be long gone before seeking hidden cameras became a police priority. Heck, it'd be too late then. The show would take the cameras down when they left.

I dropped my hands to my sides. "It's okay. I think I can handle this one my own." Vigilante style.

THE CROWD OUTSIDE Adrian's house was thinner than usual. Knots and clusters of people in black *The Watchers* shirts milled around the sidewalk and on the porch. Most shirts had STAFF on the backs. I held my head high and beelined for the door.

"Excuse me," a voice called as I cut through a small crowd of *The Watchers* staffers. I pulled out my keys and pretended as if one was to the front door.

"Ma'am."

I cringed. Thirty was too young to be called ma'am, unless that voice belonged to a baritone grade schooler.

"Ma'am."

I scrunched my shoulders to my ears and placed a hand on the doorknob. The door swung open, startling both me and a staffer I recognized. He was the little guy who'd stopped me in the street with Adrian.

"Hi, Noah." I raised a hand. "I left my…something personal in Adrian's bathroom. I just need to grab it."

He pulled the door closed, snuffing out my point of entry. "Your something personal?"

I forced a blush. "Yes. You remember me, right? I came over with Adrian Davis the other day to grab a cot from storage." I stage winked. "I left something personal last time I slept over and I need it again."

The porch was quiet. If anyone bought my acting, it didn't say much about the show. The door sucked open again and Jesse Short, the show's producer, stepped across the threshold.

I did a one-finger wiggle. "You're just the man I need to see."

The staffers shared an awkward mix of panicked and apologetic expressions. Noah turned to Jesse. "She left something personal in Mr. Davis's room."

Jesse raised an eyebrow and motioned me inside. He blocked half the doorway as I entered, forcing me to brush past him. Whether it was meant to intimidate or interest me, he failed at both. He shut the door and stared at me.

I narrowed my eyes. "Do you know what I found in the national forest today?"

"A reporter?"

My mouth fell open. "You were watching. I can't believe you'd do that. He said it was you, but I thought surely a television show would know they can't stick cameras anywhere they want. That's a national forest, not some actress' bedroom. Those trees are protected."

He glared. "Those cameras were expensive. I'm still deciding how much you owe me."

I pursed my lips and counted to three before I lost it. "That's crazy talk!"

He smirked. "You bashed my property with a tree branch. I have it on tape." His cool demeanor set off a line of bottle rockets in my chest. Cocky. Arrogant. Hollywood creep.

"You had no right to put them there. Where else are they? All around town? If you don't have a permit for them, I'll take those out the same way. Lots of tree branches around."

"Do it and I'll sue."

My jaw swung open. "You can't do that."

He swaggered closer and whispered, "Honey, I can do whatever I want. Money talks."

"Do not call me honey. I am not your honey. I am a concerned citizen who is making a citizen's arrest."

He chuckled. "A what?"

"You heard me. Citizen's arrest. You're a peeping Tom. You can't record whatever you want without warning people. This is the real world, pally. People have rights here." I shook a finger at him. "Ever heard of an invasion of privacy?"

Jesse leaned toward me in the narrow front hall, a clear warning in his eye. "Those cameras helped me capture the gripping heartbreak seen here at the memorial and then allowed me to share those raw emotions with the nation. I had more viewers that night than the halftime show at the Super Bowl. You should be thanking me for putting this little Podunk town on the map. Those cameras are staying. They're going to propel me out of the reality television hood and into primetime real estate. So keep your hands off, honey." He spat the final word and strode away.

I gripped Adrian's coat tree, willing myself not to jump on Jesse's back, screaming like a lunatic. My fingers curled and released around the fixture. I headed to the kitchen to cool down.

Water ran in the sink where a pixie-sized girl with short black hair filled a glass. "Don't take it personally. That's just him. He's a d-bag. He's been worse since we heard about Anna and Rick." She sipped the water. Her multiple face piercings and deep purple lips distracted from her wide eyes and freckles. She was at least ten years younger than me. I didn't envy her that. Settling into myself had taken time. My early twenties were a mess of emotions and bad haircuts.

"Yeah, probably worried about ratings," I grumbled.

"For what it's worth, I think you're right about putting cameras around the island. That was skeevy, even for him. The show's on the bubble, though. After all these years, people are losing interest. That's why he made the switch from observing cultures to lining up holiday specials. Halloween is a big holiday and he knew the ghost hunters would get behind it after he read this island's website and spread the word."

"How many cameras do you think are out there on the streets and in the forest?"

"Dozens. I keep mine with me, but we all have one.

Plus, the show sends scouters out to find places to set them up where they'll be safe and get good footage. I helped set a few on the beach yesterday morning. You'd have to check with the guys to see where they put theirs."

My mind swirled. "You each have a personal camera? Are any missing?" Like one small enough to hide in a ceiling fan?

"I don't know. No one said anything about losing a camera."

"Can I see yours?"

She set the glass down and detached a small camera with *The Watchers* trademark eye from her belt loop. "These are issued by the show. They're triggered by motion sensors, to save battery and memory space. I set one like this up if I plan to ambush someone with something."

"Ambush?"

"Sure. If I get a good fight on tape, I get a bonus at the end of the shoot."

I released a long breath, refusing to fixate on how low it was to set up a fight between two people for personal gain.

The camera she held looked nothing like the one from Sebastian's room at Island Comforts. Which led to another question. "Do all of the show's cameras have night vision?"

Her face split into a smile. "Of course. How else could we get the goods on who's hooking up? Every camera on the island records at night as long as something sets it off." She giggled and snorted.

I concentrated. So, the camera from the bed-and-breakfast probably wasn't issued by the show. No logo. No night vision. Motion sensors made sense. The video only began when Rick and Anna walked into the room.

My heart hammered as something else occurred to me. "The outdoor cameras must be tripped a lot at night. There's lots of activity after dark. Nocturnal creatures."

She giggled again and my tummy sank. "The forest is tricky. The batteries die in those cameras a lot." She blushed. "Very little triggers the cameras on the beach, though."

I swallowed. "No?"

She watched me squirm. Her face turned pink and she leaned in, conspiratorially. "Nope. Just the occasional nocturnal creatures having a go in the sand, on a picnic table, in a car..."

I held up a palm to stop her. Heat scorched my face. I flipped up the collar on my jacket and wrapped hands around my middle. "What?" This was worse than the dream where I went to the beach naked. In my dream, no one recorded me.

She drew in a quick breath between giggles. "The guys said I should've set more cameras on the beach, but I never dreamed we'd see much going on out there with the temperatures dropping like they are. It's too bad I didn't listen because the couple we caught was hot. The cameras were too far away to get a clear look at the good stuff, but we saw enough. They were wild, you know?"

I gulped.

She looked me over and grunted. "I guess you hear about that stuff all the time. You live here, right? I'm from New York. No beaches like this. Definitely nowhere to get it on outdoors. I give that couple a double thumbs-up for style and enthusiasm. I still can't believe it. Right out in the open."

I wheezed and wiped sweat-slicked palms over my jeans. "The national forest is closed at night." I averted my gaze. Unless they have the magic key to the guard gate like Fargas and Sebastian. "That's not something that happens a lot. You probably won't see anything like that again while you're here." Not a chance in Haiti.

"Bummer."

I zipped up and pulled my hands inside my jacket sleeves before ducking back outside, into a crowd of people who'd probably seen that tape, too. I needed to assemble a street team and take down those cameras... without being caught on camera. I ground my teeth. Someone needed to stop the madness before my first sex tape went viral.

FOURTEEN

FIRST FRIDAYS HAD become date night for Sebastian and me. No matter how busy he was, he never missed a Friday night. Originally, the mayor had suggested First Fridays as a gimmick for drawing in a few extra dollars during tourist season. I was young when the tradition started, and back then it only happened on the first Friday of each month during tourist season. The little shops stayed open an extra hour and ran specials until closing. Within in a few years, the community latched on to First Fridays with both hands. By the time I graduated high school, First Fridays had become a weekly event lasting late into the night. These street fair-style celebrations now began early in the spring and continued until the winter weather insisted otherwise. I hadn't missed a Friday since I moved home.

I squeezed Sebastian's fingers. His slow, lumbering pace put me at ease. Sebastian had loved the island from his first visit, and walking through the streets with him, sensing his contentment, sent butterflies through me. Anxiety and general malaise was a hazard of his job, but none of it showed. Tonight, he was mentally present and almost smiling. His lazy half grin kept me guessing. I fizzed inside with desire to touch his lips. The street buzzed with enough activity and excitement to set a recently-shot-at girl's nerve on edge, but beside Sebastian I felt untouchable.

He projected a steadfast confidence I'd always envied.

Sebastian treated nothing with nonchalance. He was a rock, a refuge, an unwavering solace. He oozed the very things I craved and it gave me chills to be inside his world. Sebastian let very few people past the shield that protected his work, identity, location or heart. When he touched me, I instinctively understood I'd broken all those barriers even if he didn't always give voice to the notions. He didn't talk about his feelings, and ironically, as a counselor, I appreciated that about him.

The final remnants of Indian summer were slipping away, and the night was cool. Overhead the sky twinkled with stars, as if someone had poked thousands of holes in rich velvet fabric and stretched it over the world. Everyone on the street sparkled with contagious energy. Kids noshed on caramel apples and other food on sticks from corn dogs to kabobs.

Sebastian lifted our joined hands. "Look."

Across the street, a pocket of women in stretch dresses and miniskirts circled Vance Varner as if he were giving away cash. I did a mental eye roll. "That's Vance. He's a cast member. Have you met him?"

Sebastian moved in Vance's direction, stopping within earshot. "Not officially."

"He says he was in his trailer while everyone was on the beach that night." I peeked at Sebastian, whose expression flattened. "I'm not getting involved. I just happened to see him and asked if he perhaps killed two people. He said he didn't, so I wondered if he could prove it."

We stopped a few feet behind Vance's harem and listened. He spoke above the crowd and held his shoulders in a stiff pose with his chin at a tilt. Always modeling. Maybe trying to give the crowd his best side. A woman on his right asked for an autograph, and I laughed.

Sebastian turned curious eyes on me.

"He autographed Claire's shirt. You should ask her about it."

Sebastian pulled us closer to the little crowd. "Is he posing for something?"

I followed the direction of Vance's chin. "Sebastian." I whispered, tugging him down to me.

He leaned close to my ear.

"I think you're right. Watch. He keeps his chest angled to that storefront. He's posing. I bet there's a hidden camera over there and he's trying to get face time." I'd ranted about the cameras hidden around the island for thirty minutes while I got ready for First Friday. I couldn't get enough nerve to tell Sebastian about our potential internet debut. Claire and Adrian had been in the kitchen, and it wasn't a story I wanted to share with either of them.

Sebastian released my hand. "I'll look for a camera. Settle down. Your eye's twitching."

"I'm fine."

"Stay here and try not to get arrested." Sebastian walked toward the storefront in question.

For the record, I'd never been arrested, officially, but I'd consider going to jail worthwhile if I could eliminate every voyeuristic camera on the island.

I headed for Vance. "Hi, Vance. How's everything going? Pretty night tonight."

His fans adjusted their halter tops and made room as I slid into the mix.

I looked quizzically at the storefront across the way. "You're awfully interested in that dollhouse shop. Do you know something we don't know, Vance?"

He shook his head, as if I tried his patience. "What are you doing?"

"People on this island deserve to know when they're being videotaped. I think you're setting the stage somehow because you want more time on camera." I looked for Sebastian.

"Lady," Vance snapped, "I don't need to scheme to get face time. I told you that."

People walking nearby stopped to stare.

I made my best innocent face. "The way I see it, models have a short shelf life. More airtime could help you get a role in something that pays the bills when your agent stops calling you for print ads. So, I have to wonder. Where do you draw the line? How far would you go to stay on camera?" I inched closer and lowered my voice. "I bet it's hard to get ahead on this show when the other contestants are sleeping with the host."

His nostrils flared.

"You can't compete with boobs, Vance." I gave him a two-palms-up, out-of-your-control taunt.

Vance sucked his cheeks in and puffed air like the Big Bad Wolf. A vein on the side of his neck bulged. "I had nothing to do with what happened to Rick and Anna. I get plenty of time on camera without trying. Fans ask for this." He bumped a fist against his chest. "People want to see it. They want me on camera."

"Okay." I nodded. I couldn't cross Vance off my mental list of suspects, yet his body language and pupil dilation all indicated he was telling the truth. He believed people watched the show to see him, but I couldn't get a good read on his response to the murders. All he seemed to care about was his self-importance.

In true pontificating goofball form, he stripped off his shirt despite the evening chill. A bunch of ladies swooned and squealed.

"That's ridiculous," I said. "Completely bonkers. What are you doing? It's cold. Get a jacket."

He wrapped goose-bump covered arms around two voluptuous blondes and winked at me. "Thanks, Mom."

I guffawed. A blonde in silver stretch pants laughed. "That's your mom? It's so cool you brought her along."

"I am not his mother!" He was twenty-six years old. Was she blind? I rubbed the creases on my forehead and pulled a swath of bangs down to my eyebrows.

Sebastian cut back through the crowd, carrying a camera. "Got it."

"I am not old enough to be his mother," I muttered.

Sebastian kissed my head and steered me to the cotton candy man. "You did good. One less camera in town. You want pink or blue cotton candy?"

"Blue." I took the warm spun sugar, smiled, and leaned into the curve of Sebastian's body. "Claire took all my good food and she's trying to make me run a marathon."

Sebastian stared.

"Say something."

His forehead creased. "Has she met you?"

I nodded. "She's a meanie. She took everything and left me with whole grain tortillas and yogurt."

"How does that make you feel?" He smiled at his long-running joke on my profession. He'd spent his share of time in required FBI counseling after stints undercover or discharging his firearm. The counselors all asked that question once too often.

"How do I feel about granola and low fat cheese?" I curled my arms against my chest and did a witchy voice. "It burns us."

He narrowed his eyes. "Was that a *Scooby Doo* impression?"

"Stop," I laughed. "I was Gollum."

"No. That was bad. That was like Shaggy doing a Scooby impersonation."

"It was a really good Gollum." I stuffed wads of cotton candy into my mouth. It wilted and vanished on my tongue. "You want to hear it again?"

"No. Definitely not." He kissed my sticky lips. "What are you wearing to Adrian's rally tomorrow? He said we have to come in costume."

A light flicked on inside me. "You're going to Adrian's rally? I thought you'd have to work."

He locked his hands behind my back. "Island politics are deeply important to me. What's your costume?"

"None. You can go as FBI. I'm not wearing any costume."

His lips lifted in an ornery smile. "Dirty. You'll need me for protection then. If you decide against nudity, you can always go as the new face of Extreme Island Makeovers." He turned me to face a sign on the window of Mrs. Davis' tanning salon. She'd taken a candid of me and added clip-art hair and someone else's body.

Fire scorched through my limbs. Had she lost her ever-loving mind? She couldn't do that without my permission. Where'd she get that awful picture of me? I curled my fingers into fists at my side. I looked ridiculous. My hands trembled in frustration. "I can't believe it. I mean. I can't. Can you?" I waved my arms pointlessly. What could I do about it? "She's evil."

Sebastian pulled me back to his body. "Tell me again why you moved back to a place that makes you nuts?"

Words escaped me. I thought he got it. My heart broke a tiny bit as I considered the possibility I was wrong about how he felt about Chincoteague. He might leave once Jimmy the Judge was captured. Then what? My throat thickened.

I took a deep breath. "I moved here because there's nowhere else I'd rather live." The truth of the statement settled into my core. Even with all the quirks and legends and nosy neighbors. Chincoteague was family and you didn't leave your family.

"Just checking." He grabbed my hips. "May I have a bite of that cotton candy?"

I hid the almost-bare paper cone behind my back and licked my lips. "All gone."

He moved closer, pressing his hips to mine. "That's disappointing."

I pulled my gaze from his hypnotic brown eyes to my apartment in the distance. I lifted onto my tiptoes and grazed his ear with my lips. "I might be able to locate a little more sugar at home."

Sebastian growled and lifted me off my feet. I squeaked as he tossed me over one shoulder like a caveman and strode through the crowd toward my home. Best First Friday ever.

ADRIAN'S RALLY WAS hopping when Claire and I arrived. He'd erected a stage on the site of his old boathouse. The boathouse went up in fireworks in July, but he'd rebuilt. Tables of food and arches made of balloons were set in front of a pretty new building, the future home of my counseling practice, if I ever convinced anyone to meet me in an office instead of under the guise of shopping, jogging or driving golf balls.

I adjusted sunglasses over my eyes. The sun wasn't warm, but it reflected off the harbor, bright enough to blind me. Fall hung in the air, hot apple cider lifted from steaming cups and dew-covered leaves floated to the ground with every puff of wind. The buttery scent of scallops called to my tummy. Gulls screamed overhead, circling the giant steamers where Melinda and Missy prepared fresh seafood skewers for the crowd. Random bleating of tugboats on the harbor punctuated the high school band playing our fight song. Adrian's party was magnetic. Street vendors closed in on the scene, moving their carts closer to the action and farther from Main Street. People exited shops and walked immediately in our direction.

Masses of costumed people covered the lawn. It was like attending a masquerade ball outdoors, in full daylight, surrounded by a lot of American flags.

I eyeballed Claire. "This is the strangest campaign rally I've ever attended."

Her formfitting costume emphasized the hours she spent at the gym. A set of trademark eyes printed across her shoulder blades underlined *The Watchers* logo. She'd wound a silk scarf around her head like a headband in poison green, a perfect match for her fingernails and wedges. She adjusted her gadget belt and smiled. "It's fun. I still can't believe you didn't come in costume. Party pooper. We could've been a pair of gorgeous ghost hunting besties, mesmerizing every ghost on the island with our sexy outfits and capturing them with our kickass attitudes."

"Yeah, but every party needs a pooper." I snuggled into my white wool coat and scanned the area for Sebastian. "Sebastian said he'd be here, but he was gone when I woke up this morning. Did you see him?"

Claire pointed to a figure standing next to my parents, who wore Team Adrian shirts and jester hats. "There."

A bolt of electricity shot through me. Sebastian came as FBI, like I'd suggested. "I'll be right back." I crossed the lawn with my eyes locked on familiar black cargo pants and a flak jacket. I snuck up behind him and pressed my hands over his eyes. He crouched, and I whispered against the back of his neck. "I love a man in uniform. Care if I help you out of it later?"

He spun on me in a heartbeat, lifting my feet off the ground and laughing boisterously over the deafening crowd.

Wait a minute. It wasn't like Sebastian to spin me around or laugh like a frat boy. Drat! I slapped the imposter's chest.

"Put me down." I wiggled free and straightened my coat. "What are you doing dressed like that?"

Adrian's freshly washed hair was darkened and wet. He was dressed in full combat gear.

"Where'd you get those clothes?" I demanded.

"Claire."

Of course. His new best friend, Claire. Those two were killing me. "Why are you dressed as FBI?"

"It's a costume rally, and you like a man in uniform, remember?" He pulled me against his side. "I'm hoping your other offer still stands."

"Stop. It's a criminal offense to impersonate a government agent." I shoved his hand away. He put it back the minute I let him go. I pushed it off me. The process escalated to a frenzy of hand slapping.

Mom giggled. "Just like old times. You two never could keep your hands off one another."

"Argh!" I hopped around him and stood beside my mother. I tried glaring at Adrian, but my face wouldn't cooperate and my heart thundered stupidly in my chest.

Mom stroked my arm. "Where's your costume, sweetie?"

"I'm not dressing up."

Claire's laughter rose above the noise of the crowd. She stood with Fargas on the edge of the lawn. They looked oblivious to the two hundred people around them. He handed her a red helium balloon.

"He digs her." Adrian tied a white balloon on my wrist.

"I don't need a balloon. I'm thirty."

He shrugged. "You like balloons. Plus it's cute." He tugged the string and the balloon bounced in the air above my head.

"Thanks."

His soulful blue gaze pierced mine. "I'm glad you came."

A smile curved my lips. I'd never miss a chance to support Adrian. He must've known that. I looked away. "You think they're hooking up behind our backs?" I pointed to Fargas and Claire.

"Looks like it. It's about time, too. He's had his eye on her since the day they met."

"Really?" I turned back to Adrian and regretted it immediately. His eyes burned with unspoken emotion.

"Yeah. He was just a deputy then. She was FBI. He didn't think he had a shot. Now, he's the sheriff. I think he feels like that's enough to earn her respect. Makes him a worthwhile candidate for her attention."

"That's silly. She doesn't care about stuff like that."

"She should. Care that he's trying, I mean. Women aren't the only people who like to be respected, Miss Feminist Pants. Some men would do anything to get a girl's undivided attention." His gaze drifted to the platform where he'd soon give his campaign speech.

"Adrian."

He shook his head and pursed his lips. "Don't read into that. We're talking about Fargas," He squeezed my arms and kissed my cheek. "I'd better go make nice with the citizens of this fair town before I run out of shrimp and they leave."

I struggled for a breath as he walked away. It wasn't fair that after all these years, he still took the oxygen with him when he left.

"Patience!" Claire and Fargas crossed the lawn to me. "Have you heard his speech yet? He practiced it last night on me. It's amazing. He's a great speaker."

I shook my head, fending off emotion I couldn't explain. "You knew that wasn't Sebastian when you sent me over here."

She smiled. Brat.

The microphone screeched and people covered their ears. I recognized most of the faces in the crowd. Locals, reporters, ghost hunters. Todd Ramone and the reporter with the expensive shoes stood on the perimeter. Neither seemed interested in reporting the rally. Instead, they watched the people. Looking for a juicy story, no doubt.

Adrian fiddled with the microphone. His ready smile quieted the crowd. "Ladies and gentlemen, I'd like to thank you all for coming. In light of the recent shootings, we've amped up security." He brushed invisible lint from his Kevlar vest and sucked air. A muffled set of cracks registered in my brain a split second later. Adrian stumbled forward and fell into the microphone stand. Blood poured from his mouth and dripped from his fingertips.

My heart lurched into my throat a moment before the world stopped spinning. A lifetime of memories with Adrian crowded my scrambled thoughts. *This isn't happening.* Adrenaline spiked through my system and my ears rang. *Not him. I need him.*

The crowd turned into a stampeding monster, pounding away from the scene, trampling everything in its path. I jumped into the mix, fighting my way upstream, careening around members of the crowd and bouncing off strangers. Arms slapped me and hips knocked me. I lost my footing twice, landing on my hands and knees in piles of dropped food and discarded flyers.

"Adrian!"

The area cleared out in seconds. Behind me, Fargas barked orders and distant sirens cut through the rush of voices. I looked over my shoulder for the ambulance. News reporters pushed their way forward, but my folks and Claire held them off with idle threats and determination. Flashing lights appeared in the distance.

"Adrian." I flung myself onto him. Blood coated his mouth and neck. "Can you hear me?" My tears dripped onto his cheek and I smoothed them away. "Please, say something. Don't be dead. You cannot be dead. I need you." Sobs racked my chest.

His eyes fluttered and he groaned. "I think I knocked my tooth out. Ow. Oh." He spouted profanity. I wiped tears and sat back in shock. Air shuddered from my chest. If he could gripe, things weren't as bad as they seemed. He wrapped a giant palm around his opposite arm. Blood rolled out between his fingertips and poured from his lips. The fallen microphone was painted red with it. The burn and tear marks on his vest proved its worth. It had saved his life.

"You knocked your tooth loose." I flopped my legs out in front of me. "I thought..." Tears and laughter strangled me. "When someone gets shot and blood comes from their mouth, it's not good." I wiped my eyes and nose on my sleeve. My laughter erupted.

Fargas looked alarmed but stayed in cop mode, securing the perimeter and calling people to action.

Adrian rose onto his elbows as the ambulance drove

through the littered grass to meet us. Becky, the EMT Adrian had dated a few times, opened the driver's side door and gave him a exasperated stare.

"Someone shot me." He rubbed his bloody palm over the vest. "In the arm."

She dropped to his side without speaking and dug into her bag. She checked his vitals, his mouth and his arm before loading him onto the gurney. "Looks like your lucky day." Becky looked at me. "What happened to you?"

My white wool coat was spattered in dirt and hunks of food from falling down on my way to Adrian. His blood darkened the cuffs and collar where I'd thrown myself on him.

I took his hand. Tears stung my eyes. "I'm fine."

Becky looked at our joined fingers. "Are you riding with him to the hospital?" Tension laced the words.

I pulled my hand away. "Oh, um, no. I'll meet you there." I gave him my most supportive smile.

Adrian's eyes grew round like a kicked puppy.

I stroked his cheek. "I'll answer questions here and get a cleanup crew together. Maybe we can put a positive publicity spin on this incident before any rumors get out of hand."

Becky wheeled him toward the ambulance. I waited for the taillights to disappear, then I collapsed into a pile of sobs, tears and snot. Who would want to hurt Adrian? He was an overgrown teddy bear. Everyone loved him. I'd thought. Curiosity sat me upright. An assassination attempt in plain sight of two hundred people was nuts. Adrian was running for Mayor of Chincoteague, not President of the United States. What was going on here?

Claire's shoes came into view. "You okay?"

I steadied my breaths and wiped my face. "I thought."

A nervous giggle-sob escaped. I shook off the over-whelming emotion and pulled in a deep breath. "Yeah. I'm okay."

"Good. Then try to look less heartbroken and more concerned citizen. Sebastian just got here."

I shuffled to my feet.

Sebastian led the way with two guys from the bureau on his flank, eating up the distance between a big black government-issued SUV and Fargas. Adrian had told me the FBI was coming in to investigate the island shootings. Apparently that wasn't hearsay.

Why hadn't Sebastian mentioned it?

I took a step on shaky legs and locked stares with Claire. "I need a few minutes."

She gave me an understanding nod and moved toward Sebastian and his men.

I hobble-jogged across the street for coffee and a breakdown.

FIFTEEN

I HID ACROSS the street, watching the cacophony of chaos settle into a controlled hum. I needed to get to the hospital and let Adrian know I was there. My heart ached as I leaned against the side of our town's only bookstore. My parents and closest friends stood in the littered field, acting as crowd control against an onslaught of reporters. A thousand questions formed a tempest in my brain. Had the shooter been aiming for Adrian, or did they mistake him for Sebastian? The target wasn't me or I'd be in the ambulance right now. I wasn't wearing a bulletproof vest. The wretched week had begun with a double murder in Sebastian's room. An image of Jimmy the Judge snarling down a gun sight twisted my stomach. Was one of his henchmen out there today?

Karen Holsten speed-walked toward me, yelling into her cell phone, "I don't care how it gets done. Just make it happen." Tears streamed down her cheeks. She shoved the phone into her bright orange designer handbag and screamed at the sky. I pressed my back to the wall and she marched past without making eye contact. What had put her on edge? Karen was normally as cold as a fish. Tears and public screaming were out of line with her usually well-executed facade. Unfortunately, I had more pressing issues, like finding out who was trying to kill the men in my life. My questions about Karen's kooky behavior had to get in line. For her sake, she better not have had anything to do with someone taking a shot at Adrian. If this was her cockamamie scheme to give her husband a sure win for mayor, I'd find out and she would be punished. Then, I'd call Fargas.

I took the alley behind me at a snail's pace. It was a short walk home to get my Prius. Claire would let me borrow her car from the rally if I asked, but I was halfway between the two points, and I didn't want to go back. My mind and limbs were as weighted as my heart. I pushed my feet forward but slowed at the sight of a makeshift memorial outside Island Comforts. The tokens of affection seemed to sprout overnight. Curiosity pulled me closer. Teddy bears, notes, photos and panties decorated the small fence around Mrs. Moore's azaleas.

A middle-aged man held a trash bag in front of him, stuffing the memorial inside, one item at a time. His face was red with effort and the bag dragged against his feet.

I maintained my distance as a number of ideas ran through my mind. Was this man a crazed fan? Was he a lowlife who stole tributes like these and sold them on eBay to the highest bidder? Had he rushed over here in a rage after shooting Adrian?

"What are you doing with those things?" My voice hardened with each word.

The man glared at me over tearstained cheeks. Purple crescents underlined each eye. "What does it look like I'm doing? I'm destroying this abomination. Look." He motioned to the lacy underwear hanging on the fence and goodbye notes signed with lip prints. "It's disgusting. The man dies in bed with my daughter, and women still come to leave this…this…trash for his memory." He wiped his face with a handkerchief.

"You're Anna's dad?"

"Yes." He pulled a fresh bag from the pocket of his coat and shook it open. "She was a nice girl before all this. She had real friends, good grades and a future." His voice broke on the last word. "A year after joining up with this show, she dropped out of college and moved to L.A. permanently. She traveled everywhere with these gypsies, and we were lucky to see her twice a year. At Christmas she announced her love for Rick Fitzgerald. He was nearly twice her age, for crying out loud. Her mother almost had a stroke. We said he was too old for her. She didn't want to hear that. True love, she said. She called all the time crying after she took up with him. Rick cheated on her, but she could never prove it. They'd fight and make up. We begged her to come home. She wouldn't." He shook his head and ripped notes off Mrs. Moore's fence. "Next thing you know, she says they'd made up for good, and that all the suspicions she had about him were misunderstandings on her part."

He stood poker straight and stared at the house before us. "I can't believe she's gone. That she died here, like this."

"I'm sorry for your loss." The words were stupid. Not enough. He'd lost a child and all I had to offer him was "I'm sorry." "I'm sorry" worked when you stepped on someone's foot or spilled their drink. There weren't words for what had happened to him.

I turned away, dumbfounded, and moved toward my apartment. My heart grieved for Anna's father, but I couldn't help wondering how long he'd been in town and if there was a chance he'd waited on Rick Fitzgerald in Sebastian's room that night. It was dark when the shots were fired. If he believed Rick was cheating, ruining his little girl's life, would he come to confront the man breaking his daughter's heart? Would he come with a gun? Could he have made a terrible mistake?

Flick's Funeral Home came into view and I walked

along the farthest edge of the sidewalk, unwilling to cross the street. The old empty home seemed to watch me approach. A handful of *The Watchers* staff lined the walkway to the front door. Lights were on inside the house and stagehands positioned silver canopies on the yard.

I recoiled. The little old lady who owned the place had lost her mind last month and tried to kill me. She was in jail now, but I'd seen her at a serious level of crazy. Part of me imagined she somehow got free and waited inside the funeral home for me. I'd never step foot in that place again. I had nightmares about her.

Adrenaline replaced defeat in my bones. As I turned to run, my nose bounced off a familiarly scented shirt. Todd Ramone caught my shoulders in his palms. "Slow down, speedy. Where you off to in such a hurry?"

"Are you kidding me?" I wailed. "Why are you still following me? Didn't you hear there was a shooting today?"

"Yep. Saw the whole thing, including a little blonde racing against the crowd, despite a gunman on the loose, trying to save her one true love."

I squared my shoulders. "I thought he was dead. Also, I'm not blonde. I spend a lot of time in the sun."

Todd snorted. I scooted around him on the sidewalk. "Stop following me."

He matched my pace. "What if the gunman had shot you while you were laying in a heap over your ex-lover?"

I hadn't thought of that. "I don't know. Don't call him that. His name's Adrian Davis."

"Fair enough. What were you thinking?"

How I needed him. That I couldn't lose him. To lose Adrian again would be like ripping my soul down the center. I faltered and then regained my speed. Clearly I was traumatized.

"What does your boyfriend think of your attachment to your ex?"

I hustled around the corner toward my apartment. "There was a shooting," I growled. "My love life is hardly interesting in comparison. I'm not the story here."

He laughed. Loud. "Come on. You're smarter than this. You want to know why I'm interested in your story? Let me see." He tapped his chin. "Someone's trying to kill one of your boyfriends. Three times this week, in my humble opinion. That puts you at the center of my investigation. Aside from that, your island interests me, and half the shenanigans I read up on lead back to you somehow. You're like the linchpin of all strange happenings. Where were you when Rick and Anna were shot?"

I skidded to a stop. "You think I'm a suspect? I was in the Range Rover with Adrian the other night, and I ran to help Adrian today. You stink at your job, buddy. I mean, Lou."

"Getting mad won't change the fact you know exactly what I mean and why I'm following you. Those men orbit around you like you're their home planet. If I stick to you, this story will unwrap itself and land in my lap. The icing for me is that following you is fun. Your parents are a hoot. People randomly corner you to unload personal and, let's face it, kind-of-funny stories. Some lady in skintight sequins wants you to be her spokesmodel so bad she put you on her store window. I saw you hiding at a food truck from her. Some angry guy made fun of your hair for no reason. Your life's got spunk."

He was right about that last part. My life was bananas, but they were my bananas, and I didn't want them posted online.

"Fine." I tightened my ponytail. "You'll post whatever you want online anyway. Lou." I dragged out his pen name.

"With you as my subject, I don't need to invent anything. People can't make up the kind of stuff you get into. In the interest of fairness, here's a truth about me." His voice slid into a sweet Southern drawl on the last few words. "I'm not from L.A. I'm from Alabama. Readers assume all the reporters for the Hollywood Watcher live in L.A. It's not true. I travel as needed but, for the most part, you'll find me in Birmingham."

I appreciated the honesty. "What's your real name?"

"Todd Ramone."

I raised an eyebrow.

"Really."

"Okay." I looked him over, ideas buzzing in my head. "I'm short one partner in crime and, contrary to what it looks like, I'm trying not to get involved in this mess."

Todd widened his stance and folded his arms. His blue eyes twinkled with intense interest. "Go on."

"I have a proposition. What if I buy you lunch and we trade information over a friendly meal? I'm definitely not investigating this, but you are and I really want to know what's going on. I suggest our lunch and the entire conversation should be off the record. You don't mention it online or elsewhere, and I'll keep it to myself, too."

He extended a hand. "Deal. Except, I'm buying lunch and don't give me any feminism equality business. I buy women lunch and not the other way around. My mama taught me right."

His full Southern charm raised a smile on my lips. I didn't trust him out of my sight, but I wanted to know what he knew. Bad.

I called Mrs. Davis to check on Adrian. I was that

desperate. She pointed out his shooting was my fault and then asked if I'd made a decision about her job opportunity. I hung my head and disconnected.

"Adrian's being discharged into his mom's care," I told Todd. "He'll probably be at my place when we finish lunch, so I can't stay long."

Todd pulled the door open to the Tasty Cream and stepped aside for me to pass. I chose a table with a view of my apartment so I could watch for Adrian, Claire or Sebastian's return. We ordered burgers, fries and malts then got down to business.

"To clarify—" Todd dragged a fry through ketchup, "—this is you *not* investigating?"

I nodded sincerely. My mouth struggled around the melted Swiss, onions and mushrooms on my burger. I dotted the corner of my lips with a napkin and swallowed. "I'm staying out of this."

"Denial is one way to cope with your problems." He chuckled. "Is there a reason you're staking out your own apartment?"

"Yes. I don't want to be seen with you and a lot of vigilant people are staying at my place this week. If I spot them first, I can duck." I tugged on the uncooperative straw in my malt. Working Mrs. Tucker's malts out of the cup was sometimes painful, but always rewarding, like the soreness people felt after working out at the gym. My cheeks sucked together and my brain pinched.

"All right, then. Let's get started before you're spotted sharing a meal with a handsome reporter. No need to stir up any more jealousy." He winked and pushed another fry into his mouth. "If Rick and Anna's death wasn't an attempted hit on one of your boyfriends, I think it was about the show's award money."

I put the cup down. "Thank you. There's always money involved somehow."

His eyes twinkled. "We agree on something."

"Yes." I tried the straw again, earning a little taste of the joy to come when my malt melted a bit more. "So good."

"I think there's magic in here." He tilted the cup and looked down the open end of his straw.

The chair beside me scraped back and Henry Franks fell into it, looking like he'd fallen into a vat of paint. His coveralls were splattered and doused in white. The same color was smeared across his cheeks and forehead. "Thank heavens I found you."

Todd leaned away and wedged an elbow over the back of his chair. A crooked smile lit his face.

"Hi, Mr. Franks." Awkwardness dropped over me. Mr. Franks was a client who loved his wife more than anything, but she constantly accused him of cheating, most recently with me. She was also my client, unbeknownst to him. She acknowledged her tendencies toward paranoia and anger management issues, but she sometimes egged and graffitied my car if she saw me talking to her husband. He did handyman work in exchange for our impromptu sessions. Confidentiality kept me from disclosing our true relationships to either of the Franks.

Mr. Franks slumped. He heaved a sigh and landed his weary gaze on me. "The town hired me to paint over some of the spray paint the ghost hunters and fans are leaving around the island. They keep painting those creepy eyes in glow-in-the-dark paint. It's hard for me to see it in the daylight, so I go out after dark. My wife thinks I'm cheating. She's losing her mind over it. I can't sleep when I'm home because she yells all day. At night

I comb the island looking for the eyeballs. It's giving me nightmares, so when she does let me sleep, I still don't rest."

Todd lifted his eyebrows.

"Well." I pulled in a deep breath, unsure how to proceed with an audience member who doubled as a reporter. "You need to get proper sleep. Please make taking care of yourself the priority. Without enough rest, you'll get sick easier and feel disoriented, nauseous and moody." The list sounded a lot like my life. I took another long breath. "Have you told your wife what you're up to at night? Maybe she doesn't understand your sudden change in work hours."

"I have. She doesn't believe me. She thinks I cover myself in paint as some kind of kinky role play or an elaborate cover-up. You know how she is."

That earned me another looked from Todd.

I needed to get rid of Mr. Franks before his marital troubles became a news story. "Well, have you considered taking her with you? Invite her along. Ask for her help. Maybe she wants to feel needed."

He perked up. "You think? She's been making big dinners and doing things for me, then getting mad when I can't stay awake to enjoy them."

"Definitely tell her you need her help." I sucked on my malt to consider my own feelings about being needed. The chocolaty heaven rushed to my tongue.

"You're a lifesaver, Patience. I can't thank you enough. Really. Lunch is on me. Thank you." He patted Todd's back. "Sorry I interrupted your date, buddy. She's a good one. Hold on to this girl." Mr. Franks dropped a line of twenties on the table between Todd and me, before disappearing around the corner.

Todd fingered the money and whistled. "Nice scheme you got going here."

I slapped his hand and pocketed the money. "It's not a scheme and that encounter was none of your business. Got it?" I leaned across the table with my angry face. "Also, this is not a date so don't say a word."

He stuffed a handful of fries between his lips and talked anyway. "You've got your hands full in the date department. You know what I found interesting about your advice? I learned you like to feel needed. It explains a lot, really. Counseling is the perfect profession to fulfill that internal craving, but I guess you know that. You know another way to feel needed? Crime solving. Saving the city. Superhero stuff."

"I hate you." I busied my mouth with the burger and Todd laughed. I looked out the window for a sign Adrian had returned. Nothing.

"Ah, but we're a dynamic duo. United for a common goal. We seek the truth." He smiled. "Now, who's on your suspect list?"

We agreed about the suspects, assuming the initial gunmen meant to kill Rick and Anna. Most likely: another contestant. The contestants all had alibis, except Vance. A crazed fan was less likely, but possible. Dan and Elisa both had solid motives. Elisa admitted her anger with Anna for sleeping with Rick. If Dan knew about Rick and Elisa, it was a reasonable assumption Dan would feel betrayed too. Todd and I both questioned the strength of their video chat alibi. Todd dished the inside scoop on the cast dynamics, hookups and breakups, and the ongoing frenemy status of everyone on set. Traveling and living together made them friends, but ultimately the cash prize kept their friendships in a strange limbo, where trust was always an issue. Complicated.

I told him about the hidden stairway and lack of hiding places in the room.

He already knew Anna's dad was on the island. Todd had a contact at the closest airport watching for his name in past and current logs. Mr. Copeland had arrived this morning on a direct flight from Minnesota. I sighed in relief as I mentally crossed him off the list of suspects.

Todd provided far more details than I had to offer in return. He impressed me. "You're good at this."

"I used to be a cop."

I put my burger down. "How old are you?"

"Thirty-one. I did four years in the army after high school. My parents couldn't afford college. They didn't even suggest it. I was the first in my family to go to college, but one in a long line of soldiers. I used the GI Bill for tuition. Got a degree in criminal justice, went to the police academy and was issuing parking tickets in no time." His lips turned down.

"Not what you expected."

"No."

"So, why didn't you shoot higher? Detective, or law school, or another branch of government?"

"Like the FBI?" He smiled. "Look at you. You get canned and you're still recruiting."

As human resource manager, I'd recruited college students across the country, seeking the best and brightest, and enticed them to use their powers for good. I wanted a strong frontline for our Federal Bureau of Investigation. I'd loved my job. Seeing that first glint of possibilities in students' eyes. Shaking hands across my desk when new agents were hired. Even though the bureau had nixed me, I still believed in them.

"Speaking of the FBI, it was a little humorous that

the candidate, also known as your ex-lover, dressed up as your current lover." He wiggled his brows.

Had Adrian dressed as Sebastian? FBI, yes. Did he intend his costume to be Sebastian? Maybe. Even injured, Adrian made me crazy. What was his point with that getup? I shook off the thought. Adrian's mind was a carnival. Who knew why he did anything? Besides, this particular decision probably saved his life.

I focused on the important questions. "What do you know about the insult guy from yesterday? He didn't look like a reporter. Everyone else with a press badge either dresses to fit in or is wearing a cheap suit and is followed by a cameraman. That guy had on thousand-dollar loafers."

Todd rested his elbows on the table. "A thousand dollars? Really?"

"Yeah. I'm almost positive. I'd need to confirm with Claire, but yeah."

"Interesting." Todd leaned forward and looked around us before opening his mouth.

"Patience!" Frankie dashed to my side. "Are you okay? I looked all over for you." She rubbed my back, then leaned over and hugged me.

"I'm okay. They're releasing Adrian into his mom's care." I peeked out the window again. Still no sign of my houseguests or Adrian's mom coming to blame me somehow. I turned back to Frankie and smiled. "Look at you in your uniform. I'm not used to this look, but I love it."

She stood to her full six feet, looking proud. "We didn't catch the shooter, but we know where he was standing and we confiscated about a hundred cell phones with cameras. We're comparing the footage from today with the footage captured outside Sebastian's Range

Rover the other night. I'm picking up milkshakes and heading back to look for anyone present at both shootings. Maybe we can identify the gunman."

"Talk to Jesse Short. He admitted to placing hidden cameras all over the island. He might have a camera still running over there." I blew out a long breath. If they caught the shooter, they might take all the cameras down and collect the footage as evidence, which was a good thing. If necessary, however, I'd spend a lifetime denying the footage of Sebastian and me on the beach.

Her eyes narrowed. "He can't do that."

I nodded. "That's what I told him."

"I'll have a talk with Mr. Short. I'm glad Sebastian's crew came over today. We needed the added manpower. Sebastian's been so busy running around the island lately, we weren't sure he put in the call."

I bristled. "He always does what he says he'll do." Her other words prodded my brain. "Sebastian's been here on the island? I thought he was on the mainland most of the time."

Todd let out a low whistle. "Well, that's awkward."

I gave him a stay-out-of-it face.

If Sebastian was on the island every day, why'd he take off in the morning and stay gone? What was he so busy doing? I barely saw him. Was he putting distance between us? At First Friday he asked why I'd moved home. Maybe he was having a change of heart. He'd catch Jimmy and go back to the mainland.

I swallowed a lump and pushed my half-eaten burger away. The last time he stayed away from me was because he thought Jimmy had found him and he was protecting me. All current signs pointed in that direction again. The couple in Sebastian's room. A shooting at his Range Rover. A shooting at Adrian dressed as… FBI.

Todd stood and extended a hand to Frankie. "Todd Ramone. I'm a friend of Patience's." I'd rudely forgotten to introduce them. He complimented her uniform. She blushed. His smile widened and his sparkly blue eyes darkened. They moved away from the table, chatting a little closely for strangers.

I checked out the window for Adrian again. If he was the shooter's intended target, things were bad. Adrian was running for office. He couldn't stay out of the public eye or he'd lose the election. His opponent Beau Thompson and his new wife, Karen Holsten Thompson, would love for that to happen. Hopefully they didn't love the idea enough to hire a shooter. Adrian needed to win that election. Coach Peters had a lot riding on it. I cringed. The island needed Adrian, but if he kept campaigning, the shooter would have unending opportunities to finish the job.

The Tasty Cream door sucked open and a masculine silhouette moved through the blinding light toward me in steady strides. Sebastian dropped to a squat beside my table. His careful eyes examined me head-to-toe. "Are you okay?"

If the gunman was hired to kill Sebastian, the shooter would have more chances to get at him, too. Sebastian couldn't solve the murders from a safe house. He wouldn't go to a safe house even if it was an option. Sebastian didn't hide, he barreled in, guns blazing and bad guys falling. I shivered.

Sebastian kissed my temple and slid into the seat Todd had occupied a moment before. "You disappeared. I assumed you went with Adrian to the hospital, but when I checked on him, he hadn't seen you. I worried you were abducted."

I wasn't sure if the abduction line was supposed to

be a joke. It wouldn't be the first time I was abducted this summer, or the first time he came to my rescue. His other words registered a minute late. "You went to check on Adrian?"

"Yeah. He's fine. A little too happy for a gunshot victim, if you ask me. Who's he supposed to be dressed up as anyway?"

I choked on a laugh and busied my mouth with the straw from my chocolate malt.

The odds of Rick and Anna's murders having anything to do with the show dwindled, and selfishly, I hated that truth. If some lunatic on the island was literally gunning for one of my guys, they'd have to deal with me first. Resolution straightened my spine. Before I'd let something else happen to Adrian or Sebastian, things would have to get messy.

SIXTEEN

SEBASTIAN WALKED ME across the street. No sign of Adrian or Mrs. Davis, but Maple Shuster stood up on my stoop. Sebastian turned his back on her and spoke softly. "You ready for her? If not, I can come in and do my thing."

His thing came down to silent intimidation. If he came inside with the intention of keeping Maple on her best behavior, he would succeed, but I wanted to talk with Maple and welcomed any new information she had on the shooting.

"I'm fine. Maybe she can distract me." The air was dense with tension and clung to my skin, prickling my arms and urging every instinct I had to attention. I scanned the area for danger. Paranoia was a sure sign of anxiety and sleep deprivation. I suffered from both.

"If you're sure." He turned back to the steps outside my apartment, giving Mrs. Shuster a clear view of his stern face. "I'll check in on the team and come back in thirty. I think you should take a day off."

I patted his arm and walked away. I wasn't a child. I knew what I could handle and when I needed a break.

"Hi, Mrs. Shuster." I slunk up the steps with a forced smile. "What's that?"

"Delivery." She presented a bakery box from Half Baked.

"Thanks." I unlocked the door and ushered her inside. "Everything okay?" I made room for the box on the counter and worked the tape until the lid gave way. Every flat space in sight spilled over with food truck bags. Apparently, Adrian had made his rounds before the rally. I had enough junk food to sponsor First Fridays all by myself. I smiled. Claire couldn't win this battle. Adrian hauled it in faster than she could throw it away.

"No." Maple's voice quaked. "I'm not okay at all. The reporters are all over me. I'm repeating stories I never meant to tell the first time. It's a gossip's worst nightmare out there. I'm spilling my guts to anyone who asks, and I can't stop. I'm sick. I need help."

Her wild eyes worried me.

"Here." I took her elbow and led her to the couch. "I'll make hot tea and share my treats."

She nodded and lowered herself onto the cushions. I filled the Keurig with water and dug through the cupboard where mom dropped off vitamins and other healthy things I never opened. "I have chamomile and lavender tea." The tea came in handy when I had a cold.

"What's in the bakery box?" she asked.

"You mean this isn't from you?" I stuck a tea bag in her hot water and lifted the cardboard box lid. "I wonder who sent it?"

"I hope they sent a pumpkin roll. Half Baked makes a pumpkin roll to die for."

"Well." I lifted a Halloween cupcake from the box. "They're cupcakes with a holiday theme."

"Oh, dear." She levered her body off my couch and crept over to me. "That's…nice."

The white cupcakes were wrapped in black papers. Red gel icing dripped from the top where a tiny fondant knife jammed into each cake. The overall look was professional but creepy.

I tore my gaze off the frosting. "Who sent them?"

She shrugged. "The box was on your stoop when I got here."

"I guess they're appropriate. Four days before Halloween, on an island crawling with ghost hunters. Someone probably thinks it's funny. They know I hate all the hoopla."

"You hate the hoopla?"

I backpedaled before "Patience Price hates Halloween" was tomorrow's headline. "Well, the shootings are scary."

She took the cupcake from my hand and ate the knife. "This is delicious."

"Maybe you should avoid the reporters." I unwrapped a cupcake. "If they upset you, try to steer clear."

"I have too much time on my hands. Never retire, sweetie. There's nothing to do."

No risk of that on my end.

She sipped her tea and savored the cupcake, humming with pleasure between bites. "I'm helping your parents at their shop. The reporters go there a lot. They like to ask about you. I guess I could help less at the Purple Pony until this blows over. I applied at the police station for the receptionist position. If I get that job, I'll be safe from reporters. Sheriff Fargas runs a tight ship over there."

"The reporters ask about me?"

She nodded. "The Purple Pony's more fun than the police station, though. Your dad's running for the title of Mr. T-shirt. I'm helping him brainstorm new shirt ideas. All these tourists are sending shirts back home and putting pictures of their custom shirts online. The orders never end. He's swamped. Business is booming."

"Dad's running for Mr. T-shirt? Against who?" Dad was the only custom shirt guy on the island.

"Oh, honey. It's a national contest. Don't you use the internet?"

"I have email." Who had time to surf the internet? I barely had time to watch the local news.

"Look. This one was my idea." She unbuttoned her floral blouse and stretched the fabric wide. A bright yellow shirt announced Gossips Use Their Mouths. "Do you think it's too much?"

I set my cupcake on the counter and rubbed my neck. "I think you could get in a heap of trouble walking around like that." I fought off a wave of childish humor bubbling in my chest. Half of me wanted to call and scold my dad for printing the shirt, the other half wanted to text a picture of it to Claire.

"I like it. I have it in pink and blue. Do you think these shirts are the reason so many reporters flock to me?"

You think? I focused my thoughts. "What do they want to know about me?"

Her eyes lit up. "Mostly they ask if all the stories are true. Like, if you worked for the FBI and if you solve crimes and counsel folks. They also ask if you're anything like your parents and who I think you'll end up with romantically." She wiggled her penciled-on eyebrows. "Sometimes they ask where you live."

Good grief. "You don't tell them where I live, do you?"

"No. I only say you live in one of the most haunted buildings in town. I'd never give your address." She lifted her teacup and smiled. "Do you want to know something?"

I made a cup of coffee. No tea for me. I didn't have time for feeling calm. "What?"

"Karen Holsten's pregnant. She and Beau eloped when they found out so they wouldn't end up with a shotgun wedding. They worried they'd lose the church vote if they didn't. In about seven months, she's going to have 'premature' labor." She dropped her hands after the air quotes.

Huh. It fit. Karen was emotional. Also, she didn't insult me when she had the opportunity and her waist looked less like Barbie's and more like a regular person's.

"You know what else?"

I shook my head, contemplating Karen as a mother. "No. No more gossip. You said you want to get a handle on this habit, remember?" I sipped fresh coffee and cleared my thoughts.

"Anna Copeland's father caught a cab out of town. I saw him get in when I was on my way over here. He dropped two big trash bags into the dumpster by the harbor, flagged a cab and said, 'Take me away from here. I've had enough of this town.' I can't imagine what was in those bags."

"How'd you know it was him?"

Maple huffed. "May I?" She motioned to Sebastian's laptop.

I opened a browser and sat with her on the couch.

She brought up HollywoodWatcher.com. "They've posted pictures of Anna's family online." A picture of Mr. Copeland dismantling the memorial was front-page news. "Oh. That explains the bags. Did you know he's a Baptist pastor in a little town out West? He's big on community rallies and fund-raising, things like that. I bet it killed him when Anna joined *The Watchers*. You think he hated her lifestyle choices enough to do something about it?"

"I don't think he's a killer. I think he's a grieving father."

Footfalls tromped up my steps. I opened the door

when Claire's laugh rang out. Sebastian, Claire and Adrian smiled on the stoop outside my front door. My heart soared. "Come in." I shooed Mrs. Shuster off the couch and set her teacup on the kitchen table.

She hustled out of the way. "Oh, dear."

Adrian leaned on Sebastian until they crossed the threshold. "There you are, sexy." Adrian drunk-walked to me and wrapped his arms around my head. His weight tilted me off balance and I stumbled.

He stood and wobbled backward. Sebastian had him by his shirt. "That's enough of that, lover boy." He led him to the couch and let him go. Adrian face planted into the cushions with an "Oomph."

"He's drugged. Painkillers." Sebastian looked at me under heavy lidded eyes. "I found him arguing with his mom and broke it up. Sounded like he was safer here than with her. I had no idea they had such issues."

"What kind of issues?" Maple leaned forward in her seat at my table.

Sebastian widened his stance and anchored giant palms over his narrow waist.

No one breathed for several beats.

"Well, thank you for the tea." Maple scuttled out the front door with a backward wave.

Having a scary boyfriend was handy. I loved Maple too much to ask her to go, but I needed to talk with this crowd alone. It was shameless and cowardly of me to take advantage of Sebastian that way, but still nice.

Claire headed out behind Maple. "See you later."

"Wait. You just got here," I complained.

"I needed to change shoes. I'm filming a scene for the Halloween special now. I'll be back after and we can catch up. Maybe his meds will wear off by then."

She pointed a thumb at Adrian, who was smiling at my carpet.

I gave her a quick hug. "Deal."

Claire grabbed my shoulders. "The producer, Jesse, said the camera loves me and he invited me to the Halloween bash as his personal guest. Can you believe that?"

"Wow. Hey, did you order some Halloween cupcakes?"

She gave me a crazy face.

Right. She was the one throwing out my goodies.

"Never mind. Congratulations. Have fun today." I waved goodbye as she bounced down the steps to her car.

Inside, I caught Sebastian's gaze and groaned. "I don't trust that producer or his stupid hidden cameras."

Sebastian secured the door behind me and went for the cupcake box. "These are weird." He lifted one and turned it in his palm.

"They're from Half Baked. I'm guessing they're from Missy or Melinda, but they didn't enclose a note. Missy said they use Half Baked for help on orders for baked goods she and Melinda can't fill. I saw her there earlier this week. They are weird cupcakes. In honor of Halloween this week, maybe?"

He grunted and ate a little knife.

Adrian rolled onto his side. "What'd Maple tell you? I missed her today. I like to check with her after my morning jog. She fills me in on the new gossip."

I sighed. "You shouldn't encourage her. She wants to break the habit. I think she gossips because people expect her to, so stop asking."

"Okay." He nodded several seconds too long. "What'd she say?"

I bit my tongue. Adrian would appreciate one nugget

of information more than anyone else I knew. Besides, everyone would know soon. It wasn't like she could hide it forever. I crossed the room to sit with him. "Karen and Beau eloped because she's pregnant."

Adrian cackled. "Ah, good for them, man. Good for them. That's wonderful. Beau will make an excellent father. How'd you take the news? I know how you feel about babies."

Sebastian lumbered near. "What's he talking about? How do you feel about babies?"

"Fine." My cheeks burned.

"She doesn't want kids. Never did."

My tummy knotted. He was right. In the past, I hadn't. I'd had a clear idea about life when I was younger. Before college. Before the FBI. Before moving home and meeting Melinda and her family. I didn't know what I wanted now. A few weeks without a near-death experience was on my short-term goal list. Down the road... I didn't hate the idea of having a family. It wouldn't be terrible to have a husband or push a stroller through the sand.

"Is that true?" Sebastian's voice had an edge to it I didn't recognize.

"Yep," Adrian babbled. "I'd say she was the perfect woman if it wasn't for that."

"What?" I appraised his face. His eyes were glassy from painkillers. Still, I couldn't help myself. "You never said you wanted children."

"Last time we talked about children, I was eighteen. Of course I didn't want children then. I do now." He raised onto one elbow. "Why do you think I bought a house with seven bedrooms?" He flopped back and smiled. "I'm going to teach my kids to swim and kayak and cook shrimp."

"What about football?"

He was a college football star. What about that?

"Ah. Football comes later. I don't care if they play ball. I want them to love our island, though. That's first." Adrian looked at Sebastian. "What about you, tough guy? You adding any little soldiers to your army?"

Sebastian gave him a sour look. "You should rest."

Adrian's eyes drifted shut. He looked helpless lying there and my heart tugged. I needed to figure out who the gunman's true target was and then make sure he never had another chance to hurt someone I cared about.

"Company." Sebastian nodded at the door and disappeared into my bedroom.

A two-headed shadow appeared outside my door. I rushed to let them in. "There you are." Dad hugged me and plopped a stack of shirts onto my table.

Mom opened a trash bag and shoved food truck food inside.

"Hi, Dad. What's going on? Mom, stop cleaning. That's Adrian's food. You shouldn't throw it out." I curved a protective arm around my cupcakes. She emptied the counter and started wiping it down with baking soda and half a lemon.

Dad nudged me. "I want to run some ideas past you. I'm running for Mr. T-shirt, so the ideas have to be good. I need input."

I turned my back on Mom. I couldn't stop her, but I didn't have to watch.

"Okay. Go."

Dad fanned a white shirt over his chest. Special Agents Use Handcuffs.

Sebastian snorted and coughed behind me. "Hey, Mr. Price. I saw someone on the stairs, so I got out of the way. I never know if company comes for a few private minutes of counseling or if they're here to visit."

Him and me both.

Wait. Was he explaining himself to my dad? I looked at Dad. He could care less that Sebastian came from my room or that Adrian was stoned on my couch.

"You like the shirt?" Dad shook it at arms' length, displaying his product to Sebastian, who looked uncomfortable.

Sebastian's mouth opened and shut.

"Well?" I enjoyed the sight of such an intimidating guy rocking on his heels. "Do you like that?"

Mom interrupted. "Leave the poor boy alone." Only my mother would address a thirty-five-year-old federal agent and former navy SEAL as "boy."

I stepped closer to Sebastian, unable to stop taunting him. "You do use handcuffs, right? What's so hard about this question?"

Dad giggled. "It means in bed." He tousled my hair. "It's a double entendre."

My jaw fell open and snapped shut. Really. Why did anything surprise me anymore?

I looked at Dad's eager eyes, Adrian petting my shag carpet and Mom scrubbing a lemon against my counter top, then I leaned against Sebastian's chest. "These are my people."

He wrapped strong arms around my waist and kissed my head. "I like your people."

SEVENTEEN

MOM WAS BACK first thing the next morning, buzzing around my apartment, wiping already clean counters and singing a seventies rock ballad. "How'd he do last night?" She motioned to Adrian on my couch.

"Adrian hasn't moved this morning. Claire had to sleep on the cot in his office. She didn't love it."

Mom shoved her bottom lip forward. "How'd the filming go for her? She looked adorable in her ghost-hunting gear."

I smiled. "She's ecstatic. She came home on a cloud. I didn't know being an extra was so exciting, but she kept me up until midnight talking about how good it felt to be back in the spotlight. Apparently she's a versatile actress. From princess to ghost hunter."

Blueberry syrup slid over the short stack in front of me. Dad had brought breakfast from the Baby Cakes food truck. The rich buttery aroma of hotcakes and flavored coffee made my little apartment feel homey. Sebastian forked sausage and eggs in silence. The bureau had nicknamed him the chameleon for his ability to blend in, but sitting with my parents and me, he might as well have been a six-foot dancing polar bear.

When Mom finished cleaning my apartment, both physically and spiritually, she made tea from a container of leaves she kept in her purse and poured four glasses. Sebastian tipped his cup, eyeballing the little leaves swirling in the mix.

Mom stirred her tea more often than she sipped. She kept watch on Sebastian and me, probably waiting to snag our empty cups and read the leaves. "Patience."

Dad, Sebastian and I stilled.

Mom smoothed her long gauzy skirt. "Have you made a list of all the people who might want to hurt you? I know you think the danger is focused on Adrian or Sebastian, but as your mother, I think it's wise to give this some thought. Is there any chance you were the intended victim in any of these crimes? With so many people in town, there could be more than one shooter."

"Mom." I relaxed my shoulders, hoping to convey a calm, peaceful demeanor. "I'm not sure what's going on here, but I don't think any of this was directed at me. Last time, the gunman aimed for Adrian. I was nowhere near him."

Dad made strange clucking sounds.

"What?" I lifted both eyebrows, daring him to argue.

"Well, you have a hefty list of people who might like to see you sleeping with the fishes. Also, stop looking so peaceful. It's eerie."

I stiffened my spine. "That's not true. My biggest nemesis is Karen Holsten Thompson and she's not a murderer."

Sebastian lifted his teacup to his crooked lips. "She did burn your eyebrows off."

I lifted fingers to the stubble growing on my brow bone.

Not long ago, Karen snuck over to my new office and filled a hibachi with lighter fluid, hoping to make a scene. I arrived later and added some more fluid, unknowingly. I lit a match and *FOOM*. No eyebrows. Though, they were growing back nicely.

Dad clucked some more. "She could easily dodge a

murder charge with all those pregnancy hormones flowing through her. Temporary insanity. If I ever planned a murder, I'd wait for a pregnancy, or afterward. Makes some people do crazy things."

Mom nodded in agreement.

"No. Stop it." I wrinkled my nose.

Of course they'd heard about Karen's pregnancy. Maple spent her spare time with my parents. The idea of Karen as a mother faltered in my head. How could she be a mom? I graduated from high school with her. The logical portion of my brain understood women had babies much younger than thirty, but this was a woman I'd known in pigtails. If she was old enough for motherhood, so was I. The idea both thrilled and horrified me.

"What about Mark Mathers's wife?" Dad added. "You sent her sick husband to jail. She's surviving on money from homemade jewelry now, and who knows how they're treating him in the big house."

My mouth popped open to defend Mary Mathers, but I couldn't argue. People had killed for less.

Mom set her teacup aside. "What about Mrs. Flick's family, or a member of Sheriff Murray's family? Someone you haven't met might hold a grudge about something that happened to their loved one at your hand."

My voice hitched. "Those people tried to kill me."

Dad patted my hand. "Sheriff Murray worked with some dangerous people this summer who might blame you for foiling their trafficking scheme. I think your mother's right. You should make a list."

I looked to Sebastian for help. Aside from the clenching of his jaw, he sat motionless beside me.

"Fine. I'll make a list, but first, can I get anyone a cupcake?" I hustled to the kitchen and loaded a plate with cupcakes. "Did you guys happen to order these for me?" I set the plate on the table, and Mom gaped.

"Heavens no." She leaned away from the bloody knife cupcakes. "Those are filled with processed sugar and look at the blood drizzle. Red Dye #40 is the main ingredient in that. Completely toxic. You shouldn't eat those."

I lifted one to my mouth and took a bite.

Mom sighed. "No wonder you don't sleep."

Sure. Red dye. That was the reason.

I focused my attention on Sebastian and swallowed. "They could be right. This could be about me."

He stared for several beats. "Maybe."

Dad pulled a knife off one cupcake and made little stabbing motions in the air. "Adrian was the target this time. We can't argue about that. They shot him twice."

"Who shot me?" Adrian rolled over on the couch and winced. "Damn. Someone shot me." He rubbed his chest and arm. His face crunched in pain. "Are those cupcakes?"

I carried one to the coffee table and left it with a cup of fresh tea. "You had one yesterday. Don't you remember?"

He pulled the knife from the top and made stabbing motions like Dad.

Dad laughed.

"Not really. Thanks. Yesterday's fuzzy. Whatever Becky gave me for pain was powerful. I dreamed of lollipops and butterflies." He moved in slow motion to an upright position.

His expression pained me. "Did they give you pills for today? It looks like you're in pain."

Deep purple bruises stretched and marred his lips where he'd hit the microphone with his face.

"Front pocket." He leaned back to allow me access.

I stopped to stare. The distinct bulge worried me. If I reached in there, would I find a pill bottle? I leaned forward, fingertips hovering at his hip.

He cracked a smile, winked and slid the prescription bottle from his pocket. "Stay out of my pants," he whispered.

I straightened. "You're a dork." Even in pain, his mission in life was to irk me. I considered swiping his pain pills in exchange for an apology, but something else came to mind. "I need to call Melinda and see if she or Missy sent these cupcakes." I turned toward the table where I'd left my phone. Sebastian handed me the phone and I scrolled through my contacts.

A knock on my door stopped me dialing. Sebastian moved toward the door. I let him take the lead. Who knew what lurked outside? I had enough trouble in my living room.

Sebastian swung the door wide. Irritation creased his brow. "Yeah?"

"I'm looking for Patience." Todd Ramone's easy Alabama accent filtered past the guard at my door.

"It's okay. Let him in." I waved at Todd. "I know him."

Sebastian moved to the kitchen, giving me space but staying near enough to intervene if necessary.

"Todd, this is my family. Mom, Dad, Adrian, and you met Sebastian." I pointed to each face as I announced their names.

Mom fluttered to my side. "It's nice to meet you, Todd. Can I make you some tea?"

"Thank you, Mrs. Price." Todd nodded. "That sounds perfect."

Mom cleared the empty cups from my table and took

her time looking inside each one. She frowned into my cup longer than I liked.

"Mom?" I cleared my throat. "Still making more tea?" I sent her a telepathic message to knock it off, but I hadn't quite mastered the process.

She lifted worried eyes to me and busied herself heating more water.

Todd sauntered to Adrian's side and greeted him with a complicated handshake.

What on earth? "You two know each other?"

Adrian tossed pills into his mouth and chewed them. Gross. "Ramone and I played ball together junior year at Miami." He looked at Todd with questioning eyes. "How do you know Patience?"

"We had lunch together yesterday."

My brain hurt. "You know each other?"

Adrian cocked an eyebrow. "You had lunch together?"

Awkward. I averted my eyes and admired my wall's wooden paneling. We didn't need to talk about lunch.

Todd broke the silence. "How're you doing, man?" Todd asked Adrian.

"Shot and sore, but I'm alive. Sore sounds pretty good, considering the alternative." Adrian's gaze traveled to me.

Why wouldn't Todd have told me he knew Adrian? My skin burned with irritation. He knew all about Adrian. He called him my ex-lover. My foot itched to kick Todd's shins. Lying by omission was still lying. He probably thought he could get more candid information from me if he feigned ignorance. Sneaky reporters.

I baby-stepped closer to the couch. "What brings you to my place at eight in the morning?"

Todd looked around the room. His expression was

tighter than I'd seen before. Either he had bad news or Sebastian had him rethinking his visit. "I checked out the lead you gave me."

Sebastian's heavy lids drooped lower.

I growled. What was Todd trying to do to me? "I don't know what you mean. I'm not looking into anything. No leads here." I exposed my palms in proof.

"Oh, right. Sorry. I forgot." He looked at my folks and announced in the world's worst acting debut. "I was confused, thinking of someone else entirely."

"Go on." Sebastian closed in on him from the kitchen. "You said a lead?"

"There's a reporter on the island who Patience…or someone…thought dressed a little too nicely for mere paparazzi. He has expensive shoes."

All gazes slid in my direction.

I could've claimed innocence before the shoe comment. Now, I was stuck. "They're John Lobbs." I looked from face to face for recognition. "Never mind."

"What do you know about the guy?" Sebastian asked Todd.

"Not much, except that Patience was right. His press badge is a fake. I looked for the *Massachusetts Messenger* last night. It doesn't exist. I called a few contacts in the Boston area. No one has ever heard of that paper. No web presence, blog, website or anything."

Sebastian moved to stand between Todd and me. "Did you tail him?"

Todd widened his eyes. "Yeah. How'd you know? I've been on him since we finished lunch yesterday."

"And?" A chorus of voices sang out. Mine included.

Todd looked at me. "He set up camp across the street in a Cadillac, watching your place all night. I stayed on him until a few minutes ago when he headed over the mainland bridge. I figured this was a good time to stop over and tell you about him."

Sebastian's thumbs darted over the face of his phone. "Can you identify him?"

"Yes." Todd and I answered.

Sebastian headed for the door. "Davis, keep an eye on…" He stopped to stare at Adrian, who was gripping his bruised ribs. Sebastian swore under his breath. "Don't leave."

Adrian gave him a weird two-finger salute.

I grabbed Sebastian's elbow. "Wait. Where are you going? What does this mean to you?"

"It means someone's following you." His phone rang and he stepped through the open door to answer.

Mom delivered fresh tea to Todd. "Thanks," he said.

I huffed out a breath and made plans to interrogate Todd further once Sebastian was gone. "Cupcake?" I shoved the plate of Halloween cakes in his direction. My strategy? Butter him up. Use a sugar-induced euphoria as truth serum.

Todd scowled. "Wow. Those look ominous."

I turned the cupcake plate, no longer craving the creamy frosting. What if these sweet treats were never intended as gifts? They could be threats. But what sort of twisted person threatened a woman with cupcakes? I pulled my phone free from my pocket. Missy could set this straight. Who ordered these for me? I scrolled to her cell number.

The bark of sirens from the street outside split the morning air, balking and bleating.

Sebastian took the steps two at a time. I ran onto the stoop. Ambulances, fire trucks and police cruisers blew past my apartment, driving on the curb as needed to pass halted traffic near the intersection. In the rescue vehicles' wake, a black, government-issue SUV slid into the space at the curb where the Range Rover usually stood. Sebastian ducked inside with a warning look over his shoulder.

I lifted my fingers waist high. *Yeah, yeah. Stay put. Not going to happen.*

EIGHTEEN

I KISSED MY dad's cheek, waved to mom and grabbed my keys. "I'll be back. Stay as long as you like."

Adrian blocked the doorframe with one hand across his ribs. "You're supposed to stay here."

I hated to cause him trouble, but I didn't have time to argue, and it was his idea to snoop into this. "I'm not staying here."

I poked the area beneath his arm and he groaned. "Mean."

"Yep. Are you coming? You can ride shotgun."

"Don't say shotgun."

I rolled my eyes. "Where's Todd?" I turned in a little circle. That guy was like a ninja, popping up and disappearing all over town.

Adrian gave me an angry face and moped out the door. "Todd passed you on the stoop. He's probably already at the scene of whatever's happening."

"Be safe," Mom called from behind us. "Remember, use your phone if you need to." She dragged the word phone into three syllables. Right. The Taser phone Dad bought on eBay. How could I forget? I'd been afraid to touch it since she assured me it worked but wouldn't say how she knew.

I swung the passenger door of my car open before rounding the hood to the driver's side. The world outside my apartment smelled like a county fair, minus the animal barns. It was a wonder I didn't need stretch pants. A family of five carrying bucket-sized lemonades and caramel-covered apples meandered past. The apples were the size of softballs and one was covered in broken pretzel pieces and M&Ms. I mean, come on. These food trucks were killing me. I started the engine and tapped my toes, waiting for Adrian to cram his body into the seat beside mine. He winced a few times fastening his seat belt.

Finally.

I pulled into traffic and turned to Adrian, avoiding another look at the caramel apples. "How do you feel?"

"Like balls."

I fixed my eyes on the road, refusing to consider what that meant or what Freud would say about the reference. Freud, the father of psychology, not my cat.

Adrian groaned as I accelerated. "Nice car. Green this time. Funny."

I thought so. Fuel efficient. Clean running. A Prius was as "green" as cars got in my price bracket.

The closest parking space to the fire trucks and ambulances was two blocks from Adrian's house on the marsh. Wooden sawhorses blocked the street and federal agents polka dotted Adrian's yard. When we arrived in the mix, Fargas stood at the open front door talking with big hand gestures.

An agent I recognized from the bureau blocked our path. I put on my hey-there-old-buddy face and used my most professional voice. "What's going on here, Agent Fellows?"

He looked me over. No sign of recognition.

I extended a hand. "Patience Price. Human resources. We were on the same softball team. We kicked John's Gyros' butts in the playoffs last fall. Remember?"

A crooked smile split his face. "I remember you. You

look different. Whatever you're doing, keep it up." He whistled and nudged me with an elbow. "What've you been up to?"

Adrian nosed in. "What did you say is happening in there?"

Fellows dropped his congenial expression. "Do I know you?"

"No. I'm Adrian Davis. This is my house. *The Watchers* rented it for their Halloween special."

Fellows hooked his thumbs into his belt loops and turned his face to me, ignoring Adrian. "Can you believe this show? It's like the whole production's cursed."

I nodded. I didn't believe in curses, but it certainly looked like a curse the way the week had unfolded. "Did something else happen?"

He lifted his chin. "Anna Copeland's dad has the producer hostage. Anna died earlier this week. A real shame."

"Oh, no." I hurried around Fellows and across the lawn. I powered past a line of agents on the sidewalk and landed on the porch beside Fargas.

Fargas rubbed his face with both palms. "Patience, what are you doing here? We've got this covered."

"Mr. Copeland," I called. "Mr. Copeland? Can we talk?"

Fargas shook his head at me. "Are you insane? He's got a gun."

"Who is that?" A voice called from beyond the door.

I cleared my throat and leaned my head through the open door. "Patience Price. We met yesterday when you were cleaning up the mess outside the bed-and-breakfast. I thought you took a cab home last night." Mrs. Shuster said she saw him hail a cab and tell the cabbie to get him off the island, but here he was, holding the producer hostage.

Mr. Copeland's eyes and forehead appeared around the inside corner. "I remember you. What do you want? You didn't come here to save this guy, did you?"

"Jesse Short? No. I think he's an awful person."

Fargas slapped my arm. "What are you doing?" He whispered through gritted teeth.

I whispered back. "He is an awful person. A really, really bad one."

"So, why are you here?" Mr. Copeland asked.

A Sebastian-shaped silhouette moved across the wall in Adrian's kitchen. The shadow had his gun drawn. I pressed my nose to the screen door. "May I come in?"

Fargas grabbed my elbows to restrain me, but I wriggled free. A hand clamped down on my shoulder, and I shot a glance back at Adrian. I'd forgotten about him. I flicked his hand off me. His chin swung left and right. I nodded.

"Okay." Mr. Copeland's voice startled me. "Come in, but only you. No cops."

I ducked inside and stopped in the archway to Adrian's kitchen. Jesse Short was bungee corded to a chair, with socks in his mouth. His bare toes curled against the marble floor. Gross.

Mr. Copeland wiped his brow with one wrist, waving a handgun in the opposite shaky fist. "I hate this guy. He ruined my daughter's life. She was a good girl before she met you." He spat the last sentence in Jesse's face. "You took her from us. You killed her."

Jesse wiggled his head *no, no, no.* His wide eyes tracked the gun's every movement. Soft grunts accompanied the panicked expression.

It was a little evil, but I wasn't in a hurry to free him.

He should stew a while. He should know his ruthless methods of climbing the television ladder harmed people, maybe even killed people. Mr. Copeland wouldn't hurt him.

Sebastian moved on silent feet through Adrian's thick living room carpeting. He locked his gaze with mine and cursed silently. I read his lips and pursed mine. Mr. Copeland couldn't see Sebastian, but he could see me.

"Mr. Copeland, you don't want to hurt him. I read about you online. I know who you are."

His expression changed to shock. "What do you mean? What are they saying about me online?"

"Nice things. I read that you're a youth pastor, a philanthropist and someone who supports his family. You're a pillar in your community. Lots of people look up to you, Mr. Copeland, and this—" I waved my arm toward the gun in his hand, "—this isn't you. It's not admirable, and it's not what Anna would want. You were her hero."

"You can't know that." His voice cracked on each word.

"Yes, I can. I do know."

He blinked through tears and lowered the gun a few inches. "How?"

I moved closer. "Because I have a dad too. We don't always see things the same way and he doesn't always agree with my choices, but he always loves me, and I know that. He's my hero, like you were Anna's. You can't do this, Mr. Copeland. She wouldn't want you arrested for her. It would break her heart. She wouldn't want you remembered for one act of violence when you've done so many acts of kindness."

He sucked air and wiped his face with his unsteady fingers and a sleeve. The whimper in his chest grew into a series of sobs.

Elisa French slunk from another room and stopped in front of Mr. Copeland. "I'm really sorry about Anna."

To my surprise, he hugged her and she cried. "We weren't always close, but I loved her too, you know? I'm really sorry. I know Patience is right. She wouldn't want this for you. You should listen to her."

Elisa repositioned her arms, burying her face in his neck, and the gun clattered to the floor. Sebastian swept it off the ground, shook his head and secured it in his waistband. Fargas caught Mr. Copeland by the wrist in a silver cuff. Cameramen swooped in, angling their equipment at our faces, capturing reaction shots. Boom mics floated in the air, ready to record the smallest sound. Surprise, surprise. Vance Varner materialized with a verbal play-by-play of the standoff, which he'd witnessed from a safe distance. Convenient.

Against my instincts and despite personal opinion of the creep, I helped Sebastian untie Jesse. My fingers shook with memories of time spent in a similar situation. People fluttered around us, knocking into me as I balanced on my knees.

Jesse's mouth moved the minute Sebastian pulled the socks free. "Can you believe that guy?" He stood and brushed himself off as if Anna's grieving father had given him cooties. "Did you get all that?" He looked from camera to camera for assurance. One cameraman gave a thumbs-up.

"Hold it." I waved my hands. "I don't want to be on your show, so make sure you cut me out of any footage you captured today." I leveled my stare at the cameraman, assuming my odds at intimidation were better with him than Jesse.

He lowered the camera. "Just today?"

Sebastian crossed his arms and moved behind me. "What do you mean by that?"

Jesse and his enormous ego joined our conversation. "Anything taped inside this house is fair game. There's a sign on the porch. You come inside, you join the show."

My tummy coiled. How many times had I been inside the house this week? Too many, if he was telling the truth. I ran down the hallway, turning sideways and galloping between staff and crew.

Fargas read Mr. Copeland his rights on the porch. I stroked Mr. Copeland's sleeve as I passed them.

"Sorry," I whispered.

"Excuse me." Free from the crowd, I tapped Noah, the blue Mohawk guy, on his shoulder. "Is there a sign out here saying anyone inside gets taped?"

"Yeah." He pointed to the wall behind a line of ghost hunters.

I pushed my way into their group. "Excuse me. Sorry. Pardon me. Dang." There was a sign. No one could see it through the perpetual crowd, but I doubted that mattered.

Adrian followed Fargas and Mr. Copeland to the cruiser. I changed trajectory. Adrian gave Fargas a business card and leaned close to his head.

I marched onto the sidewalk and grabbed Adrian's elbow. "What was that about?"

Beads of sweat darkened the hair at his temples and glued a few sparse bangs to his forehead.

"Wow," I said. "You don't look too good."

Adrian shrugged and flinched. "I gave Fargas my attorney's business card for Mr. Copeland. He'll get him out of jail before dinner and on a plane home by sundown. Copeland's got a wife somewhere who's mourning their daughter and probably wondering what happened to her husband."

"You're a good guy, Adrian Davis."

He raised stormy blue eyes to mine, with a deflated expression. "Yeah. It's too bad about nice guys. I hear they never finish well."

I slid an arm around his waist and pulled him to my side. My shoulder fit into the curve under his arm. "I'm sorry I dragged you here. You need rest."

"Good. Let's go home."

We ambled onto the porch. "Excuse me. I've got a gunshot victim here." I shooed away a few loiterers and dropped Adrian into one of his rocking chairs. "I'll be right back. I want to talk to someone and let Sebastian know we're leaving."

Adrian leaned his head over the back of the chair and stretched his long legs out in front of him. "Hey, Patience."

"What?" My palm wrapped around the doorknob.

He pointed at the sign on the wall behind him as a reminder.

Right. Once I crossed the threshold, I was fair game for taping. Again. I pulled in a long breath and headed for my target. Vance blathered in the kitchen, posturing for the cameras, wiping fake tears and arranging his limbs so that flexing might seem natural, but didn't.

"Cut," I called.

Everyone looked at me. No one cut. Sebastian snorted in the next room.

Vance gave me an evil stare. "They don't listen to you. You're not the director, and you can't walk in here and pretend like we didn't just experience a trauma. That man was going to kill us all." He looked blatantly into the camera with wide, childish eyes.

Sebastian leaned around the corner with a gun in his hand. I stopped breathing. He pulled the trigger, and water sprayed through the air, fell short and sprinkled onto Vance's bare feet. "This is the weapon I retrieved," Sebastian said.

I raised my eyebrows. Mr. Copeland had a water gun. "Unless you're related to the Wicked Witch of the West, you weren't in danger, Vance." I aimed a bright smile into the nearest camera. "Vance was afraid of a water gun."

"What's your deal, lady?" Vance snapped.

"Let me see your phone." I opened and shut my fingers in the universal sign for gimme.

Vance made a big show of being a victim but gave me the phone. His wallpaper was a shirtless shot of himself. Shocker. I looked through his call log.

"You made quite a few calls to this number: 757-555-6519." I turned the screen his way. "Then you stopped calling that number the day Rick and Anna were attacked."

"So?" He grunted and leaned one elbow on the island behind him.

"So, whose number is it?"

Vance grabbed the phone. "I'm not telling you anything. Give that back."

"Fine. I'll find out for myself." I looked into a camera. "I wonder if it was Rick's or Anna's phone number he called so many times."

Vance squeezed between the camera and me. "Knock it off."

"You were losing face time to the women on this show. You couldn't compete for Rick's attention anymore. So, what'd you do about it?"

Elisa stormed into the room, wailing. "Leave him

alone. It's *my* number, okay?" Her boyfriend, Dan, trailed her.

Sebastian collected Vance's phone and read the call log for himself while Vance made a series of desperate stage-expressions.

Dan glared over Elisa's head at Vance. "What were you talking to my girl about all those times, Varner?" The mild-mannered surfer's face took on a menacing expression. He jerked Elisa's arm. "What's up, babe? What's going on here? Tell the truth. Are you cheating on me with this turd?"

"Take your hand off her." Sebastian seemed to grow before my eyes. His shoulders squared. He anchored hands on his hips, filling the room with warning. His fierce expression electrified the air.

Everyone froze.

Dan dropped his hands to his sides.

Vance ran upstairs. Dan and Sebastian faced off over how he could or couldn't touch his girlfriend. Elisa cried. The cameramen split up to cover the action.

Todd reappeared from the next room and elbowed me in the ribs. "I think your work here is done."

Right. Time to go home and plan my next move.

NINETEEN

LATER THAT NIGHT, Sebastian greeted me with a stern look. "There's cold pizza on the counter," I said. It wasn't my most stellar attempt at a peace offering, but he accepted.

He went straight for the kitchen.

I pressed pause on the television remote and followed him. "I didn't expect you to be back tonight."

Sebastian leaned against the counter, appraising me. "You walked into a hostage situation today. The police were there to diffuse the situation, and you still pushed your way into a room with a gun-wielding lunatic. I don't have any idea how to process that." He swigged the beer I handed him. "You seemed so much more stable seated behind a human resources desk." He took another long pull on the bottle and exhaled. "Here, you're like out-dated dynamite. I have no idea when you might detonate next, and you're killing me. You know that, right?" He rubbed his chest with one hand. "I've been to war and came back stronger, better. We've dated three months and I have an ulcer."

I frowned. "Mr. Copeland hardly qualifies as a lunatic, and he had a squirt gun."

Sebastian nodded silently, at what, I wasn't certain. Despite the nodding, he didn't seem to agree. He stared at the couch where I'd been sitting when he arrived. "Where's your sidekick?"

"In bed."

He wiped his downturned lips. "In your bed?"

I didn't like the implication or his attitude. It took what little strength I had left not to fight with him for calling me old dynamite. "Yes. In my bed. He was shot. I think that earned him a bed."

Sebastian dropped his empty bottle in the recycling bin and opened my refrigerator. He uncapped another beer and sucked the contents half empty before joining me on the couch. I had no intention of speaking to him ever again.

I pressed Play and watched as Vance Varner escorted two Italian women to *The Watchers* rooftop hot tub. The women giggled and chatted at top speed. He told the cameraman he had no idea what they were saying, and he didn't care. Anytime the camera came close, he made licking motions and tugged the girls closer to primetime humiliation—a topless dip in the petri dish *The Watchers* called a hot tub. After what went on in the season one pool, I'd never swim again. Watching the threesome sink into the bubbling pit of bacteria, I squeezed Purell onto my palms and shivered.

"What are you watching?" Sebastian peeled his work boots off and stretched back against the cushions.

"*The Watchers*. They went to Rome for season two. Vance is even more of a pompous creep overseas."

"Have you been watching these all day?"

"No. I started about three hours ago. Season one was only twelve episodes and without commercials, they went fast. Before that I went to a cooking class. I thought the cooking lady invited me over under the guise of cooking but really wanted an undercover counseling session. Turned out, she really was worried about my ability to feed you."

"Feed me?"

"Yeah. We made pumpkin rolls. She said the way to your heart is through your stomach." I gave him a dirty look. He'd tricked me into talking to him.

Sebastian looked at his shirt stretched over hard six-pack abs and turned to me. "Nope."

Good thing. I hated cooking. All things domestic eluded me. I killed plants, burned toast and bought an endless supply of long-lasting toilet cleaner cubes so I rarely had to scrub.

"After cooking, I went to a free line-dancing class, so I wouldn't hurt the feelings of the person who invited me. Line dancing also turned out to be an undercover session. I hate never knowing if I'm on duty or not. How can I bring my A game if I have no idea when there's a game?" Not to mention I nearly broke an ankle tripping on my borrowed boots. My lack of coordination surpassed all understanding.

Sebastian rolled the cold bottle against his forehead. "How was the pumpkin roll?"

I sighed and fell sideways against his chest. "I left it at the line-dancing studio."

"Really? That was nice."

I rolled onto my back and dropped my head into his lap. My bottom lip popped out as I gazed up at him. "I didn't mean to. I forgot it."

Sebastian patted my head. "One question."

"Fine. What?" I hated his questions. They always ended in me squirming and backpedaling out of trouble.

"I know you aren't looking into the murders because you promised me you'd let me do my job this time without any meddling."

I nodded, eyebrows scrunched. I didn't hear a question.

"Why the sudden interest in watching all *The*

Watchers episodes? Why show up at the scene of another crime today?" His dark eyes dared me to lie.

I spun into a seated position and crossed my legs on the couch. Adrenaline pumped through me. I pulled the little gold pillow Claire bought me as a housewarming gift onto my lap and faced Sebastian. "Who do you think is committing all these crimes? One minute I'm sure Vance is behind everything, trying to create more hype for the show, or more drama for his life. The next minute…"

Words caught in my throat. I couldn't say the alternative. My brain scrambled away from the thought whenever it came back to the forefront.

Sebastian took my hand in his. His wide thumb traced the length of my finger. "You think Jimmy the Judge has found me."

I stared, unable to think, speak or breathe. That was exactly what I'd worried about every second of the past three months.

Sebastian waited. In every other situation, I lost at these kinds of challenges. I liked motion and words and things that made life progress. Waiting and silence were foreign concepts, alien notions and virtues unknown to me. Except now. When Sebastian voiced my greatest fear, every fiber of my body stopped to hold a collective breath. Saying it out loud was like setting the idea free into the world where it could come for us.

He fiddled with my fingers. "I don't know if you're right or wrong. I need to go to Vegas and follow up on some leads, but I can't leave you right now. You keep getting shot at. Fargas needs the extra help here and there's currently another man in your bed."

Selfishly, I was glad he wasn't going after Jimmy in Vegas. I could keep an eye on him here. Jimmy the

Judge couldn't take Sebastian from me. I didn't want to know a world where Sebastian didn't exist.

"Don't go." The whisper escaped my heart before I could think better of it. On impulse, I kissed him, hoping to cover my raw plea. I pressed my lips to his with a lifetime of desperation and recklessness.

A growl rolled deep in his chest as I climbed into his lap, positioning myself to face him. His arms wrapped protectively around me and he deepened the kiss, sending electricity through my body, down the length of my back and into my socks. My toes curled. Heat in my cheeks spiraled to my tummy and a little lower, setting my hips into a slow tilt. Sebastian's intoxicating mix of cologne, spice and testosterone turned my bones to jelly. Under the heat of his tongue, the usual flicker of desire I had in his presence flamed to combustion temperatures. I moaned against his lips.

Sebastian broke the kiss, eyes wide and fiery. "Adrian's in the next room."

Dang it. Adrian's name was ice on everything I had going. I slid off Sebastian's lap, crossed my legs against the disappointment and sucked in short rapid breaths. Stupid homeless politician.

"Claire's back." Sebastian adjusted his posture and his jeans before the door opened.

Claire stopped short of hanging her coat on the rack beside the door. "Oh. Did I interrupt?"

"Nope." Sebastian finished his beer. "That was all Adrian."

Claire looked adorable in her vintage pinafore dress and kitten heels, but her lipstick was lighter than usual and her hair was pulled back in a casual comb-and-go style, not in keeping with the rest of her look.

I smiled. "Where were you?"

She looked at Sebastian.

I looked at Sebastian. "Do you know something?"

"Yeah. I need my own place. One that's not a crime scene."

My brain split. What the heck did that mean? My place was fine. If you didn't mind a small crowd. Claire tiptoed toward the bathroom.

"Hold it." I cleared my throat. "You were going to tell me all about your night."

"I was?"

I patted the cushion beside me.

Sebastian levered his giant body off the couch. "I'll let you two talk. I need a shower."

Oh. I hated to make matters worse. "Give it a few minutes to heat up. The hot water heater's on the fritz again."

Sebastian kept moving. "Sounds perfect."

Claire took Sebastian's spot. "Were you two…" She trailed off suggestively.

"No. Adrian's in the bedroom."

She quirked an eyebrow.

Maybe my apartment wasn't ideal for every situation, but it was all I had that hadn't been blown up or shot at lately, so I wasn't complaining.

"So, dish," I said. "Where did you go all dressed up and what happened to your lipstick and hair?"

Claire touched her lips with one hand and smoothed her ponytail with the other. Her chin jutted forward. "I was with Max."

My brain blanked. Did I know Max? The name carouselled in my mind. Max. Max. Max. "Fargas?" Maxwell Fargas was his full name, but no one called him Max, did they? Until recently, I'd called him Deputy Doofus. "Max?" The word felt awkward on my tongue.

"Yes. Fargas. We had dinner and talked about school. Did you know Max has a degree in criminal justice, and he's getting his law degree online? He takes classes on the mainland when he can, usually in the winter when tourist season dies here for a few months. The rest of the year he takes the courses from home."

I blinked. You think you know someone.

"Is this official? You're dating Fargas?" I knew she downplayed her attachment to him. I wanted to know how much.

She fluffed her skirt. "That isn't the point here. The point is that Fargas is going to be a lawyer soon. He's studying for the bar. There's a lot to Max you don't see. You don't see because you don't look."

"Wow. That was very Confucius of you. How is the fact you're dating Fargas not the point? There is no other point. How did I not know this? Why don't I have more details? Have you kissed him?"

Her cheeks reddened. Normally her light mocha skin hid blushes while mine gave me away. Not this time. Claire took sudden interest in her manicure.

I gawked. "Are you kidding me? Tell me more. How long has this been going on?"

She shrugged her narrow shoulders, looking as guilty as a child caught with one hand in the cookie jar. "I told you when we met I thought he looked like Clark Kent."

"Yeah, the journalist, not Superman."

She turned her large brown eyes on me. "I prefer brains over brawn."

I wrinkled my nose. "What about the SWAT guy? He was huge."

She nodded, somehow managing an exasperated expression. "And smart as a box of hair. Nice. Polite. Cute.

Yes. If I wanted to talk football, hamburgers or horse-power for the next fifty years, he'd be the one for me."

I slouched against the couch. "Fifty years? What is happening?" I looked around us, at the floor and ceiling. She didn't date seriously, let alone talk about having a future with a man. "I think I'm sleeping and this is some weirdo dream. This whole week is made of things I don't understand. Please help me understand. Am I in a coma?" I gripped her arm. "Am I dead? I blew up with the office, didn't I?"

She shook me off. "Stop it. I like Max and he likes me. There. I tried talking about it with you sooner, but you're always busy or there's a crowd around you, or both."

"This is what you wanted to talk to me about?" Thank heavens. "I thought you had a shopping addiction or nine months to live."

She blew raspberries. "Max and I are getting closer and I needed to talk to you. Things are changing in my life and I worry. I'm happy now, but I sometimes want other things, too. You know?"

I knew. I wanted the crime spree on my island to end. I wanted Jimmy the Judge captured. I wanted a peanut-butter-and-chocolate Sophisticake to help me handle this conversation. "I know."

"Did you hear about Karen and Beau? They're having a baby." She looked impressed. "A few years ago, everyone I knew was having babies and I didn't care. I wasn't ready. I had other goals on my mind. Then I heard about Karen this week and I wondered…am I missing out on something bigger than what I already have? Do I really need a second bedroom for a closet or could I use it for a nursery?"

"A nursery!" I jumped to my feet and the world spun.

Adrenaline and I didn't mix. "Hold on." I went to get a glass from the kitchen and poured wine halfway to the top. I sipped it and waited. Nothing. Drinking wasn't a good idea in general. Alcohol consumption lowered inhibitions and I liked my inhibitions. Fortunately, it also loosened tongues and I couldn't have this conversation without a little help. I sipped again. Nothing.

"Are you coming back?" Claire asked.

I took a big gulp that heated my tongue. "Yep. On my way. Sorry."

She eyeballed my glass.

I eased into my seat beside her. "I'm glad you're happy. I wish you would've told me right away, but it's fine. I understand and I'm happy for you" I took another long drink and held up a pointer finger, signaling I wasn't finished. "I feel the same way about Karen's marriage and pregnancy."

Claire's somber face smoothed into a grin. "Really?"

"Of course."

"You don't like change, though. If I'm dating someone, I might not be around as much."

I laughed, the effects of wine touching my fingertips and belly. "You'll probably be here more if you're with Fargas."

Her head moved slowly left and right. "Fargas is leaving once he passes the bar. He's looking at jobs on the mainland, and he has an interview in D.C."

"You're not moving to D.C." I'd be heartbroken.

"No. I'm not saying that. I'm just saying there's change afoot. You'll need a new sheriff, no matter which job Max takes, and if he takes a position closer to me on the mainland, I'll be dividing my time after work between here and there." She wrinkled her little nose.

"Don't you ever wonder where I disappear to when I'm staying with you?"

I hadn't. Claire was athletic and independent. I assumed she had things to do, like jog or shop.

"Hey." I narrowed my eyes. "Did you tell Sebastian about Fargas before you told me? I saw that look you two exchanged."

The blush on her cheeks returned. "Of course not."

I sipped the wine and pointed at her face. "You and Sebastian shared a look. I saw it. It was right after you told me you were with Fargas tonight. Sebastian knows something I don't. Doesn't he?"

She pursed her lips and shut her eyes.

"You can tell me." I patted her leg. "Come on. I won't tell."

She blew out a long breath. "This is awful. I tell you everything, but I wouldn't tell you this for like five years if I could avoid it." She smoothed her skirt and shifted in her seat to face me. "Okay. No judgment."

I nodded in agreement. For good measure I locked my lips with an invisible key.

She rolled her eyes. "Did you know *The Watchers* have cameras set up on the seashore?"

I blanched. "What?"

"Sebastian confiscated all the footage from *The Watchers* hidden cameras after Max arrested Mr. Copeland today. Some reports were filed about the cameras and Sebastian knew they bothered you, so he pushed. Max and Sebastian were going through the footage at the station when I went to pick Max up for dinner."

I covered my face and peeked between fingers. "They saw the tapes?"

"Yes. They promised me they fast forwarded through the, um, personal parts, but yeah. They saw."

I flopped backward on the cushion beside her. "I'm going to die."

"Why?" She peeled my hands away from my face. "Did you know about the tapes and not tell me?"

"I didn't want anyone to know. It was my first sex tape. I was cooking up a plan to get back there and destroy them. Plus, the girl said you couldn't see any faces."

"Well, you didn't have to see our faces if you knew about my Disney tattoo."

We stared wide-eyed at one another, pointing fingers.

"*Your* tattoo?" I said as she asked, "*Your* sex tape?"

It wasn't me caught on film. It was Claire. With Fargas. I squealed and clamped both palms over my mouth.

"Stop it." She knocked her knee against mine. I shot upright and bounced silently beside her in my seat. I buried my face in the gold pillow. Tears of joy and relief ran over my cheeks.

"Stop celebrating. I'm humiliated."

I tried to straighten my expression and pulled the corner of the pillow away from my face. "Sorry." A giggle-snort erupted through my composure. I tried again. "Sorry. I'm really sorry."

"I'm not talking about this anymore." She turned her face away. "What about you? You said you might envy Karen a little too? That's a pretty serious diversion from the girl I met five years ago."

My humor fell away. "I know. Life's moving so fast. I don't want to miss anything. For the first time, I think I might like to be a mom one day. Buy a house. Find a Mr. Patience Price to mow the lawn and change tires, take out the garbage or whatever husbands do."

"Your husband?" Claire leaned her head on my shoulder. "He'd better be rich or have some legal pull. He'll probably spend a lot of time bailing you out."

I laughed. "Maybe I'll settle down one day and focus my curiosity on things like finding the perfect cannoli recipe or organic herb gardening."

"Maybe." Claire tucked her legs under her. "You have any more wine in there?"

I hoisted my body upright and carried my empty glass with me to the kitchen in search of a bottle and another fancy glass. My heart thudded as Sebastian's reflection came into view. Across the narrow hallway of my too tiny, too crowded apartment, the bathroom door stood open as Sebastian rubbed a towel over his shower-dampened hair. Embarrassment tightened my chest. How much of our conversation did he hear? How loud had I been speaking? Did he know I wanted things bigger than I'd ever admitted to anyone before this night? I fumbled the wine bottle onto the counter and took a slow calming breath before lifting my eyes to his again.

The reflection of Sebastian in my bathroom mirror winked. One corner of his mouth pulled slightly in the almost-smile I loved.

And my heart blew into confetti.

TWENTY

I WOKE WITH a groan. After an hour of debate and several wine-hazed rounds of rock, paper, scissors, I'd won the couch for my bed. Seven hours later I doubted "won" was the right word. Claire's floor bed of pillows and quilts was neatly folded and stacked in the corner. Her heels stood against the wall and her cross trainers were missing. Exercise people exhausted me. Claire, like Adrian and so many others, jogged every morning. Adrian had missed a couple of days due to a gunshot wound, and he complained endlessly. Lucky for me, he had food truck people to occupy his free time before sunrise. Waking me wasn't a smart option, and he knew it.

"Morning." Adrian approached on slow feet, carrying two mugs of coffee and sporting a clean shave. He set one cup on the coffee table and backed away. Wise. I wasn't a morning person.

"Ha-ha." I rubbed my forehead. "Mornings are not my friends. Morning people are unnatural." I lifted a tired eyebrow. "How long have you been up?"

His dimple caved in. "Couple hours. It's a beautiful day." He whipped the curtains open, and I swatted the air, hoping to give the sun a black eye. If I hit Adrian instead, so be it.

"Where is everyone?" I swung stiff legs over the cushion's edge and forced my body into a seated position.

Adrian sipped his coffee and smiled over the rim.

"Claire went out for a run over an hour ago and Sebastian left after you fell asleep. He woke me around midnight and let me know I was in charge of you for the night." He wiggled his eyebrows. "I guess he opted to go back to work, given the one bedroom and four adults sleeping here. I offered him the cot in my office when I saw Claire on the floor, but he wasn't interested. He stopped to check on you this morning then left again."

"When?" I perked up, sucking down hot coffee. My fitful sleep wasn't solely due to the crappy couch. Nightmares of Jimmy the Judge hunting Sebastian had kept me tossing and turning all night.

"I don't know. Not long. Maybe five or ten minutes ago."

When Todd said the mean old reporter followed me around the island yesterday, Sebastian had practically turned purple. If Sebastian was in search of the reporter, then Sebastian was probably somewhere on the island and I could catch up to him. Most likely, Meanie read the Hollywood Watcher website and had the same reporting strategy as Todd, i.e. "follow Patience because she's where the action is." This theory meant Meanie was harmless. I liked that option. Of course, the idea Meanie might be a gun for hire kept me awake half the night. I decided around two in the morning if I caught Meanie pointing a gun at Sebastian, he'd get a load of me. Okay, the expression "get a load of me" was all I'd come up with while I tossed on my couch. I didn't have a plan, but I definitely couldn't do nothing.

I launched from the couch, yanking off clothes as I dashed down the hall to my room. I pulled on a fresh pair of jeans from the stack on my dresser and a Chincoteague High School sweatshirt off the floor. Adrian waited outside the door and followed me to the bathroom.

"What are you doing?" He stared at my reflection as I brushed my teeth at warp speed.

I raked a brush through my hair and twisted the poofy, sun-streaked mass into submission. Voilà! Ponytails: masking my lazy hair days as an intended casual look for twenty-five years.

"I'm going to find Sebastian." One quick swipe of lip gloss and mascara. Boom. Ready to go. If I didn't think about my outfit, face or hair too long, I looked great. No need to waste time. Denial was my favorite mental crutch. My pants often "shrank" in the dryer, and I went over budget on shoes because the prices kept going up. These things were out of my control. Denial worked. See?

Adrian trailed me to the kitchen. "Why are you following Sebastian?"

"Never mind." I poured a to-go cup of coffee and struck a confident pose. "I retract that statement. I'm meeting a client, so I can't talk about it. Counselor-patient confidentiality." I shrugged and pulled my lips to the side, giving him my best those-are-the-rules face. "Thank you for the coffee."

"Shouldn't you dress more, I don't know, professional, if you're meeting a client?" He leaned forward with his I-see-right-through-your-bull face.

I wouldn't give in to the pressure. "No. I'm not supposed to look like I'm counseling. It's very low-key." Adrian needed to drop his inquisition. He didn't need any more trouble.

He pursed his lips.

I took that as my cue to skedaddle. "See ya. Try to get some rest."

I bounded out the door and down the steps to the sidewalk, ignoring the crowds and unprecedented island traffic. Sunlight twinkled over the little circle of broken glass in my windshield. Someone had shot my car.

My stomach churned on black coffee, too little sleep and too much wine. I looked over my shoulders at the parade of people, living their lives oblivious to my mini panic attack.

The curtain inside my living room window dropped shut. I doubted peeping Adrian could see what I saw. His angle was bad, but my view was perfect. I ran a fingertip over the smooth glass outside the splintered hole and cringed. Who would shoot an empty car and why hadn't I heard the shot? I'd slept on the couch under my front window. I curled shaky fingers. This wasn't a drive-by shooting. The car was perfect, save for one bullet hole in the windshield on the driver's side. I stared through the hole. Inside, a matching hole tore through the fabric on my headrest. My heart hammered painfully and instinct insisted I run back to my apartment, barricade the door and embrace agoraphobia. The infuriating, super-stupid part of me insisted if I did that, I'd never know if Sebastian was safe.

Was he following a strong lead right now? His FBI buddies were here for a reason. I hoped the reason wasn't new intel about Jimmy the Judge dispatching a hit man to Chincoteague.

I slid behind the wheel and inhaled the new-car-and-cranberry-air-freshener smell. I exhaled with less chest pain, but now a new problem occurred to me. I couldn't drive my car around town with a bullet hole in the windshield. Bullet holes were conspicuous and I was undercover. Not to mention, Sebastian's Range Rover was still impounded. If the police took my car too, I'd have to borrow the pony cart from Mom again, beg the love bus from Sebastian or walk. I drummed my thumbs against the wheel, praying for a moment of brilliance. It hit me.

Ha! The prayer worked. I jumped out and ran around the back of my car to the trunk. Dad had made an emergency car kit for my birthday. I popped the trunk and dug into the little purple crate. Protection stones. Ashes. Water. Condoms. Aha—duct tape. I ripped off a silver hunk and slapped it over the hole in my windshield. I pressed another piece to the headrest for good measure and dusted my palms together.

Back in business, I started the engine and scanned the street. *Where are you, Sebastian Clark?* I sent the telepathic query into the cosmos and waited for the force or a tingling in my nether regions to guide me. Hey, the prayer for brilliance had worked. Telepathy could work, too.

This time, I got nothing.

Fine. I didn't need divine intervention. I scooted lower in my seat to see under the duct tape. If Sebastian was still on the island, I'd find him. There wasn't much ground to cover. I started with the police station. Three black SUVs and two cruisers. No obnoxious blue-and-white love bus. Next stop, Main Street. I crawled along the busiest blocks, watching fans and ghost hunters spill in and out of my favorite shops.

Bingo.

The love bus sat at the curb outside Island Brew. I parked at the open meter beside Puff-n-Stuff, a cigar shop with a questionable back room. The pipe smokers who emerged from there rarely smelled like pipe tobacco as much as incense and pot. I'd spent my high school career trying to get a look in that back room. The owner protected it like the Holy Grail was housed inside. Someday I'd make it a priority to soothe my curiosity. Meanwhile, I slipped onto the sidewalk and crept along the edge of Island Brew, peeking between giant block letters painted on the storefront window. Inside, a little blonde poured coffee and laughed with an older woman I recognized as the shop owner. Sebastian sat against the wall with a stranger. Two manila files rested on the table. Sebastian shook hands with the man, who was wearing a rumpled suit, and accepted a stack of papers from him.

Was this a sting operation? Who was that man? I looked around for Sebastian's team, but he appeared to be there alone, aside from the suit.

The men stood and turned for the front door. Busted. I scrambled out of sight, tripping over my feet to get around the corner. My back scraped against the building's rough stone exterior. My left ankle stung where my right foot landed on it as I trampled myself getting to safety. I wiggled my sore foot and tried not to think too hard about the degree of unhealthiness in my behavior. Boyfriend stalking wasn't something I normally condoned, but this was different.

See? Denial won.

Sebastian moved toward the love bus, and I baby-stepped farther into the narrow alley between shops. A huge smile split my face. Maybe I could be an agent, if I wanted to, which I didn't. Still, I impressed myself. Who knew I was so vigilant and stealthy? I licked a fingertip and dragged it through the air in a score-one-for-me tally mark.

"Ah!" I squeaked and slapped a hand over my mouth. Adrian leaned motionless against the opposite alley wall, watching me mark my awesomeness in the air. Jeez.

He pried his body off the wall with a little cringe and closed the distance between us. "What are you doing?"

I huffed and crossed my arms. "Meeting a client. I already told you once. Did you forget your meds? Are you feeling confused?" Turning the argument around was a great debate strategy, unless you'd had five million arguments with the same person and he knew what you were doing.

"I'm taking Extra Strength TYLENOL not LSD." He walked to the end of the alley, looking both ways, and then returned to me. "You're following Sebastian."

I let out a long sigh of irritation. "Yes, Mr. Nosy. I'm worried Todd was right about that reporter following me and that Sebastian might be following him."

"Why do you care? That's a good thing."

"Not necessarily. If that guy was sent by Jimmy the Judge to find Sebastian, then I don't want Sebastian following him."

Adrian rolled his eyes. "That's his job, Patience. I don't know if you've seen the guy lately, but your boyfriend's kind of scary. Some dude posing as a reporter isn't much of a match for Seb. Anyway, Todd's always been a drama queen. I'm sure it's nothing. You're getting your panties all knotted for no reason. Let Sebastian handle this and let's go home."

I pulled my chin back and arched a brow. "Excuse me? Don't talk about my panties. Also, I don't overreact. Todd might be a drama queen, but I'm not. I'm following my leads. Todd says this guy's shady, so I'm checking him out. If he's just a reporter, or a fan posing as a reporter, fine. If he's dangerous, I want to know. Sebastian's always saying Jimmy the Judge would come at me to get to Sebastian if he knew where we were."

Adrian shook his head. "Well, you aren't following the reporter. You're stalking your boyfriend."

"Am not. Whatever. You know what the problem is?

You don't understand logic." He also didn't have all the facts. I grabbed his sleeve and pulled him close for a whisper. "Someone shot my car this morning. Maybe all this is about me. Maybe Jimmy's taunting Sebastian, and Rick and Anna were in the wrong place at the wrong time. You said Sebastian left five minutes before I got up, and I left ten minutes later, so in that little timeframe, someone marched right over to my car in broad daylight and shot it. Whoever did that knew Sebastian was gone and I was home." My voice cracked.

Adrian's eyes bugged out. He grabbed my elbow. "Someone shot your car today? Why didn't you tell me?"

I slapped his hand, but he didn't let me go. "I am telling you. I don't understand your protest. You were the one who wanted to look into this."

"I wanted to look into Rick and Anna's deaths, not get you involved in some mob guy's vendetta against your boyfriend." He towed me out of the alley by my arm. My feet twisted and I stumbled behind him. When we were fully exposed on the sidewalk, he stopped. Several cars down the block sat my Prius with a six-foot-two guard dog leaning against the hood. The duct tape from my window stuck to his thumb.

I snatched my arm free and straightened my spine. "Traitor. You saw him there when you looked a minute ago, didn't you?"

"Yep." Adrian walked to Sebastian's side and angled his back to me. I dawdled on the sidewalk.

"Where's your Jeep?" Sebastian watched me as he spoke to Adrian.

"In the alley."

Sebastian nodded. "Take her home. I'm taking the car to impound. This is officially a crime scene." He huffed and shoved black Ray-Bans over his cool brown eyes.

I sighed and tossed my keys to him. He opened the door and ran fingertips over the duct tape on my headrest before ripping the tape off. A string of words harsh enough to make Coach Peters blush rumbled out on one long breath. His blank agent face contradicted the wild frustration in his words. The momentary untamped emotion sent tingles over my skin. Sebastian was mad and I was the reason. Again. As if I had anything to do with what happened to my car. I was the obvious victim here.

Adrian returned to my side. "Come on. Let's go home."

Sebastian folded his body behind the wheel of my new car and powered down the window. "This crime scene is ruined. You stuck tape over the holes." He glared through my windshield.

I narrowed my eyes and sucked in my cheeks, waiting for my car to disappear around the corner. I whacked Adrian. "Fink."

"Ow!" Adrian rubbed his arm where I slapped him. "I'm trying to help you."

"Are not. You're trying to make me crazy. Why are you driving me home? He could've at least offered me the keys to the bus."

"Yeah, right. So you could follow him some more?" Adrian tossed his keys into the air and caught them in one hand. "I don't know if you've noticed, but your track record with cars sucks. Anyway, my ride is so much sweeter than that love bus."

"Stop talking like that."

Adrian lifted his foot behind us and kicked my bottom.

"Stop." I shoved him. "I swear. You're twelve."

"You're twelve." He kicked me again.

"Stop it." I cracked a smile. Adrian was impossible,

but I couldn't stay mad in his presence, which said a lot because I could hold a grudge like a champion.

He flipped the hood on my sweatshirt. "You look like you did in high school wearing this." He tugged the hem. "You wore this hoodie to all my games. Remember?"

I remembered. "Well, for old time's sake, can I drive your sweet ride?"

Adrian chuckled darkly. "Baby, you never have to ask for my sweet ride. Ow!"

"Don't call me baby. Give me the keys."

"Mean."

"Dork."

TWENTY-ONE

ADRIAN SHOVED ME across the threshold at his mom's tanning salon. "Mom?"

"What are we doing here?" I asked for the tenth time. "I want to wait in the car."

He caught my wrist as I spun to leave. "I told you. I need to drop something off." He tapped the little silver bell on the counter.

"I'm coming!" His mom hustled to the counter with an exasperated expression. "I heard you the first time. You don't have to yell. That's what the bell's for." Her attention moved to me. "What's this?"

Adrian swung the keys to his Jeep around one finger, smiling. He whistled a tune I didn't know, but it sounded a lot like neener-neener.

His mom fluffed her big pageant hair and moved to my side. "Why, hello, Patience. What a lovely surprise. What brings you here?"

What brought me here? Adrian Davis the lying liar who lied, that's what. He'd lured me to the salon under the guise of "dropping something off," but his hands were clearly empty. I bit my tongue.

Adrian rocked on his heels and his smile widened. "I'm dropping her off."

I clutched his sleeve. "No. Adrian." I curved my lips into a begging frown and widened my eyes, trying to look as pitiful as possible.

He kissed my head. "Sorry, sugar, but you can't be

trusted and I need to meet with the mayor to finalize some last-minute campaign issues. Having his endorsement is huge. I can't miss this meeting, but I can't take you with me, and I can't leave you alone."

I fumed, running through possible escape scenarios and weighing how much I truly cared if his mother hated me or not.

Mrs. Davis pulled the band from my ponytail and ran her fingers through the thick of my hair. "Good thing curlers set better on dirty hair."

I jumped and ground my teeth. "Good thing." I gave Adrian a telepathic you-will-pay message.

"How long do you need, Ma?" Adrian rubbed his mouth with one hand, nearly choking on his laughter.

Why did I want her approval? She was mean. We always argued. That was our thing. A couple of near-death experiences this summer and suddenly I felt compelled to make nice with everyone. What was wrong with me?

She sighed. "Oh boy. I don't know. Give me two hours at least."

"Two hours!" I lunged for Adrian as he ducked out the door. My head snapped back when Mrs. Davis didn't let go of my dirty hair.

"Come on. We've got lots to do. Let's start with a spray tan while your curlers set."

Oh my Lord in Heaven, kill me now. I rolled my eyes to the ceiling, but lightning didn't save me. My heart drooped. Death by electrocution sounded far superior to what I faced. Beyond the front room, a line of beauty shop chairs stood like dance hall girls before a wall of mirrors. The mirrors were illuminated by a thousand lights. The temperature was at least ten degrees warmer than it had been in the reception area. I tugged the neckline of my sweatshirt.

"I don't know, Mrs. Davis. I'm feeling a little nau-seous. I should go home and eat something. I can come back later." Or never. Whichever.

"Nonsense." She pushed me backward into a big pink swivel chair and sprayed a cloud of perfumed droplets over my face, pumping the bottle wildly with her dim-pled fingers.

I coughed and waved my hands over my face. "What is that?" My mom would have a stroke and keel over dead if she walked into a room with so much product of any kind in the air. Her perfect skin would turn gray and sag on contact with Mrs. Davis' beauty shop of horrors.

She clucked her tongue. "It's conditioner, so I can comb through this mess. Surely you know what con-ditioner is." She grappled with the brush in my newly wetted mane. "Or maybe not."

"Gah." I opened and shut my mouth, tasting the con-ditioner with every breath. "Ow!" I grabbed my head as she brushed the strands flat against my ears and hefted another can into the air. "What's that?"

She rolled her eyes and slapped a *Cosmo* on my lap. "Read this. It'll keep your mind busy. Take the 'Are You A Hot Lover Quiz' on page fifty-seven. I think it's bull, but maybe you'll score higher, considering all your practice lately."

I shut my eyes hard enough to cause a headache and counted to two hundred. I'd have counted higher, but by then it was time for my spray tan.

ONE HOUR AND forty-seven minutes later, the little shop bell dinged. Mrs. Davis went to greet the newcomer while I held my breath and zipped an electric-blue se-quined spandex mini-dress over pasties and Spanx. The Spanx were made for a toddler. Everything I had stung from lack of circulation, except the girls up top who were puckered and fighting off the pasties I'd glued over them. Adrian was never sleeping in my bed again. He could take his injured heinie somewhere else for comfort. I wobbled out of the dressing area on five-inch stilettos. Lights from the mirrored wall reflected off my dress, throwing rainbows over everything in sight. I blinked through the spots in my vision. Giant spider legs came into view with each movement of my head. Mrs. Davis had glued false eyelashes with rhinestone tips on my eyelids. The lashes were so heavy it was a wonder I could open my eyes, let alone see where I was going. The thick liquid eyeliner made me look like a living piece of anime.

I inched my way toward the front, hoping Adrian was back so I could kill him. My natural gait was truncated by layers of elastic at mid-thigh. Diamond-shaped cutouts in the dress at my breasts and tummy were nothing compared to the enormous V down my back from shoulders to tailbone, barely concealing my low-rise thigh squashers. The front diamonds let in enough cool air to keep the girls suffering under their bandages. I stopped at the last mirror and gaped. My hair needed its own zip code. I looked as if I belonged in a boxing ring, carrying a big number over my head. Worst makeover in the history of makeovers.

Voices carried through the door separating the back room from the front. Adrian chuckled. I pressed my glossy red lips into a line. Just the man I wanted to see.

I shoved the door open, and a blinding flash stopped me in my tracks. A round of giggles joined Adrian's laughter. Claire and Fargas stood beside Mrs. Davis at the door. Adrian tapped on his phone screen.

"Aw, honey." Claire rubbed my arms. "You okay?"

"No. I am not."

Adrian hugged his mom. "Thanks for keeping an eye on our girl. I sent a picture to Sebastian. He'll thank you for this one, Ma. She looks great."

Mrs. Davis patted Adrian's cheek and beamed with pride. How did one person look at something and see beauty, while another person looking at the exact same thing, at the exact same moment, saw a train wreck of sequins and shame?

Claire touched my hair and turned to Mrs. Davis with a fierce look in her eye. "Did you bleach her hair?"

"Not yet. This is a rinse. I can make it permanent anytime, though. Let me know." She winked.

I tiptoed to the door, careful not to slide on the silver sticks propping my shoes at a full tilt. Another flash lit the room. Adrian laughed. "I love the back of this dress. What do you have on under there?" He whistled long and low.

Fargas held the door for us.

I couldn't bring myself to look him in the eye. "You don't want to know."

On the sidewalk, everyone stopped to stare. All sound ceased and I thought I heard my mom having a coronary somewhere. Maybe it was all in my head. I couldn't be sure after the amount of product I'd inhaled in the last two hours.

"You look like Dolly Parton." Adrian bounced along beside me.

I glowered. "I hate you so much."

Claire touched my hair again with tentative fingers and hummed. "The tan's a little much."

"A little much? I look like an Oompa Loompa."

Adrian scoffed. "Maybe if Oompa Loompas were hot leggy blondes."

I averted my eyes as we passed Mr. and Mrs. Franks on the sidewalk. This was not the professional impression I wanted to give my clients. I stepped around Adrian to hide.

Mrs. Franks hit her husband with her purse anyway. "Stop looking at her, Frank!"

My head fell forward. "Please, take me home, Adrian. I beg you."

We all climbed into the Jeep. I turned to Claire and Fargas in back. "You came here together?"

Claire stroked my shoulder over the seat. "Adrian promised us a sight we'd never believe or forget. Is that shimmer powered? Oh, honey."

"Don't forget dinner," Fargas added.

"What?" Panic zipped through me.

Adrian flipped on his blinker and slid into traffic. "I'm taking you all to the Tasty Cream for dinner."

"I need to go home first and change. Where are the clothes I had on before?"

He glanced at my dress. "Looks like you forgot them."

"Well, I'm freezing."

"Yeah, you are." His smile widened.

I turned my face away from him and crossed one arm over my chest. My skirt crept farther up my thigh every second. When the freckle, only previously seen when wearing swimwear, came into view, I clamped my fingertips around the hem of my dress and held it in place. True to his word, Adrian pulled into the Tasty Cream lot instead of up to the curb outside my apartment, where Claire's car and Fargas's cruiser sat.

Claire hopped down from the backseat of Adrian's giant Wrangler and looked at my place across the street. Her gaze slid over my new look. "We could make a run for it."

My ankles wiggled. If I took off my shoes, I could run, but by the time I got across the street, my dress would be around my waist like a belt. "I can't run."

Adrian slung a heavy arm across my shoulders. "Chin up, buttercup. I'm buying, so order anything you want."

As if I could eat in this modern-day undergarment death trap. Still, I hadn't eaten in hours. "Excuse me."

I baby-stepped into the restaurant and shuffled past the counter. Mrs. Tucker covered her mouth with both hands. Someone took a picture. I kept my head down and moved as fast as possible on stilettos to the bathroom. My mouth watered as I passed tables full of Mrs. Tucker's food. My brain took inventory of the smells mingling in the air. Salty fries, greasy burgers and rich chocolate malts. My tummy groaned as I locked the bathroom door and wrestled free from the Spanx. I dropped the garment into the trash and inhaled. Air whooshed into my lungs. I leaned against the wall to enjoy the sweet rush of freedom.

Finding my friends in the crowded restaurant was easy. I followed the familiar laughter. Despite my morning ambush, I smiled. Whatever else happened, I had great friends. I had a hideous outfit, but a good life.

"Here she comes," Adrian belted out, "She's Miss America." He stood and dragged the chair beside him away from the table.

I yanked the hem of my dress as low as possible and sat in the chair, scooting my bare thighs under the table and covering them with an open napkin.

Claire looked compassionate. If anyone understood how awful I looked, she did. "I ordered you a chocolate peanut butter malt."

"Thanks."

I lifted a menu to my face, hoping no one else would notice me. No such luck.

Todd Ramone wove his way through the crowd, swiping a chair from a nearby table. He turned it around and straddled it. "I've got news." He leaned both elbows on our table and greeted us by name, except Fargas. He called him Sheriff.

"Go on." Fargas gave Todd his full attention. His congenial expression was instantly replaced by a look I recognized, one Sebastian wore often. Maybe there was more to Fargas than I'd noticed before.

Todd's eyes twinkled as he locked his gaze on me. "I don't know what happened to you, but I'm sorry I missed it. You were in the salon so long, I went looking for another lead and ended up at the hospital." He rocked on his chair, inspecting my face and hair long enough to make me squirm. "The new pathologist gave me a firm warning about you and a detailed account of how her predecessor was axed when you finked on her."

I stared. His words weren't registering. My right pasty had detached along the bottom edge. I could only imagine what would happen next. I appraised the distance between me and the bathroom. The crowd was thick and my heels were higher than my hair. I couldn't make a run for it, so I wiggled in place, pressing my arm to my chest, hoping to right myself without a scene.

Fargas cleared his throat.

"Right," Todd said. "Well, what I found out was completely off the record and I can't use it in my article, but, according to toxicology reports, Rick Fitzgerald had cocaine in his system at his time of death."

Adrian slapped the table. "One of the food truck guys said Rick was an addict. I figured the guy was being dramatic or fishing for attention."

The wheels of my brain shifted into gear, processing the new possibilities. "If he had an addiction, he could've owed someone money." The hit might've been meant for Rick after all. Relief washed over me. I'd overreacted again. Maybe Rick's murder wasn't a case of mistaken identity by one of Jimmy the Judge's goons. Maybe the murderer was someone else's goon, and Sebastian was safe on the island.

Still, Rick's bad habits didn't explain why someone shot my car, or Adrian.

Fargas stood. "I'm going to look into this and see if someone over at *The Watchers* knows anything about the allegation. The cast seems pretty close. One of them has to know if he had a problem or if someone might've come looking for him on the night of his murder."

The waitress delivered our drinks as Fargas was getting up from the table. "Leaving so soon, Sheriff? Can I get you anything to go?"

"No thank you." He dropped his wide-brimmed hat on his head and tipped it to the waitress.

She promptly blushed and Claire's smile grew.

Todd followed Fargas to the door.

"Can I get a to-go cup and an order of fries?" I asked.

"Good idea." Adrian rattled off his to-go order after mine and a few minutes later we headed for the Jeep.

When we parked in Adrian's drive, Fargas's cruiser was nowhere around. I wiped the grease off my fingers and sighed contentedly. Adrian poked my exposed belly button.

"Stop." Stupid sequin cutouts. "I should've changed when we left the Tasty Cream."

Cameras rolled as we approached. Vance and Elisa rocked in the chairs on Adrian's wide wraparound porch.

Jesse Short stood in the grass, observing and rubbing his chin.

Elisa's voice rose over the low buzz of offstage voices. "I think this island really is haunted." She rubbed her arms and widened her big blue eyes for the camera.

Vance joined her at the porch railing. "Don't worry. We'll be gone soon."

Hallelujah.

"Mr. Short?" I moved into Jesse's line of sight and a wide wolfish smile stretched over his face. Two seconds later, recognition dawned over his features and the smile fell with a huff. "Patience Price. To what do I owe the honor?" Sarcasm dripped from each word. He held up a finger. "Wait. Let me guess. Your sheriff just left, so I suppose you want to know about all Rick's bad habits, too."

Adrian nudged me. "Go on."

I straightened my spine and wrapped both arms over the peek-a-boo holes in my dress. "Rick had bad habits?"

Jesse snorted. "Yeah. Just a few. Alcohol, coke, gambling, women…that guy was a disaster, but people loved him. He was the life of any party, even if he did owe half the West Coast money."

"For drugs and gambling debts?"

Jesse shrugged. "I don't know. We weren't that close. He didn't tell me any personal details. He had a few high-ticket projects go belly up though. Everyone knew that."

"Did anyone ever come to the set and try to collect?"

Jesse looked as if I'd asked the most absurd question ever uttered. "Guys in fancy suits showed up from time to time when we were filming. They invited him out for lunch or drinks. He'd come back all roughed up. That kind of crap screwed with our taping more than once. Black eyes, busted lips, fractures, hangovers. We spent half the makeup budget on his pretty face." He sighed. Both hands fell from his chin to his hips. "Excuse me. Cut!"

Jesse barked orders and corralled the crew onto Adrian's porch, leaving us alone on the grass.

Adrian helped me into the Jeep. "That was insightful."

"Well?" Claire poked her head between the front seats.

"Did you wait in the car so you wouldn't be seen with me in my new Extreme Island Makeover?" I caught a glimpse of my giant eyelashes in the side view mirror and laughed. Maybe laughing was the right response. I pressed the straw from my malt against my lips and coaxed the ice cream into my tummy.

"Of course not." She looked guilty. "I didn't want him to get mad at me for asking questions and cut me out of the scene I'm in. There were plenty of extras. He could easily replace my two minutes of fame with someone else's. Besides, I think you look wonderful, and I need multiple pictures as soon as possible."

I choked. "Promise me you won't take any pictures, and I'll tell you what we learned."

She smiled. "No promises. Tell me anyway. I know you want to."

True. "He said Rick owed people money, and what do I always say about money? Whatever bad thing is happening, it's almost always about money."

Adrian started the Jeep. "Now we need to find out if Rick owed someone enough to be killed for it." .

TWENTY-TWO

LESS THAN TWENTY-FOUR hours until Halloween, and I was holed up in my apartment waiting for it to pass. A steady stream of onlookers had filed over the bridge into Chincoteague all week. The island was over capacity, engorged to the point of bursting. RVs and minivans lined the ball fields and families had set up tents over every square inch of grass. Hundreds of fans had partied day and night for two days straight, tailgating in celebration of the big event: *The Watchers* Halloween special. Ghost hunters came in droves from all corners of the world. Candlelight vigils for Rick and Anna were an ongoing and sometimes impromptu event. I'd stop inside a shop for something and come out ten minutes later to a flash mob of candle-toting mourners.

The previous buzz of controlled chaos had grown steadily into a roar. The little voice inside said there was a lion behind that sound. *The Watchers* would stop at nothing to secure ratings, and the thickening crowd made a proper investigation nearly impossible.

When my parents invited Sebastian and me over for dinner and Sebastian agreed to go, I breathed easier for the first time in days. I needed a respite from my apartment, my transient roommates and any talk of gunmen for a few hours. I craved normal. My parents were consistent, reliable and predictable. Everything else in my life was fruit loops.

The love bus rattled to a stop outside my parents'

house on the harbor. Bamboo and evergreens lined the drive, separating it from the neighbors and providing a semblance of solitude on an island bursting with activity.

"Can you smell that?" Sebastian opened his door and hesitated. "That smells amazing. Remind me why we don't eat here every night."

For starters, Sebastian didn't come back most nights, but probably his question was rhetorical, so I went with a less pointed response. "I don't know, but we should definitely come here more often."

The warm buttery scent of seafood hung in the cool night air. Tendrils of smoke from Dad's grill wafted into the sky above their house, mixing muted gray with soft shades of lavender and moonlight. This time of night the moon looked large enough to touch. Inches over the horizon, it floated on gently rippling waters, making its heavenward ascent. Silhouettes of gulls lined the roof. They flapped their wings and craned their necks toward dinner cooking on the deck below. The birds took turns squawking and complaining, or maybe calling dibs on the feast under dad's grill lid.

My parents' house, like all the others on the harbor, stood atop enormous six-foot poles. The poles protected waterfront homes from the angry waters of a coastal storm. Island kids spent hours under their homes, playing in the sand and shade, drawing tic-tac-toe boards with bamboo rods and carving their initials into the sturdy poles.

"P. P. plus A. D. forever." Sebastian ran his fingertip over the heart linking my initials to Adrian's.

I remembered the day Adrian carved those letters. Twelve years later the images were fresh in my mind, bright, vivid and powerful. Frustrating.

I tugged on Sebastian's arm. "Who knew forever lasted so long?"

Sebastian's attention fixed on the initials.

I kissed his cheek and tugged on his arm again. He followed me under the house and onto the rear lawn where a dozen wooden steps led to my parents' deck.

I forced out memories of my childhood with Adrian. Partly because the idea that I'd made the wrong decision pushing him away stung my heart like a jellyfish. My brain knew I was happy with Sebastian. Adrian was my past. Sebastian was, possibly, my future, but was I thumbing my nose at destiny? Did I believe in destiny? Does anyone really meet their soul mate in preschool? Were soul mates a real thing? I inhaled to clear my head. No. Those were my parents' ideas, not mine. First loves were supposed to end with high school, not return ten years later, all rich and handsome, to sleep on my couch and confuse my brain.

Sebastian touched my arm. "There's something I want to tell you."

"Peepee!" Dad waved his arms in air circles large enough to land a Cessna. "You're here!"

His enthusiasm was contagious. I smiled. My awkward romantic issues could wait. I needed a hug from my dad. It took incredible self-restraint not to run to him.

Dad wrapped his arms around me and kissed the top of my head. "Good to see you. You look amazing. How you doing, big guy?"

Sebastian shook Dad's hand. "Glad to be here."

Fresh shrimp and scallops swam in a bubbling butter and herb bath, and veggies from Mom's summer garden steamed in a pot on the side burner. Her centerpiece of fruit and dinner rolls adorned the table beneath a giant wide-mouth vase. Mom turned the glass upside down to protect our appetizers from the swarms of gnats and other bugs that hovered close by. When you lived on an island, cooking outside was an at-your-own-risk behavior.

I slipped my hand under the glass for a handful of blueberries and popped them into my mouth. Sebastian opened the Igloo on the floor by the table and twisted the top off a beer. His expression wasn't right. His body language seemed normal, but his eyes were on alert. If he sensed danger, he wouldn't have a beer, though. Right?

He set it on the table without taking a drink. Crap.

"Everything okay?" I intruded on his personal space. "You're acting hinky. Something's off tonight."

He pursed his lips and shook his head. "We need to talk."

Crap. Crappity crap crap. A colony of bats dove past the moon like harbingers of doom. No girl ever wanted to hear those words from the man she share a bed with— on the nights he bothered to come home so she actually had a clue where he was. My attitude kicked into defensive mode.

"What is it? Tell me now and be straight about it." I wrapped hands with electric blue fingernails around my hips. It had taken a thirty-minute shower and a bottle of shampoo to undo the damage inflicted during my ambush makeover, but I didn't hate the nails.

Sebastian sucked his teeth. "The team got new intel on Jimmy the Judge that suggests he's not in Vegas. Jimmy's my assignment. I need to check out the lead as soon as possible. The agents in Chincoteague will remain here another forty-eight hours until *The Watchers* pack up and head out, or longer if Fargas needs additional help with the murder investigation." He glanced away. "I'm leaving for Norfolk in the morning."

My mouth fell open and a bug flew in. "Gah!" I swatted the air and rubbed a napkin over my tongue. "Wah?" I gagged and grabbed his beer for help. I sucked in a mouthful of bitter liquid. My eyes watered. The bug tasted better.

Mom slid the door to her kitchen open and glided to my side. "There you are. I thought I heard you two. I made your favorite." She frowned at the beer in my hand and offered one of her signature Mai Tais instead. I passed the beer back to Sebastian. Mom's frozen cocktails were amazing, packed with fruit skewers and blended with ice.

A few swallows later, I came up for air. "I ate a bug."

Mom nodded. "It happens." She patted my shoulder and went to help Dad at the grill.

I collapsed into a chair at the table and stared at Sebastian. "You're leaving in the morning."

"Yes."

"You know where Jimmy's hiding?"

"The bureau got video confirmation of him downtown yesterday."

"Downtown?" My skin iced over. "You mean downtown Norfolk. He's gunning for you. That's why agents are on the island. They suspected he was close before the video confirmed it." These weren't questions. The truth was in his expression—a strange mix of grim and eager.

Sebastian confirmed my statements with a stiff dip of his chin. "We think he's planning something. The agents on the island are watching for signs of Jimmy's known associates. We don't know what he's up to in Norfolk, but we have him on street cams, and we assume what he's doing involves me. He might have no idea I'm living here. Whatever plan he's hatching, I need to make sure he and his people stay far away from here. From

you. My team's strategizing right now. I told them I
needed tonight."

My heart unfurled a tiny bit. "You did?"

He slid an arm around my waist and pulled me near.
"Yeah. I did." Sebastian lowered his lips to my ear. "I
don't want you to worry. I know Jimmy. I worked with
him for eight months undercover, remember? He's an old
dog. No new tricks. My team is smart and swift. Jimmy
in Norfolk is a good thing. He's on our turf. Arrogant son
of a bitch. The whole frigging bureau is gunning for him,
and he came to us. We're going to get him tomorrow."

Sebastian had taken out five members of Jimmy's
crime family a few months ago. Jimmy couldn't have
trained a new load of thugs so fast, could he? Whoever
he had working for him was new and they weren't ready
for what the bureau had under its shield. Sebastian was
fierce. He was a leader and he was a bulldog who didn't
stop coming until the enemy was behind bars. For the
first time in months, the weight of Jimmy the Judge
lightened on my shoulders. Sebastian could handle this.

"This time tomorrow, the nightmare will be over." I
whispered the words against his chest. When did I grab
on to him so tight?

"That's the plan, boss."

"What about all the Vegas tips?"

"Bogus. He probably called the tips in to throw us off.
I'm embarrassed to say it worked. We were canvassing
footage of Vegas street cameras all last week for nothing. Do you have any idea how many cameras are in
Vegas? You'd hate it."

Probably. "When will you be back? Will you call me
when you get him?"

Sebastian leaned back. "Yes, but when I get back,
we're making some big changes here."

I stepped out of his grip, ready to pounce. "I'm sorry, what?" I didn't need to make any changes.

He took a step forward. The look on his face said "shut up and listen."

I fought a smile. Goose bumps ran down my arms.

"When I come back, you're going to the gun range with me twice a week and you're learning to use a handgun. I want you to get your concealed carry license."

Nope. I shook my head as he continued his ridiculous set of demands.

"You're also taking self-defense classes. From me. Not those lame-ass, get-away-and-run-for-help classes they give twice a year at the bureau. You're taking the shove-his-nose-bone-into-his-brain-and-kill-him-for-touching-you, Sebastian Clark class. These demands are non-negotiable."

"First of all, ew. Second of all, I don't believe in violence. Third, everything is negotiable, unless it's an ultimatum."

"I don't believe you'll ever stay out of harm's way or keep a promise to let me handle my own investigations, so this is happening."

A standoff. We stared at one another until my cheeks burned with indignation. "You're not the boss of me."

"Yeah, well, you're going to be the death of me unless I have some thread of hope you can save your life if necessary."

I mulled that over. "It's a common opinion that self-defense and weapons training only provide a false sense of security and hinder a woman in the event she needs to use either."

Sebastian cracked a smile. "That's the bull criminals want you to believe so they don't have to work so hard."

Mom honked the air horn at gulls swarming over the

open grill, and I squeaked. Very brave of me. Sebastian shook his head. Dad hoisted trays of food off the grates and ran for the house, while birds dove and circled overhead and Mom laid on the horn.

I jumped inside after Dad and took a seat at the table.

Mom looked at Sebastian and me as she piled shrimp, scallops and steamed veggies on our plates. "Something wrong?"

I lifted my fork. "Sebastian gave me an ultimatum."

Sebastian's jaw clenched. The little vein in his neck pulsated. "I gave her an order."

"Oh, that's so much better," I scoffed. "Do you hear this guy?"

Mom leaned across the table. "Did she tell you about her new cell phone?" She whispered the last two words.

Sebastian looked at me. I shook my head.

Dad shoveled scallops into his mouth. "What're the demands?"

"Dad! Not the point. He can't make demands."

Dad shrugged. "Depends on the demands. Maybe you were going to do those things anyway. Then you aren't obeying. You're living your life and he's blowing his horn."

I liked that. Maybe I'd planned to get my concealed carry license. It didn't mean I had to carry a gun. It only meant I could if I wanted to. I believed in exercising my freedoms.

Sebastian watched me during dinner. My parents watched him. I prayed for invisibility.

Mom and I cleared the table after dinner, and she put on a pot of coffee to go with the baked apple pie Melinda had sent over. I stepped onto the deck while the coffee brewed and dialed Melinda's number.

Melinda answered on the fourth ring. "Hello?" Children argued and squealed in the background.

"Hey, it's Patience. I'm at my mom's and I wanted to thank you for the pie."

"Oh, did you try it? Is it good?"

"Not yet. Mom's making coffee first."

Melinda didn't speak for a long beat. "Coffee at nine? No wonder you don't sleep well."

The swig of beer and half a Mai Tai should cancel the coffee out, but I didn't mention it. "Hey, I've meant to call you for a few days. I got a delivery from Half Baked. Was it from you?"

"No. Just the pie. Why? Was it bad? Oh my goodness. Please tell me their quality is good enough to substitute for ours. All our customers are getting stuff from them this week to help fill our orders."

The door behind me slid open, and Sebastian approached with a tray. He had two cups of coffee and two pieces of pie.

"Everything's delicious. Sebastian's here with my pie. I've gotta go." I disconnected and set my phone on the table. The evil-cupcake situation worried me. So did the look on Sebastian's face.

"Are we okay?" He pulled out a chair for me.

"Yeah." I dared a glance his way. Though I hoped for the best, he was facing off with a killer tomorrow, and I shouldn't rock the boat.

Words loaded my tongue. A few popped loose. "I'm never carrying a gun." There. It had to be said. Boat rocked.

"I figured."

I shifted in my chair for a better look at him. "You did?"

He blew out a long breath and cocked a grin.

My shoulders relaxed. He wasn't bossing me around, and he knew me well enough not to expect me to change for him. Smart man. A little smile formed. "I haven't decided about the nose-pushing self-defense class yet. I like the get-free-and-run method the bureau teaches."

"Fair enough. We'll start small. Aim to immobilize the attacker without killing him." He reached for my hand and squeezed my fingers. "There's something else I want to talk with you about."

Jeez Louise. First he told me they found Jimmy the Judge and he's leaving in the morning. Then he demanded I carry a gun and kill with my bare hands. I shuddered at the thought of what came next.

Sebastian sat beside me at the table and tapped his pie with a fork. "I saw the look on Adrian's face the other night when he said you didn't want kids, and I heard you and Claire talking about the same thing."

I studied the moon over the ocean. Where was the rest of my Mai Tai when I needed it? "And?"

"Where do you see yourself in five years?" He pushed a forkful of apple pie between his lips.

I'd asked him the same question at his FBI interview a few years back. I gave him the same answer he gave me back then. "Here."

He smiled. That word had got him the job. Would it get me off the hook?

I cleared my throat. "Maybe we could talk more about incapacitating villains."

"Not yet. When you say 'here,' do you mean in your apartment? In a house? Alone? With a family?" He laced his fingers together at the back of his head and waited.

"I don't know." I fidgeted with the hem of my shirt, unsure what to say or how to react. I couldn't read him. What answer did he want or expect? Did it matter?

He dropped his forearms onto the table and adjusted his position, leaning toward me, intimidating me. "You don't know or you don't want to say? If it's the latter, then why not? Are you unsure, indifferent or ashamed of the answer?"

I pulled my feet into the chair with me and wrapped my arms around my knees, no longer interested in pie or coffee. No one lied to Sebastian, not successfully anyway. It was his job to know people. I let out a breath. "I'm not great at being vulnerable. Telling people personal things gives them power over me. I know it sounds dumb."

"It doesn't sound dumb." His words nearly overlapped mine, as if he'd anticipated my response.

I laid my cheek against my knees. "What about you? Big white house, little picket fence, two point three minions running around?"

Sebastian didn't move a muscle. For a moment, I worried I'd offended him somehow, though the words were harmless enough. Cool night winds blew hair across my face. I tucked the strands behind my ears and waited. I couldn't have been the first to ask him those questions in one form or another. People had asked me on a regular basis since puberty if I wanted children, how many, if I'd marry, where we'd live, etc.

"If I get Jimmy tomorrow, I might retire."

I blinked. What? "You're thirty-five. You can't retire."

He raised his eyebrows and stared into my eyes, daring me to say he couldn't again.

"I was thinking more along the lines of leaving the bureau for a new career. Something with better odds of coming home at the end of the day."

Leaving the bureau? He lived for the chase. Didn't he? My mind scrambled and flailed. "Like what?"

"I don't know. Open a dojo. Maybe teach self-defense." He smiled the crooked almost-smile I loved. "I hear the position of sheriff is coming available soon, too."

My heart fluttered. "Fargas's position? You'd be happy as a small-town sheriff? Nothing ever happens here."

He snorted.

"Nothing used to happen here."

"I think I could manage." The seriousness in his tone implied dozens of things I couldn't say out loud for fear words would ruin them. He wanted to be safe. Why? Was he planning a family to come home to at night? He'd avoided my question about minions. Part of me worried for America if he quit his job at the bureau. Special Agent Sebastian Clark stopped more crime and serial killers per year than any other agent. He had more recognition, awards and articles than I could count. In fact, I'd started a new file just for accolades when his personnel file maxed capacity.

I cleared my throat. "If I changed jobs, I'd work with teens. I always thought the island needed better prep programs for high schoolers. I never considered college until Adrian left for Miami. I wasn't alone. Most families here don't teach kids options. The men here are fishermen. Boys grow up expecting to follow in their father's footsteps. Girls expect to marry their high school sweetheart, buy a house and have kids. It'd be great to reach out to juniors and seniors and tell them there's a big world out there. My favorite part of human resources was recruiting. I went to colleges and spoke with graduates. I told them about the infinite options available to them. Kids can leave Chincoteague and do anything they choose. Then, when they're ready, the island will be here for them to come home." It took me ten years to figure it out, and I wanted to share.

"Where do you stand on minions?" he asked.

"You really shouldn't stand on minions."

He groaned. "Patience."

"I don't know. I'm afraid I'd ruin them. I'd probably turn my offspring into neurotic, distrusting, danger magnets."

He nodded.

"Wow. You don't have to agree with me."

Sebastian lifted my hand to his lips and kissed my fingertips. "Well, if that happens, you can always send them to my dojo." His eyes twinkled. "It's not a no on kids for you then?"

"No." I whispered. "Not a no, just a lot of worry."

Sebastian leaned across the space between us and pressed gentle lips to mine. "I think that goes with the job description."

TWENTY-THREE

SEBASTIAN LEFT FOR Norfolk before dawn, and I faced the longest day of my life. I'd worried for his safety all night and made plans to continue the process until he called to say Jimmy the Judge was in custody. Until then, any horrible thing was possible and my imagination was in full swing creating awful scenarios. As a bonus ulcer, Halloween arrived right on schedule. Three hundred sixty-four other days to face off with Jimmy the Judge, but today was the day. Halloween made all the most sinister ideas seem possible.

I shivered and stuck my empty mug under the Keurig for round four. Shadows climbed the walls around my windows and door. Thanks to the mayor and *The Watchers*, Halloween had taken on an anything-is-possible Hollywood feel. Ghost hunters wandered the island at all hours, dressed in black and toting night vision goggles. People continued to flow over the mainland bridge into our little town, amping up tension and reducing breathing room. Fortunately, like the stress with Sebastian, *The Watchers* drama would be over in twenty-four hours. The countdown was on. Today was a big day.

The bathroom door opened and Claire stretched in the hallway. My tiny apartment filled with a burst of steamy air scented with shampoo and hair products. She approached me with an over-the-top smile. "It's Halloween."

"Yep." I sipped my fresh coffee and glanced at the clock. If all went as planned, tomorrow would be the start of a peaceful existence.

Claire fluffed her bangs. "Have you chosen your costume yet?"

"I'm not going to *The Watchers* party. I know you love that show, but I plan to party on the couch, eating cheese doodles and counting the hours until they leave town."

She snagged a bottle of water from the refrigerator. "Sebastian will be okay." She patted my shoulder.

My throated tightened. I refused to give in to my imagination. He was fine.

I motioned to her little cream-and-lavender dress. "What? No running today?"

"Not today. Today I'm helping at the Purple Pony. Just. Like. You." She touched the tip of my nose and I swatted her away.

My parents had talked me into helping while we ate dessert on their deck last night. They expected a crowd. Claire was more than happy to assist. She got to paint faces. I had to read palms. Mom insisted I'd keep my mind off things better if I stayed busy. What better way to pass my time than by telling a line of impatient tourists they had good fortune in their future? Only twenty-five bucks a pop. Come on down.

"Here." Claire shoved her hand across the counter toward me. "Brush up on your skills. What does my palm say about me?"

I rolled my eyes and played along, rubbing my thumbs over the creases and lines of her palm. "Ahh, I can tell you use a high quality moisturizer, have a desk job and spend enough on manicures to feed a third world country."

"Ha-ha." She flipped her hand in mine. "Do your thing."

A buzz of electricity zipped through my wrist and a flash of terror sent my heart into a tailspin. I jerked my hand free.

"Hey!" She shook her hand out at the wrist and frowned at me. "If you don't want to do it, just say so."

"Sorry. I didn't mean to…" I inhaled long and slow. Exhaling the same way, I forced a smile. "I'm being ridiculous."

She lifted one perfect eyebrow.

"I'm glad you're here," I said. "I'm going to get changed and we're going to show some tourists the time of their lives." A shuddered breath rocked past my lips.

"Attagirl."

I moved to my bedroom with purpose. *I don't have psychic powers. Psychic powers aren't real. I experienced a jolt of fear because I'm afraid. My imagination is out of control.* I ran the statements on a mental loop while I dressed. Then I rejoined Claire in the living room.

Time to go to work.

WE ARRIVED AT my parent's shop on the heels of the sun. Bright orange light illuminated the harbor and everything on Main Street. Sunrises in the fall were the best. The brilliant crimson and gold rays cast a magical filter over the rainbow of autumn-dressed trees near the water. Fallen leaves still damp with morning dew painted sidewalks in various shapes and colors.

Claire slowed her steps several feet away from the shop door and faced the harbor. "This looks like a Thomas Kinkade painting." She wrinkled her nose. "Except for the hobos."

JULIE ANNE LINDSEY 267

I nodded. Fans. Hobos. Potato, potahto. Brightly colored tents polka dotted the sidewalks, housing ghost hunters and *The Watchers* fans who'd arrived too late to find housing or space in the parks for their tents. Frankie spent her nights as deputy sheriff shooing vagrants off lawns and private property. Apparently she'd given up on clearing the sidewalks.

I crossed the street when I spotted the Baby Cakes truck and ordered a short stack of blueberry pancakes for distraction and inspiration. Claire ordered a fruit and yogurt parfait with a side of granola. Her breakfast inspired me to order whipped cream on my pancakes.

Dad was outside the Purple Pony when we carried our breakfasts back across the street.

"Hello, pretty ladies." He kissed our cheeks and held the door for us. "Your mother told me you were here. I came out to check. I didn't see you at first, and I thought she'd lost her touch."

"Silly." Mom cooed from behind the beaded curtain.

I propped breakfast between my elbows on the counter where Dad stacked and folded shirts. We had forty-five minutes before the store opened. I could get a lot of worrying done in forty-five minutes. My mind zipped back to the slap of fear I'd felt when Claire showed me her palm. Nothing like that had happened in years. I didn't like it back then and I full-on hated it now. Stupid Halloween. Dumb stress. Nutty psychic mom genes. I forked a mouthful of breakfast and relaxed. Sweet blueberries danced and burst over my tongue with each bite of rich buttery pancakes. I exhaled. How bad could things get when there was a truck called Baby Cakes serving little stacks of heaven right across the street?

Six hours later, I wished Baby Cakes delivered. I'd read twenty-four palms and assured twenty-four lovely individuals that their loved ones were faithful, safe, "crossed-over" or whatever else they wanted for their twenty-five bucks. Hey, people didn't pay to hear bad news. Luckily, not a single palm had stunned me the way Claire's had. It seemed boredom knocked the imagination right out of me. The frightening zip of fear I'd felt earlier was clearly a result of an overactive imagination coupled with the worst holiday of the year for scaredy-cats.

After a morning filled with palm reading, my vast arsenal of generic, applicable-to-anyone-with-a-heartbeat lines had dried up like the marsh in July. I'd started repeating lines from earlier fortunes and hoped the clientele didn't compare notes. For the last half an hour, I spouted lame clichés like, "I see romance in your future," "Looks like someone loves you very much but doesn't tell you as often as they should," and my favorite, "You'll remember this trip always and return to the island soon." The last one was good for business.

Mom stood outside the beaded curtain and turned the little sign over. Time for my lunch break. I headed for the kitchenette in the back room and scrubbed a zillion germs off my hands.

Mom floated over to me. "How are you holding up?"

"Good." I checked my watch and smiled. Mom was right. If I'd stayed home, I'd have watched the clock and obsessed over Sebastian's safety. Instead, the day was already on the downswing. A few more hours at the Purple Pony and the sun would set. Claire and Fargas would leave for the big Halloween bash, and I'd enjoy peace and quiet in my apartment while all the tourists flocked to Adrian's neighborhood, vying for a peek at an island ghost or semi-celebrity appearance. I had plans for a long soak in mom's herbal bath salts and a Reese Witherspoon movie marathon.

If Sebastian didn't call by midnight, I'd text him for an update.

Mom rubbed my shoulders. "Claire's having a great time out there. She's wonderful with children. They all think she's a princess."

I smiled. "She is."

"Your dad went to visit a few food trucks and haul some lunch back for us. He took the wagon." She meant a literal red wagon. The same Radio Flyer wagon they pulled me around the island in twenty-five years ago now made runs to the farmers' market and harbor every Tuesday morning. Apparently, it also visited food trucks when a reality show invaded our town.

"Thanks, Mom." I patted her hand, and she went back through the beaded curtain to mingle with customers.

I slipped back into my seat and laid my head on the table. I sent Dad a telepathic plea for chocolate. I didn't care what form it came in.

The chair across from me scraped away from the table. Men's cologne clogged my nose. I lifted my head with zero enthusiasm.

The mean reporter with too-expensive shoes and stalker tendencies soiled the seat across from me. I nearly swallowed my tongue.

He smiled. "You look like hell."

My heart beat double-time. I composed my thoughts before speaking, squaring my shoulders. Who did this guy think he was? Diving across the table and demanding an explanation of what he was up to crossed my mind. "Come for a palm reading?"

"Nope."

"Good, because I'm terrible at it, and I'm hungry."

The smell of freshly printed T-shirts and patchouli made my empty tummy squirm. I sent another wish for chocolate into the ether.

Meanie stared. His black beady eyes never blinked. The expressionless look on his face worried me. When Sebastian looked that way, I knew he was formulating a plan, strategizing or reading my mind. Frustration boiled under my skin. I had enough to worry about without this goon darkening my day. "If you don't want your palm read, and I know you aren't a real reporter, then what do you want?" I presented a brave face. If he was up to no good, I had a room full of witnesses on the other side of a beaded curtain.

"Just looking for you."

"Yeah? Well, congratulations."

He chuckled, a deep throaty sound that made the hairs rise on my arms. He shoved his chair over the floor and stood. "Where's your guard dog?"

My thoughts scrambled. Did he mean Sebastian or Adrian? Heck, he could've meant Todd. Had he seen Todd following him?

"Out." That covered all the possibilities.

His lips turned down at the corners. "Out where? Chasing leads?" His dark laugh returned, louder this time.

"You first. What are you doing here?"

"My job." He stood and glared down at me. If his job was intimidation, he nailed it. Big promotions were in his future.

He shook his fat head on the way back through the curtain. I jumped to my feet and peered through the curtain as he slithered out the front door.

Chasing leads. Was that comment aimed at Todd or Sebastian? News leads or crime leads? What did he mean? I sent a quick text to both Todd and Sebastian, then one to Adrian for good measure. Just checking in.

Todd responded with two texts. On set. And Vance Varner is a douche.

I smiled.

Adrian sent me a picture of his face. Eyes crossed. Lips puckered. Dork.

Sebastian didn't respond.

I paced the floor, ideas swarming in my mind. How could the killer have waited on Rick in the secret passageway if no one knew Rick would be checking in? The room had been rented to Sebastian. Why would a guy with as much experience around cameras as Rick had hook up a camera to record his sexcapades and not pick a unit with night vision, or at least leave the light on? Sure, the camera used motion detector technology like the others *The Watchers* posted around town, but most cameras had that feature, and a motion detector would come in handy more for long-term surveillance, not one night of hanky-panky.

I looked at my phone again, hoping I'd missed a return text from Sebastian. Suddenly, from where I sat behind the beaded curtain, all signs pointed more than ever to Jimmy the Judge putting a hit on Sebastian. Sebastian's room. His Range Rover. Adrian dressed as him. My car. The meanie who watched me and called it his job. My throat went dry.

Dad burst through the curtain, sending ropes of beads dancing against the walls. "I brought the chocolate you wanted!"

"Ahh!" I clutched my chest.

Holy cannoli. Maybe I was psychic.

TWENTY-FOUR

BY EIGHT THE streets were deserted. Even the food trucks had moved closer to the big bash at Adrian's. The night was cool, quiet and normal, except Fargas picked Claire up in his cruiser, dressed as Superman. Claire wore the ghost hunter costume she'd worn as an extra. I had a feeling that would be her costume for the next several Halloweens.

I scraped my spoon around the bottom of a chocolate peanut butter ice cream container and groaned. The kitchen was so far away and my blanket was so snuggly warm. I paused the DVR, weighing my need for comfort food against the energy required to retrieve a snack. Undecided, I looked to my frozen screen. Reese Witherspoon's eyes brimmed with unshed tears. She knew what it was like to go home after being away all those years. Whoever wrote the script for *Sweet Home Alabama* probably came from Chincoteague. Next time I went online, I needed to look that up.

"Honey, I'm home." Adrian's voice carried down the hall from my bedroom. He insisted on using the secret staircase.

"I thought you were at the party."

"I'm going. You can't rush perfection." He walked into the living room with a wicked gleam in his eye. "What do you think?"

His sleek black tuxedo accented every angle of his ridiculously fit body. The bow tie and pocket square were perfectly cut. The ensemble was obviously high quality and custom-tailored for him.

My traitorous heart skipped a beat. "You look nice."

He pivoted on shiny black shoes and adjusted one cufflink. "Bond. James Bond."

"Of course." Adrian earned his 007 nickname from me after helping me stick my nose into multiple crimes that were none of my business.

He sashayed to the couch and took my empty ice cream container. "I brought you something."

"Great." I swung my feet over the edge of the couch and braced myself.

Adrian dipped into my bedroom and returned with a small box. "I got you a costume."

Stupidly, I opened it. "This isn't a costume. This is underwear and a big knife."

He beamed. "It's an official replica swimsuit of Honey Ryder, the original Bond girl. It's perfect because she set the bar for every Bond girl who followed. You get it?"

I didn't like the highly applicable analogy to our lives.

"I'm not going to the party. Not to mention it's fifty degrees out there." I fingered the soft white material. "This outfit is super cute. Can I keep it?"

His eyes twinkled.

"I'm not role playing with you, so put your dimple away. You can keep the knife."

He kept smiling. "Try it on."

"No!" I shoved him and he didn't budge. I licked my lips as the butterflies took off in my tummy. "No, thank you."

"Come with me. I know you're worried about Sebastian and this is sad." He pointed to the junk food scattered on my coffee table. "Let me take your mind off things for a while. Sebastian will call you later. I promise." He drew an *X* over his heart with one finger.

"You can't know that. What if he never calls? What if something awful happened already? I texted him hours ago. He never texted back. Something's wrong."

"Nothing's wrong." Adrian extended a hand to me. "Come on. Let me make you smile for a while."

I smiled. "You rhymed."

He lifted one dark brow. "I like to rhyme. I do it all the time."

"Dork."

Adrian lifted the remote and hit play. "I love this movie." He backed his rear onto the arm of my couch.

The actor beside Reese looked wistfully at his soul mate. He told her she could have roots and wings.

I looked up at Adrian's clean-shaven face. "You think she makes the right decision in the end?"

He paused the movie again and looked at me. "Yeah."

"Really? I'm never sure." Her character had her choice of two perfect men. One she'd known all her life, who knew all her awful secrets and loved her anyway. The other man loved her for who she currently was and he openly accepted her past, even if he hadn't lived it with her.

Adrian dropped the remote on the table. "I don't know. Maybe I'm wrong. I never related to either of those guys."

I gawked. "One's a hometown golden boy. The other's a successful politician."

He snorted. "Right?"

"Yes. Right. You're *both* her choices." My voice rose to a squeak.

He put his palms up. "Well, then I guess I was right. That lucky girl didn't have a bad option."

I flopped my head against the back cushion. "Never mind. Enjoy your party. Keep an eye on Claire. Fargas might be dressed as Superman, but I still think he's more Clark Kent than Kryptonian."

"Kryptonian? Who's the dork now?" He checked the door and window locks. "Fine. I'll go. Keep your phone with you, and I'll call and check in later."

I waved my phone. "Got it." I hadn't let the phone out of my sight since texting Sebastian from the Purple Pony earlier. Every time it buzzed, I jumped out of my skin to get it.

Off-key singing started outside the window behind my couch. I turned on my knees for a look.

Adrian moved back in the direction of my window. "Carolers on Halloween?"

"No."

"Drunken ghost hunters?"

I made a crazy face and went to the door. "Yep. Drunken carolers singing 'I Got You Babe.'" I pulled the door open. "Also known as my parents."

"Hey!" Dad adjusted his brown leather vest. Fringe bounced against his oversized turquoise belt buckle. For once, his salt-and-pepper ponytail added to his look. "Guess who we are?"

Adrian beat me to the answer. "John Smith and Pocahontas."

Mom kissed his cheek. She swung uber long, flat-ironed locks over one shoulder. "Silly. We're Sonny and Cher." She puckered her lips and made weird eyes at us.

Adrian hugged her. "I was teasing. You both look amazing. Patience and I are going as Honey Ryder and James Bond."

"Dashing." Mom patted Adrian's cheek. She gave me a once-over. "Those are pajamas."

"I'm not going."

Mom laughed. "Yes you are. We're here to make sure you don't sit around working yourself into a tizzy until Sebastian calls."

I looked to Dad for help. He'd stolen my seat on the couch and restarted my movie.

"Fine." Not really, but I needed to get rid of everyone so I could wallow in worry all alone.

"That's the spirit."

Adrian offered my parents something from the kitchen as if he owned the place. "You forgot your costume," he called after me.

"I'm not Honey Ryder." I sulked down the hallway. Forced to jump through hoops so I could eat ice cream in peace on Halloween. Unfair. Unjust. Crappy karma. This was probably payback for all the unenthusiastic palm readings I'd performed.

I stared in my closet. Blue sparkles on the nightstand caught my eye and I formed a brilliant plan. I pulled on the shiny little Band-Aid dress from my extremely awful makeover and smiled. If Adrian could dress as Sebastian for his political rally, I could dress as his mother for the Halloween party—which I wasn't attending, but he didn't know that. I swapped the awkward stilettos for knee-high white boots and sucked in my gut.

In the bathroom, I piled on the makeup and teased my hair until it screamed. A bottle of aerosol hairspray and two giant rhinestone-tipped eyelashes later, and voilà! Mrs. Davis.

"Ready!" I struck a pose in the doorway to my living room.

Adrian blanched. "You hate that outfit."

"Yes, but it's Halloween, so I'm going as your mother."

"Ew."

"Come here and give Mama a big kiss." I strutted to his side and wrapped my hand around his chin to squeeze his cheeks.

Adrian jerked his face away and grimaced. "Ah, jeez. Why'd you have to do that? You've ruined me. I'll never feel like a man again." He shivered and stuck his tongue out in a gag. "I'm leaving."

"You can't leave." I grabbed his hand and heavy fingers curled over mine on contact.

He turned a hopeful face to me. "What?"

I suppressed a smile and did my best Mrs. Davis impression. "Where you going with my kiss? You're my widdle angel baby boy." I puckered my lips and closed my eyes.

Adrian huffed. I peeked with one eye. He looked torn between leaving and chasing me across the room with something heavy. I smiled and shut my eyes again.

Footfalls padded against the carpet before his soft lips pressed mine. Adrian's signature scent of shampoo and mint enveloped me. Hot, familiar palms encircled my arms. My head tilted back to accommodate our height difference. The chaste press of our lips lasted a few beats too long. Not a quick peck on the head or cheek. There was definite lingering.

I pulled my chin back and sucked air. "Oh my goodness." My chest heaved with pent-up emotion.

My parents were gone. Vanished. Poof. How fast were they? I turned at the waist, confirming we stood alone in my living room.

"Patience." Shame and guilt marred Adrian's perfect face. "I'm sorry. I didn't mean to… I mean, I thought… I didn't think you'd…" He pressed hands to his hips and crunched his eyebrows. "You were supposed to push me away. Now look what you did."

My breathing slowed as I gathered my thoughts and processed his expression. "What?" Anger scorched my skin. "Look what I did? That wasn't my fault! You kissed me!"

He pursed his lips. "You lingered."

Ah! He thought so too. I touched my lips with both sets of fingertips. "Did not."

"Did too, and now I'm a colossal asshat who kissed another man's girlfriend. Dammit, Patience." Agitated fingers scraped through his hair and ruined the sleek look. He gave me a long sideways glare before producing his phone and touching the screen.

"Stop." I jumped in his direction. "What are you doing?"

"I'm texting Sebastian. If I don't tell him, you will, and I'll look even worse. I didn't mean for that to happen. I respect Sebastian. And you." He swore some more while I jumped around trying to liberate his phone.

"You can't tell him."

His eyes were wild with emotion. "I'm not *that guy* anymore. I don't do shit like this. Jeez, now I'm swearing. You make me crazy."

"Ha! Me? You! You! You!" I nabbed the phone and the screen went black. "What happened? What'd I do?"

Adrian took the phone back with gentle hands. All his charm and charisma were gone. Deflated. "The battery does that sometimes. I cracked the backing when we fell on the sidewalk last month."

"When your office caught fire?"

"Yeah."

He fiddled with the phone and looked at me with sad eyes. "I'm really sorry."

"Me too."

After a few long breaths, he moved to the door.

"Look, I better get going. You don't have to come with me if you don't want to. If you don't, I'll understand, but please believe I won't ever touch you like that again." He lifted his palms as if I might arrest him.

I nodded and bit back a tear. That thought broke my heart, which just made me mad. He had no business touching me like that, so it shouldn't matter to me that he wouldn't.

The smile felt awkward on my face. "You go ahead without me. I need a minute."

He opened the front door without another word. I jogged to his side. "Adrian. Wait."

I wrapped my arms around his middle and pressed my cheek to his chest. He froze under my touch. Too many emotions boiled in my heart and head. Too many to sort. Too many to process. "I love you."

He patted my back and pressed his lips to the top of my head. "Back at you."

I wiped my eyes and straightened his jacket before I stained it with mascara and makeup. "Okay. So, we're cool?" If any two people could get past a little regrettable lingering, it was us. I hoped.

Adrian's cocky, lopsided grin returned. "Very." He turned on slick designer shoes and sauntered down my steps into the night.

A pint of ice cream churned in my stomach. I needed actual food. And a lobotomy. Kissing Adrian? What was I thinking? I blamed stress and sappy movies and a sugar buzz. Definitely that. Too bad Sebastian would blame me and our romance would implode. Except, there was nothing to tell because it hadn't been an actual kiss. There had been extremely limited lingering. None, really. A misplaced cheek peck that bounced right off my lips and wasn't awkward at all. It basically never happened.

I grabbed my keys and moped across the street to the Tasty Cream. Mrs. Tucker met me at the door.

"What can I get you, sweetie?" Her round cheeks were dotted with eyeliner freckles. Her red wig was braided into pigtails, standing left and right of her head with the help of some barely visible wire.

I laughed. "Are you the sign from Wendy's?"

Her smile drooped. "I'm Pippi Longstocking. Who are you supposed to be?"

"I'm Mrs. Davis."

A deep belly laugh rumbled and filled the empty room around us. "Well, what can I get you to go with your fabulous new dress?"

"Salad."

Her face crinkled. "Salad? What happened?" She poured a cup of coffee and pushed it my way. "Come on. It's okay. You can tell Pippi."

"I'd rather not talk about it. It's too horrifying, even for Halloween."

I sipped the coffee and enjoyed the scenery. "Monster Mash" played on the speakers overhead. Faux cobwebs hung from everything and family-friendly decorations adorned every surface. Smiling spiders and witches crashing brooms into walls. Mrs. Tucker always made the Tasty Cream feel like an extension of home.

The bell over the door jingled and Karen Holsten Thompson walked in. So much for feeling at home.

Her smile faded when she saw me.

I wiggled my fingers. "Hi."

Mrs. Tucker rang Karen up at the register and hoisted a large brown bag onto the counter. The bag was filled to the brim with Styrofoam containers, and grease circles stained the sides. My gaze fell to Karen's middle, where her fingers lingered on her abdomen. She dropped the protective hand to her side and gave me a dirty look.

I had a thought. "I don't suppose you sent me any cupcakes with tiny daggers?"

She rolled her eyes and left with her ten-pound bag of food.

I looked at Mrs. Tucker. "She sent me dead birds once. Why not some threatening cupcakes?"

Oh my goodness. Of course. "Those cupcakes *were* a warning. A threat." My bones chilled. "I ate threat cupcakes."

Mrs. Tucker wiped a rag over the counter. "Were they any good?"

"Delicious." I shivered the thought away. Sebastian and his team had their finger on Jimmy the Judge. *The Watchers* were leaving in the morning. Midnight was coming up fast. The awfulness of my week would be over soon. Meanwhile, I was safe inside the Tasty Cream with good food and great company. I ate salad and laughed with Mrs. Tucker until my butt fell asleep on the little red stool at her counter.

The clock on my living room wall said ten-thirty when I opened my front door. Sebastian should've called.

Time to see how things were going at Adrian's. I pulled my laptop onto my legs and tuned into the live feed from the Halloween party. A thousand faces I didn't know clogged the screen as cameras panned and changed from one angle to the next. It was like watching New Year's Eve live in Times Square, only echoes of the island party several blocks away penetrated my walls from time to time, with a blast of microphone feedback or a random air horn blowing.

I cued up another movie but couldn't steady my mind after all the coffee Mrs. Tucker had plied me with. I opened a search engine in a new window. If Sebastian wouldn't fill me in, maybe some online reporter would have new details about the Jimmy the Judge case. I found nothing current, so I read dozens of articles from the past decade. Most of the stories I knew from my time at the FBI. I ran my fingertips over pictures of Jimmy the Judge. He was a portly, black-haired thing. He couldn't outrun Sebastian, but he was shrewd and nefarious. A shoot-them-in-the-back kind of guy. The next article was about someone called Leo the Lucky. According to the report, Leo got off of airtight laundering charges in Boston when his dear friend Jimmy stepped in with his team of crooked attorneys. Behind Jimmy in the photo, surrounded by men carrying briefcases, was a face I recognized.

"Oh no."

My hands fumbled blindly over the couch, searching for my phone. I couldn't drag my gaze from the screen for fear it'd change or disappear while I wasn't looking. The man in the picture was a few years younger and a dozen pounds lighter, but he still wore John Lobb loafers. I skipped texting Sebastian and dialed his number instead. It went to voice mail.

Mr. Meanie was Leo the Lucky. I hadn't been over-reacting earlier. It wasn't my imagination doing double-time today. There was a hit out on Sebastian, and Leo the Lucky was here to get the job done. My tummy coiled into my spine. He'd sat with me today and asked about my guard dog. He told me he was doing his job.

I tried Sebastian again.

Email dinged on my phone. I logged into email on my computer, hoping it was a message from Sebastian. I redialed his number. If he didn't answer in five minutes, I'd call dispatch. Maybe they could get a hold of him or tell me he was safe. I had one new email from DoYouEverWantToSeeYourFriendAgain@email.com. My hands shook hard enough to loosen my grip on the phone. I pulled in a breath. Inside the email was a link. No further message.

I clicked.

Dark video footage played on the screen. Claire screamed and the camera honed in on her as she ran through a maze of hallways. Heat shot into my hair. She was at Flick's Funeral Home. The one place on the island I'd rather die than step foot in ever again. My stomach knotted. I threw my purse over one shoulder, dialed Sebastian one more time and ran for my car. No car.

I swore and took the steps two at a time back up to my apartment. Claire's keys lay on the counter. I grabbed them and went back to the street.

I gunned the Jetta to life and roared into the empty street.

"Clark." Sebastian answered the phone I forgot I was holding.

Relief flooded over me. I sobbed. "He's got Claire and he wants me to get her. They're at Flick's Funeral Home. Where are you? You're in danger. It was all Jimmy!" I blurted words trying to convey all I knew about Leo the Lucky while driving through town. Tears blurred my vision as I turned up and down a half dozen alleys, taking every shortcut possible to the funeral home. Shivers racked my body.

"Patience. I want you to listen. *Do not* go into the funeral home. I'm calling Fargas now."

"Didn't you hear me? Jimmy's after you. His guy, Leo the Lucky, is on the island. That's the guy Todd saw following me. You have to be careful."

I jammed the car into park and ran for the front door of the creepy old house.

Sebastian growled. "You aren't listening. I know all about that. I followed him to Jimmy this morning. Jimmy's in custody and Leo's in the hospital. I caught him an hour ago."

My feet planted in the overgrown grass outside Flick's front door.

An ambulance blared through the phone. "Where are you?"

A car door slammed. "I'm leaving the hospital. I'll be there in an hour. Stay put and wait for Fargas."

"Are you hurt?" Panic shot through me. Claire was held captive. Sebastian was at the hospital.

"A couple bullets grazed me. I got a few stitches. I'm fine. Where's Adrian? He's supposed to watch you."

My tummy knotted. That was a whole other mess I didn't want to talk about. Snapped back to reality, I ran to the front door and tuned the knob.

"Claire's at Flick's. Send Fargas fast." Unless he's trapped in there, too. "Wait. Sebastian? I just got the email five minutes ago. When did you say you caught Leo?"

Who else was in the funeral home?

The call broke into static and disconnected. I looked at my phone, remembering the same thing had happened to me this summer when a killer wanted me cut off from the world.

Cell blocker. Shoot.

I hesitated at the threshold. Go inside and look for Claire, or wait for backup? I reached a palm around the door's edge and flipped the light switch. Nothing happened. I guessed no one paid the bills when a home was in foreclosure.

A blood-curdling scream split the darkness inside, and I jumped through the doorway without another thought. "Claire?" I dragged one hand along the wall for balance and waved the other in front of me. "Claire?"

Behind me, the door slammed shut, followed by the unmistakable snap of a lock.

TWENTY-FIVE

"HELLO?" I QUAVERED into the dark room. "Is someone there?" Ugh. I sounded like a horror movie cliché.
I rolled my shoulders back, summoning courage. Of
course someone was there. The door hadn't locked itself. I gulped. Had it? It was a funeral home, after all.
Plenty of bodies passed through these halls over the
years. What if one of the souls didn't go into the light
or get snatched up by the smoke goblins in time to leave
Earth or whatever happened to spirits when bodies died.

The floorboards creaked beside me. I pressed my
back to the wall, sticking tight to the shadows. If I didn't
see the thing moving nearby, maybe it couldn't see me—
whatever *it* was. I strained sore, tired eyes to find something in the darkness besides my fear. Bouquets of the
dearly departed tickled my nose. Decades of old women
in floral perfumes and boatloads of carnations had permanently seasoned the carpets and walls. A gag built
in my throat.

I tried my voice again. "Hello?"

Air rushed past me, stirring stale scents of the home's
emptiness into the mix.

Claire spoke in hushed tones somewhere deep in
the cavernous house. Her words carried through the air
vents, reverberating off the bare walls around me. "No,
no, no, no. Please, don't. Please."

"Claire!" I tipped my head back and screamed into
the air. "Claire. Where are you? What do you see?" The

jolt of pain and fear I experienced while holding her hand came rushing back. My heart squeezed tight. I didn't believe in those things. Did I?

"Don't do this," she begged. "Please." Her voice cracked and my heart broke. Whoever aimed to harm her would need to go through me first. I turned my head toward the front door one last time. Was it locked? Had I heard right? Did it matter? I wasn't leaving without Claire.

"I'm coming! Hang on, Claire. I'm here. I'm coming!" Following the wall with one hand, I ran in the direction of her screams. The hall stopped near the rear of the home, past offices I'd once sat in making small talk with killers. Heavy fabric over the windows limited incoming light from the moon and streetlamps. *The Watchers* had probably tamped out the light to tape their scenes earlier. My fumbling fingertips found a doorknob on the wall.

A shriek of horror shattered my world. I couldn't see what happened, but Claire's scream left no question as to whether or not she was okay. I yanked the door open and barreled blindly inside.

Two rampaging strides later, stars appeared in the blackness. My knees wobbled and I fell into waiting arms. My head throbbed and my ears rang. I counted out rescue hero as a possible career choice. Cologne filled my nostrils. My feet fumbled under the guidance of male arms until my knees gave out. Pain shot through my temples and rang in my ears. I slid to the ground and leaned against the wall. Everything in the room was slick to the touch.

Shafts of light shone through an open door on the far side of the room. I worked to focus my eyes. A shadowy figure moved into view. My head ached as I searched for Claire. The room was covered in plastic. What kind

of mold or bacteria required this kind of measure? Did
the movers do this as they emptied the home? Did *The
Watchers* crew cover things to protect their equipment?
I slid sweat-slicked palms over the floor around me.
Through squinted eyes, I made out the shapes of cab-
inets in the walls, each with a little cardholder. Fear
wedged in my throat. This was where they'd kept the
bodies. I yanked my palms off the plastic-covered floor
and rubbed them against my legs.

The silhouette approached again and stepped into the
shafts of light from the door. Jesse Short pushed night
vision goggles onto his forehead. A smug look dawned
over his face. "I knew you'd come. Everything I read
about you said you would. You hear someone's in danger, and off you go on a rescue mission."

"You," I spat. My head pounded. I pressed a palm
to the ache. "What the hell are you doing? Let us go!"

"Look around, darling. There is no us. There's only
you." He opened his palms and bowed like a magician
on stage.

"Claire!" I screamed.

"She's at the party like everyone else in this back-
woods Podunk town. Everyone but you." He lined some
dangerous looking tools on a table beside him. I hoped
they were props. A few looked a little sharp and too re-
alistic.

I forced my gaze back to his face. "Don't lie to me.
I heard her scream. Now, let us go. I told Sebastian I
was here. He's contacting Fargas now. You're done for,
so you might as well try to get a head start out of town
because…"

Jesse stuffed a wad of cloth into my mouth. "That's
enough out of you. Do you think I've gotten this far in
life without being prepared? Fargas's phone was lifted

from his pocket in the crowd about an hour ago. The radio in his car is having some trouble, as are his walkie-talkies, thanks to this." He twisted a gadget in his hand, presumably another cell blocker. "His deputy is a big fan of my show, like your friends Claire and Adrian. They're all gathered around punch bowls and big screens, having the night of their life, while you're having the last night of yours."

Confusion rocked me to the core. I'd heard her yell. Had he killed her? Why was he lying?

She screamed again, and I twisted in the direction of the sound. Her scream sounded less authentic. More… recorded.

"Your little friend is quite the actress. Eager to help out too." He played the scream again. A tablet appeared before me, glowing, in his monstrous grip. He played the clip from my email. "She taped this scene in case we needed it. She was conveniently cast as an extra when I saw she posed great usefulness to me." He dropped the tablet onto the table with the line of realistic-looking saws, clamps, scissors and scalpels. My gaze darted over the room in search of help. My purse lay near the wall two feet away. Bingo.

Jesse paced before me. "It's ridiculous…being cast as an extra on a reality show. How did she think that would work out? The show *is* reality." He broke his final word into syllables.

I inched my fingers over the cold plastic-covered floor and tried not to think about all the odds and ends around me. My tummy clenched at the creepy things left over from days when the room housed corpses instead of crazy television producers and idiotic island counselors. The purse's strap caught on the end of my finger and I dragged it closer.

"Your island was the perfect location for this epi-sode. All the clever folklore and superstition. I knew this town was the one way before Rick got onboard. While reading everything I could about your island, I found an interesting series of articles on local crimes, and guess whose name kept popping up?" Jesse lifted a long metal file off the table and moved it in the air, as if he directed an unseen chorus. "When I heard about you, you sealed the deal. You're a writer's dream. All savior-complex and no sense."

I raised my eyebrows, hoping to look innocent. My fingertips froze at my side, though they itched to rip the cloth from my mouth, to dive into my purse for help.

He chuckled and tapped the file against one open palm. "I realized I could make this season the best one ever. Islanders already thought their town was haunted. All I needed to do was convince America. I contacted all the ghost hunter websites and got them riled up, then I made a trip out here to look at possible shoot sites. I read up on the architecture and found hidden staircases, Un-derground Railroad tunnels and all sorts of fun things."

"Unduhgon Ailode?" I repeated through the gag. I had no idea. How cool was that?

Also, where was my backup? Sebastian was thorough. If he couldn't reach Fargas, he had other FBI agents to contact on the island. Someone needed to get it in gear before I found out what that big file was meant for.

He chuckled at something I'd missed. "Right? When Rick called to brag about sleeping with Anna, I saw my opportunity. Island Comforts was one of the homes with little nooks and crannies, so I thought what the hell, I'll give it a shot." He chuckled again at his play on words. I didn't laugh. I stared at the night vision goggles strapped to his big head. Now I knew how the killer was able to see in the dark.

"I was already on the island. He was looking for a place to stay, so guess where I recommended, based on all my research? Yep. You guessed it.

"The rest of the cast was sloshed on the beach. They'd never miss me. They don't pay any attention to me off set. Now, the room situation was pure luck. Rick's car was out front, so I slipped into the cellar, found the covered staircase and headed up. I had nothing to lose. Worst case scenario, I wouldn't find him and I'd plot another island haunting." He shrugged. *Kill, don't kill. Que sera, sera.*

"With step one complete, I made sure all the reporters mentioned island ghosts in their articles about the murders." He smacked his palms together in a thunderous clap.

My fingers froze on my purse strap.

"Rick and Anna died at the hands of a ghost. No one else entered the room." He made nutty ghost sounds and waved his hands.

I worked trembling fingertips over the lip of my purse and searched inside.

"Do you want to know what I'm going to do with you?" He turned dark crazy eyes on me. I pulled my hands into my lap and nodded.

"I've come up with the perfect finale to Halloween week. I want this house to gobble you up."

My jaw dropped. What? The cloth had attached itself to my tongue. Fear dried my mouth and created a disgusting paste. I couldn't swallow. Another gag climbed my throat.

Jesse tapped his chin. "I remember reading something about people being chopped into bits on this island. I love the animalistic twist. Stabbings and hangings are so overdone. I thought it'd be fun if the ghost chopped you up too. Don't look at me like that." His shoulders slumped. The excitement slipped from his tone as he stared at me. "You should've died this summer and you know it. The way I see it, your time's up. I just hope I can get this thing figured out."

He set the file down and lifted something else from the table. A soft hum grew to a buzz in his hand.

My eyes stretched wide as he marveled at the tool shaped like a small power saw. Crikey! I'd rather take my odds with the big file. The little saw revved in his palm, and the plastic-covered room took on a whole new meaning. Oh, hell no. Mental alarms gonged in my head. *Not a prop! Not a prop!*

I readied my hands for combat.

"You're my grand finale. My crowning achievement. This funeral home is haunted and I'll prove it. *The Watchers* were here when Rick and Anna were killed at a haunted bed-and-breakfast and *The Watchers* were here while you were mutilated by the ghosts in this house. I'll make up a catchy name for the ghost before we air our footage next week. It's prime time gold.

"The Halloween party is broadcasting live, but the week we spent here will go on for six episodes. Once your death's announced, we'll hype the clips of you for all their worth. Ratings will soar, and I'll finally get a gig I deserve. Sorry the finale has to be you, but from what I've heard, you're kind of a black cloud and, like I said, your time's up. Finding you dead won't surprise any locals. In show business, sometimes you have to take one for the team."

My eyebrows hit my hairline. I wasn't taking anything for his team.

Jesse shut the saw off and listened. "Did you hear that?"

The back door crashed open and Claire stumbled inside, giggling. With Todd. I watched in silent horror as they kissed and pawed at one another like animals.

A moment later, relief flooded through me. She was safe. Kind of a wild kisser, but safe. I pulled the rag from my mouth. Jesse could suck it. The game was three against one now. "Claire!"

Jesse's face contorted with shock to have a weapon turned on him.

I pointed my new stun gun cell phone at him. I didn't have a clue how to use the thing, but I figured when there's a button, press it. I pressed, and little wires shot out and attached to his pant leg.

"Ah!" He swatted the probes.

Todd jumped on him and they rolled over the plastic-coated floor, wailing on one another.

Claire dashed to my side. "You okay?" She dragged me to my feet.

The back door burst open and a man stormed inside like the Terminator. "Freeze! FBI!" Adrian's voice perplexed my aching head. He extended a child's plastic sheriff star.

Todd released Jesse's shirt and backed away.

Jesse yanked something off the stand beside him and the familiar hum of the little saw started again. "Shut the door." His crazed expression said he'd cut us all into pieces if he had to. He had a ghost to fabricate. My little circus of friends wouldn't stand between him and his dream. "Everyone shut up!"

Adrian inched forward. "Put the saw down."

Claire turned to me. "We couldn't reach Sebastian."

I shook my head. "No. He's hurt and he's an hour away." I swallowed worry for Sebastian and blew out a cleansing breath. One trauma at a time.

Worry creased Claire's brow. Was Fargas not outside the door? Where was the cavalry?

Jesse waved the saw in the air. The engine hummed louder. The crazy in his eyes spread over his features as he stepped off the mental ledge. No turning back. His eyes glazed over and his lips curled in a creepy smile. He'd gone to a place reason couldn't reach. I could almost hear his internal monologue as he accepted his fate and changed the plan to fit the circumstance. Heck, he'd planned to dismantle one person tonight, what was three more, really? I mean, he'd already prepped the room.

Adrian pressed one hand against his side arm. "Put the saw down. We've got you surrounded."

"With what?" Jesse scoffed. "Two helpless women, one reporter and a fake cop? Yeah. I recognize you, Adrian Davis. We've met, remember? You aren't fooling anyone with your water gun and kiddie badge. You probably bought that gun at the same sad little shop where Anna's dad got his."

With surprising speed, Jesse snapped a hand out and hauled Claire against his side. He poised the saw at her chin and pressed the button. "Now, if everyone would please take a seat, I can get started."

A sudden twitch in his limbs maimed the final word. His saw jutted upward, catching Claire's throat. Blood shot from her body, dashing the plastic covered floor. She screamed and stumbled back. Rage shot through me. I tackled Jesse. The saw clattered to the floor. Adrian and Todd piled on in a heap of bodies and flying hands.

Jesse shook beneath us and a zing of current sent me scurrying backward.

Claire pressed a palm to her jaw. "Who's helpless now, bitch?" She kicked Jesse with her cute leather boots and dropped her stun gun.

I crawled through rivulets of her blood to retrieve my gag rag. Claire eyeballed the cloth before pressing it to her chin. "I'm going to need a six pack of tetanus shots."

Panic and exhilaration ignited sheer joy inside me. "I thought he cut your head off."

She frowned. "He nicked my jaw." Blood soaked the cloth, but it didn't faze me. She was alive.

Wait a minute. "Why were you kissing him?" I pointed to Todd.

He beamed. "I told you. You're where the story is. I heard you on the phone and watched you go inside. You said Claire was in here, but I'd seen her at the party, so I called her to check it out."

"You choreographed my recue?"

Claire adjusted the towel on her jaw. "Fargas went for his cruiser. Adrian and I ran here."

She lifted a hoity eyebrow at the mention of running. They were in shape, so they ran all the way from Adrian's. Yee-haw.

The rag darkened with her blood. "We needed a plan to stall for time. This was all we could come up with."

"Police." Fargas charged through the open door, gun drawn. He surveyed the scene and gave Claire an accusatory look.

She cocked a hip. "What?"

He rolled Jesse onto his side and cuffed him. "I asked you to wait outside."

She rolled her eyes. "My best friend was in here."

He turned his steely gaze on me, and I stepped

back. There was a fire in Fargas I'd never seen before. I pointed at Claire. "I thought she was in here. Jesse sent me a video from her stint as an extra." I hated to be the one to break that news to her. Extras on reality television? Not a real thing. Who knew?

Spotlights danced outside the open door. A camera crew marched past Todd and Adrian. Women in suits described the scene around them in overdone campfire voices. The creepy room got smaller. A slew of ghost hunters powered up tiny devices and waved them in the air.

Fargas dropped Jesse on the floor. "Back up. Outside. Move it. This is a crime scene. Get out. Now."

The reporters shoved microphones in his direction, asking questions as he shoved them back through the door.

I swallowed a laugh. People were ridiculous. I looked at Fargas. "What happened to all the added security for tonight?"

He huffed. "You should see it over at Adrian's. It's a cluster…mess. You can't get in or out of the neighborhood. The roads are jammed with people and food trucks." He rubbed his neck and turned to Claire. "What happened in here? Does anyone have a cell phone that works?"

The lawn filled with voices. A line of spectators extended their phones toward the open door and window glass.

They could help us. "Call an ambulance!"

Sirens split the night before I stopped speaking.

Strangers peered in through the doorway. "We did that. What else?"

Frankie elbowed her way past the crowd. "Sorry. I got here as fast as I could."

Fargas nodded to Jesse. "Wake him up and read him his rights. Then knock him out again with something heavy, like a truck."

"Yes, sir."

Fargas stepped past me and wrapped his arms around Claire. He hugged her to his chest as if they could somehow snap together into one being if he held her tight enough. The expression on his face amused and stunned me. He loved her. Fiercely. I'd seen that look before and there was no doubt I was right. Huh. He whispered into her ear and stroked her hair with gentle hands. She shook her head and pushed him away. He didn't budge.

"Yes, I am." He scooped her off her feet. "You're too damn stubborn to argue with, you know that? The ambulance is right outside and you're bleeding." His words grew soft as he moved through the crowd outside the door.

My bottom lip quivered. Tears spilled over my eyelids onto fire hot cheeks. Adrian caught me in his arms and held me tight. Tears turned to sobs and I fell apart in his embrace. My knees buckled, but he held me up, pressed me to his chest and shared his strength with me when I had no more.

"I'm gonna go," Todd mumbled.

"I thought he cut her throat." Tears poured out in an unstoppable deluge. "I thought he had her captive in here, but it was only a video, and I was so thankful she was safe. Then she showed up anyway and he held that saw…" I choked on the words. "The blood."

"Shh." Adrian stroked my hair and leaned over me, pressing his cheek to mine. He tucked strands of tear-soaked hair behind my ear. "Fargas will protect her. You don't have to worry about Claire anymore."

Lights flashed through the open door and the sounds outside increased steadily by the decibel.

"But I do." I hiccupped the words. "I worry about everyone. I want you to be happy. I want them to be happy." I waved an arm toward the ruckus outside. "I love them."

Adrian's chest bobbed with humor. "They love you too. Come and see."

I moved on unsteady feet with Adrian as my guide. We stopped at the open door and I squinted into the night. Hundreds of faces packed the yard before me. Ambulances, food trucks and news vans sat at hasty angles in the grass. Clusters of people chattered and snapped pictures of one another. They took notice of me, a few at a time, tapping one another and motioning my way. The roar of voices lowered.

"She's okay." Adrian lifted one of my arms over my head, like I was a child.

A round of cheers went up loud enough to split an eardrum. I pressed my face to Adrian's chest. Whistles and hoots turned to a steady rhythmic chant. *Patience. Patience. Patience.*

"Told ya." Adrian squeezed me to his side.

I tilted my head back for a better view of his face. Soulful blue eyes glossed with emotion. He nodded. No words, just the reluctant acceptance of a man who loved me enough to do the unthinkable. I couldn't blink or turn away from the expression on his handsome face. A hundred flashes captured the moment. Adrian was ready to let me go.

I wiped tears and tracked a spotlight through the night sky. "Do you see that?"

Adrian loosened his hold on me and chuckled. "It looks like a sightseeing helicopter."

The spotlight drew patterns over the crowd. "Is that a news chopper?"

The steady thrumming of chopper blades moved nearer, dousing us with raging wind. *What the hell?* The vehicle moved into the intersection beyond the lawn and people dashed away from the beating wind. The spotlight raced paths through bystanders. I shielded my eyes with half the town as a silhouette emerged from the vehicle. I'd recognize his determined stride anywhere. "Sebastian."

The chopper lifted up into the night and disappeared, taking the hurricane with it.

Sebastian took a direct route to my side, parting the sea of people between us. He nodded to Adrian, who stepped away. "Thank you."

I dashed my arms around his neck. "What are you doing here? You said you couldn't get here. What happened?"

"I commandeered a helicopter."

Adrian chuckled behind me.

Sebastian shifted under my weight, favoring one leg.

I jumped back. Fresh panic sent my pulse into a sprint. "Oh my gosh. I'm so sorry. Are you okay? Let's sit down. You're hurt. You're shot."

He pressed warm palms to my wind chilled cheeks and stared into my eyes. "It's nothing."

I wiggled in his hands, trying to see the extent of his injury.

He wouldn't allow it. "Hey. Look at me." He kissed my forehead, my cheek, my lips. "You're safe and I'll heal." Sebastian leaned closer, pressing his forehead against mine. "I'm so sorry I wasn't here for you."

"You're here now."

He rocked his head left to right. "I'm not sure that's

good enough for me. I should've been here for you, not chasing a mobster and his goons."

I wrapped my arms around his waist and snuggled into him. "I love what you do. You protect the country from bad guys." Sebastian had accepted the FBI position over a coveted Secret Service position years ago—another reason I loved him. He was the best at what he did.

Sebastian led me towards a waiting ambulance. His limp increased with every step. "The country's a big place. I'm thirty-five. My world's changing. I'm not the guy you interviewed anymore."

I let him help me into the empty ambulance. He climbed in behind me with effort. The EMT gave him a quizzical look. Sebastian motioned to me. "I don't think she's injured, but take a look anyway."

"Yes, sir."

I ran my fingers over the FBI emblem on Sebastian's coat. "Remember when you took this job? You said you wanted to protect the American people. You could've worked with the Secret Service. That was an amazing once-in-a-lifetime offer and you passed it over. You said the Secret Service would've assigned you one or two lives someone else deemed top priority, but you thought all lives were all important. You were made for this work. The country needs you."

Sebastian watched the EMT check my vitals.

The EMT turned to Sebastian. "You don't look well, sir. I think you should lie down and let me look you over."

"He was shot," I interjected before Sebastian played it off.

"Sir?" The EMT grabbed supplies with one hand and motioned for Sebastian and I to trade places with the other.

I pulled Sebastian onto the gurney. The EMT helped him out of his jacket.

My heart stopped beating. Blood soaked his shirt. The EMT cut it off. A red bandage beneath was also covered in blood.

The EMT went to work cleaning the area and replacing the bandage. "You need to rest until this starts healing. You're lucky the stitches are still in place."

I pointed to his pants. "He was shot in the leg tonight, too."

The EMT dragged his attention from Sebastian's shoulder to his leg and finally to me. "How is he functioning?"

I sniffled and laughed. "He's stubborn."

The EMT moved Sebastian's feet and cut the length of his pant leg while I held Sebastian's hand.

Emotion brewed beneath his carefully guarded expression. His Adam's apple bobbed.

My heart broke for whatever thoughts he was battling with. "Hey. You can tell me."

His dark eyes pleaded with me. "If you're ever in danger again, I promise to be here."

"Okay," I whispered.

Sebastian gave one sharp nod in agreement and just like that, I knew he'd move mountains to see he kept his word.

TWENTY-SIX

I STEPPED OUT of the shower into a steam-filled room and smiled at the glorious quiet. In the four days since November began, *The Watchers* had packed up and taken their hoopla back to the mainland, Claire had gone back to work, and Adrian had moved back to his house on the marsh. Life was good. Peaceful. Solitary.

My toes caught in the discarded outfit on my floor—jeans and a Vote for Davis shirt. I'd handed out more political propaganda in the past eight hours than I'd ever seen in my life. The election booths were open until seven, but Adrian's rally at my new office building started at five. If I hurried, I could dress for his victory dinner now and vote on my way there.

A smile spread over my face. Adrian Davis could be the mayor in a couple of hours. I shook my head. The kid who made mud pies with me under my parents' house might run the town. What was the world coming to? Up was down. Left was right. I snagged my phone off the counter when it buzzed.

Four messages. Jeez. How long had I been in the shower?

Adrian: Results are pouring in. I'm ahead by 4

Claire: Meeting Max for drinks. See you at the big dinner.

Adrian: Beau's pulling ahead of me. Where are you? Call me. Bring liquor.

Sebastian: Finalizing some paperwork. Meet you at the rally.

I dashed a towel over my hair and squeezed the excess water out before dialing Adrian, setting the phone on speaker and tossing it onto the counter. I raked a leave-in conditioner through my hair while the call connected. He didn't answer. I redialed and moved on to makeup application.

Five rings later, Adrian answered in a panic. "Patience?"

I pinched my lashes in the evil grip of a metal curler. "The one and only."

"Where are you? I need you."

"Well, I walked the streets all day, handing out your buttons and bumper stickers. I came home for a shower, but don't worry. I'm on my way as soon as I get ready for the dinner and go vote."

He groaned. "You didn't vote yet? Why didn't you do that first?"

"Why don't you thank me for smiling and being nice to people all day?"

"That's your job."

I dropped the eye shadow pallet on my counter. "That is not my job. That was me doing you a favor."

"For saving your life."

I pursed my lips and curled my fingers at my sides. "Did you ask me to call so you could pick a fight? If you want, I can stop getting ready, put on my jeans and continue this stupid conversation all night." Wouldn't be the first time.

Silence.

"Well?" I ran lip gloss over my lips. I had him.

"Just get here. You don't have to thank me for saving your life again. If you did that every time I saved you, we'd never have time to talk about anything else."

I hung up on him and finished my makeup before blowing out my hair. Tonight was a special occasion. No ponytails allowed. I pinned crystal-encrusted combs into the hair over each ear and created soft spirals in the length with my giant curling iron. Sexy. I approved. Now for the dress.

Claire had picked the dress out for me. Without her there to approve it, I'd never have left the store with anything so expensive. Claire made me brave. Brave in the confident, feminist heroine way, not the run-headlong-into-danger way I was known for. That wasn't brave. That was impulsivity with a dash of hardheadedness. After seeing my best friend cut by a lunatic wielding a cranial saw in an abandoned funeral home, I'd gained a measure of perspective on the difference between the two. When Todd called it a cranial saw, I'd almost vomited. Brave and stupid were very different.

I dusted powder over my face and texted Claire. Have fun. Can't wait to see you two.

I meant it. Seeing her was wonderful. Seeing her with Fargas was refreshing. I didn't understand where their relationship came from, but it looked good on them. She was radiant in his presence, and he was confident in hers. They gave me hope.

I slid the dress off its hanger. The soft lining caressed my body. The midnight blue color had dazzled me from the moment I saw it in the store window. Claire coerced me into trying it on, despite the hefty price tag. The gentle shine of material twinkled when I moved. Sheer layers danced over my thighs, hanging a touch longer than the slip underneath. My favorite part was the halter neckline, where a small keyhole at my breastbone made for easy cleavage appreciation. Thanks to modern-day undergarment technology, my bosom appeared more ample than the usual borderline sufficient. I danced through a few sprays of perfume on new heels. Wide black ribbons tied around each ankle like a dark fairy tale. They were the perfect addition to my dress. I blew a kiss to my mirror.

Time to go. The Prius was released from impound after Leo the Lucky admitted to shooting my windshield. That was the only crime he admitted to, probably because he was caught on camera, thanks to *The Watchers* ridiculous number of hidden devices. Once the agents finished sifting through all the captured footage, they'd have enough to put him and Jesse away for a long time. Jimmy the Judge would probably get a triple life sentence with the file of warrants they had on him. Sebastian would go to court and testify against both in cases he worked while undercover for Jimmy's crime family.

All in all, after a wretched few months, we were all out of danger and things had finally set up to be the island life I expected when I moved home.

THE LINE FOR voting was short and, after pulling up to the curb three blocks from Adrian's rally/dinner, it was easy to see why. Most of the island was already there. The sun had set before six, leaving a gorgeous and unseasonably warm night in its wake. Twinkle lights lined my new office, the stage and the perimeter of the yard. Melinda and Missy were decked out in cutie-pie Sugar & Spice aprons, dishing out the most delicious smelling food ever. I drifted toward them.

"Wow." Melinda's mouth dipped open. "You look like a movie star."

I laughed. "Then you don't get out enough."

She frowned. "That's kind of true."

I hugged her and then Missy. "Look at you two, running a successful business, catering to politicians."

Missy smiled. "Don't look now, but here comes our beloved mayoral hopeful."

My eyes scanned for him. A few feet away, Adrian moseyed past a group of women in cocktail dresses. His gaze drifted over my bare shoulders and down the line of my body to my shoes. I returned the gesture. He looked like billboard fodder, instead of some small-town mayoral candidate. I perked with pride for knowing him. Sometimes being in Adrian's life felt like an honor. More often, it felt like we were stuck on a playground, but tonight, I was honored.

"There you are." He kissed my cheek. "Watch yourself," he whispered. "No lingering."

I whacked him with my clutch and narrowed my eyes. I'd cornered him outside Flick's Funeral Home and threatened his life should he ever mention his imagined lingering, the fact that our lips had touched this decade, or anything else that could scare Sebastian away. Anyway, there hadn't been any lingering on my part. He'd imagined it. I'd assured myself of this thought so often, I almost believed it. Denial was wonderful like that.

His dimple caved in, and his eyes twinkled with mischief. "I know something you don't know."

I eyeballed him as he led me away from my friends. "What do you know?"

"It's a surprise."

I rolled my eyes. Not this again. "Your last surprise

was a television show that brought chaos to this island and nearly got me killed. So, dish, or I'll pull your hair."

He rolled his eyes. Mocking me or having picked up another of my bad habits, I couldn't say. "This one kills me a little, but you're not in any danger." A crooked smile changed his face. He nudged me with his elbow. "You'll like this surprise. I promise."

"Fine. What is it?"

He shook his head and did a big stage sigh. "Not my secret to tell."

I whacked him.

"Ow."

"What'd you bring it up for then?"

Adrian laughed a big belly laugh. "How many times can I tell you, sweetheart? I love to get your goat."

Fire bloomed over my cheeks. "Stop calling me pet names." Why did I let him get to me? We needed a change of subject. This was his night, after all. "How are the numbers looking?"

He checked his phone. "Pretty good. I'm not sure how long until the final votes are tallied, but right now it's close. I have a small lead at the moment." He indicated a small measure with his thumb and first finger.

I patted his shoulder. "Don't worry. You've got this. Look around. This fancy-shmancy party is all for you. All these faces are your constituents. You like how that sounds?"

"Constituents." His smile grew. "Man, I really want this. More than anything else right now. I know I can do the job. I love this place and these people." His gaze moved over the crowd. For a moment, he looked like the Adrian I knew, the one few other people saw. The playful showman stepped away for one heartbeat and a sincere, caring, tenderhearted Adrian took his place.

Pride graced his features. Not pride for himself, but for them. The islanders.

The look on his face was the reason I'd done nightly calls to everyone on the island the last few days, made trips to the hospital and nursing homes in his name and delivered gifts from my parents' shop as little enticements to help undecided voters see things my way. I believed in Adrian, and the few citizens who were still undecided, for whatever reason, seemed to believe in me, so I intervened to bridge the gap. If he found out about all my unsolicited efforts, he'd make a huge deal out of it, so I kept it to myself.

"Ah." Adrian made a funny face. "I'm going to go see if I can get more updated numbers from someone. Just so you know, I may throw up from nerves soon. If I do, can you cover for me?"

I tried to look serious. "Absolutely. If you get sick, I'll announce you've suffered silently from the flu all day but put on a brave face, despite your illness, to come and show your devotion to this island."

He pointed at me. "That's brilliant. Please say that."

I laughed. "Whatever. Go puke."

He grabbed my hand and squeezed before walking away. "Here comes your surprise."

Weird.

Sebastian's voice startled me. "It's shockingly easy to find you in a crowd this size. I simply look for Adrian."

"He is tall." I swiped a drink off the tray of a passing hostess and took a gulp. The night felt hotter.

He rested his hands behind his back. "Nice dress. You look beautiful."

A blush warmed my cheeks. Compliments from Sebastian were few and far between, but when he uttered them, he meant them. The fact he mentioned the dress meant he liked it. A lot. I smiled. "You think so?"

"No." Seriousness flattened his features. He extended a hand and pulled me close. His voice lowered to a heated whisper. "I think you look more than beautiful, and the dress..." He traced the line of my side with the back of his fingertips. "The dress is sinful. It's a good thing I brought my gun. I can think of a few men I might need to fend off before the night's end."

"Right." I caught his lapels in my fingertips. "You don't look too bad yourself."

"Not if you don't mind a guy with a limp."

My fingertips grazed his hip. He'd lied to me on the phone Halloween night. He wasn't nicked by a couple of bullets. He was shot three times. The bullet in his shoulder barely missed a major artery that would've ended his life in minutes. The hit he took to the thigh tore through muscle and ligaments that might never heal properly and would surely cause him endless pain in physical therapy. I could've lost him, and I had no idea how to deal with that. If he wanted to leave the FBI, I wouldn't cry for long. A selfish thought, given the number of people he'd saved.

I stared into his dark eyes, hoping for a clue as to how he really felt about his life. We hadn't talked about his job or future since the night he was shot. Emotions were high that night. People often think irrationally under stress that intense. He loved protecting people, putting criminals away and defending our laws. Despite my own qualms, I wanted Sebastian to be happy.

"Hey, you!" Claire arrived on Fargas's arm. She was stunning in her fitted yellow maxi dress. She pointed a fabulous toe from beneath her long hem.

"Ohhh." I gawked at the pretty blue heel. Reflections of twinkle lights danced off its shine.

We'd seen the shoes at the mall when I bought my dress. "I thought those were too expensive. Did you change your mind or come into some money this weekend and not mention it?"

Her lips curved into a very ornery smile. "Remember when I collected signatures from *The Watchers* cast for handwriting samples?"

That we never needed. "Yeah."

Fargas jumped in. "She sold the shirt to a fan for two thousand dollars."

Claire smiled. "You can worship my brilliance later."

"Can I borrow the shoes?"

"Maybe." She looked at Sebastian. "Where'd you disappear to today? I looked for you."

I anchored a fist against one hip. "I thought you were at work today."

Sebastian frowned at Claire before looking my way. "I didn't say that."

"Yes, you did. You said you had to do paperwork at the office."

"No. I said I had to finalize some paperwork."

"Whoa." Claire fanned her face, despite the cool night breeze off the harbor. "Who needs a drink?"

Fargas raised a hand. "We'll be back." He escorted Claire away.

I didn't say goodbye. I aimed my best liar-liar-pants-on-fire face at Sebastian and waited.

His lips quirked. He scanned the crowd and rolled his shoulders back. "I wasn't going to do this here, but I don't think you'll let this go."

I raised my eyebrow. Darn skippy. He lied. There was no backpedaling out of it. He'd claimed he was late due to paperwork, but Claire said she hadn't seen him at work. I wanted the truth. He seemed to be unaccounted for too often lately. Before, whenever he wasn't around I'd assumed he was chasing leads, but now the leads were caught. Why the secrets?

Sebastian dipped a hand behind the material of his jacket and retrieved a small velvet box. My heart stuttered a moment before taking off double-time.

I pointed at the box. "Whatcha got there?"

He placed the box in my hand and covered my fingers with his. A small tremor played over my hands and Sebastian pulled his fingers away. A tiny gasp escaped me. The tremor wasn't mine.

He pulled in a deep breath and released it slowly. Was he nervous? If he had what I thought he had in this box, he should be nervous because I couldn't handle a proposal. He cleared his throat. "With Jimmy behind bars, I don't need to stay here anymore."

My mind raced. Adrian had looked at Sebastian when he arrived and told me my surprise was here. Did Sebastian tell Adrian about this? My gaze darted over the crowd. My folks laughed and held hands, dancing with others to the small band on stage. Adrian stood near the microphone, ready to make an announcement. He winked. I snapped my eyes back to Sebastian. Oh no.

"I don't want to leave," he said.

"What?" I focused my attention on Sebastian. What did he say?

"I like it here. I like being near you, and I'm not ready to leave."

"I don't want you to leave." I squeezed the box in my hands. "Stay."

"Patience."

Breath caught in my throat.

"This is probably a little soon. I'm not sure about relationship protocols. This is the first time in years I've given them any thought." He huffed, reorganizing his thoughts. I recognized the expression. Words weren't easy for him. That was okay.

I stroked his sleeve. "Take your time." I meant that on so many levels.

He nodded. "I know things are complicated right now."

So far, this was the worst proposal ever. I looked at the stage. Adrian smiled wildly at a paper in his hands.

Sebastian gripped my fingers again. "Open the box. If it's too much, I'll take it back until you're ready for it."

I opened the box lid with shaky hands. The top clicked into position, revealing a pink key on a red ribbon. I lifted my gaze to him in confusion.

"I bought a house. I want you to feel free to come and go anytime and as often as you like. You've been nothing but accommodating to me since the first day I came to the island. You let me crash on your couch and infiltrate your life without question, and I like it." He stepped into my personal space. "I like us. A lot."

"You bought a house?"

"Yes." He laughed. His wide arms wrapped around my waist. "I bought a house here. I can't imagine staying anywhere else, and I hope you might spend more of your time with me."

My brain whirled with hope, joy and possibilities. "You're moving to Chincoteague?"

He kissed my nose. "Yes." He kissed my forehead. My temple. My lips. "Patience Peace Price, will you accept this key?"

My head bobbed. Sebastian had bought a house on my island. He wanted to be here. Not for me, but for him. He saw what I saw when I looked around. Home. Friends. Community.

"Hello, Chincoteague." The microphone screeched with feedback. Adrian handed the microphone to our current mayor.

I swung my face back to Sebastian, whose eyes trained on mine. "Yes." A tear spilled over my lid. "I accept the key."

His eyes drooped at the corners. "You're crying."

"I'm happy."

"Happy?" Sebastian's face lit in a truly rare smile.

"Kiss me." I bounced on my toes as he leaned down and pulled my chest against his. My arms wrapped instinctively around his neck. My fingers burrowed into his hair.

Sebastian straightened, lifting my feet off the ground without breaking the kiss. Instead of the normal passion-laced growl, he smiled as he kissed me. I made him smile. Confidence burned through me. Pride filled my heart.

"I love you," he whispered against my lips.

I deepened the kiss. Cheers went up around us. For a moment, it felt like the island was celebrating the milestone with us. He bought a house!

Sebastian pulled back an inch and squeezed me to his chest.

A montage of Americana songs, from patriotic to Bruce Springsteen, blared through a series of speakers overhead. "We are the Champions" bled into "Celebration" by Kool and the Gang. I laughed. Confetti rained down over us. Popping champagne corks punctuated the high energy tune.

I turned toward the stage. Sebastian wrapped strong

arms around my waist and rested warm hands across my middle. "Looks like your boy won."

I took in the scene around me, pulling back a step from my personal relationship victory. "He won!"

I jumped up and down like a child. Sebastian hooted and pumped a fist in the air beside me. On stage, Adrian chugged champagne and sang into the microphone with each changing song.

I waved my arms and squealed in delight. My feet disappeared beneath me. Sebastian hoisted me up like a college cheerleader. I just managed a seated perch on his shoulder. As a general rule, women shouldn't stand over men's heads in tiny skirts. Call me a feminist, but they had to work for the money shot.

"Adrian!" The moment I spoke, his head turned my way, as if he'd heard me over everything else, despite all the racket. "Way to go, Mayor Davis!"

He smiled and waved a bottle of champagne.

Sebastian dropped me back on my feet. "Would you like to see the house?"

I beamed. "Yes."

He removed the key from its box and pressed it into my palm. I didn't get a proposal. I got something better: a key that I imagined opening the door to many unbelievably fantastic adventures in my future, with Sebastian as my sidekick.

* * * * *

REQUEST YOUR
FREE BOOKS!

2 FREE NOVELS
FROM THE SUSPENSE COLLECTION
PLUS 2 FREE GIFTS!

YES! Please send me 2 FREE novels from the Suspense Collection and my 2 FREE gifts (gifts are worth about $10). After receiving them, if I don't wish to receive any more books, I can return the shipping statement marked "cancel." If I don't cancel, I will receive 4 brand-new novels every month and be billed just $6.49 per book in the U.S. or $6.99 per book in Canada. That's a savings of at least 19% off the cover price. It's quite a bargain! Shipping and handling is just 50¢ per book in the U.S. and 75¢ per book in Canada.* I understand that accepting the 2 free books and gifts places me under no obligation to buy anything. I can always return a shipment and cancel at any time. Even if I never buy another book, the two free books and gifts are mine to keep forever.

191/391 MDN GH4Z

Name _____ (PLEASE PRINT)

Address _____ Apt. #

City _____ State/Prov. _____ Zip/Postal Code

Signature (if under 18, a parent or guardian must sign)

Mail to the **Reader Service:**
IN U.S.A.: P.O. Box 1867, Buffalo, NY 14240-1867
IN CANADA: P.O. Box 609, Fort Erie, Ontario L2A 5X3

Want to try two free books from another line?
Call 1-800-873-8635 or visit www.ReaderService.com.

* Terms and prices subject to change without notice. Prices do not include applicable taxes. Sales tax applicable in N.Y. Canadian residents will be charged applicable taxes. Offer not valid in Quebec. This offer is limited to one order per household. Not valid for current subscribers to the Suspense Collection or the Romance/Suspense Collection. All orders subject to credit approval. Credit or debit balances in a customer's account(s) may be offset by any other outstanding balance owed by or to the customer. Please allow 4 to 6 weeks for delivery. Offer available while quantities last.

Your Privacy—The Reader Service is committed to protecting your privacy. Our Privacy Policy is available online at www.ReaderService.com or upon request from the Reader Service.

We make a portion of our mailing list available to reputable third parties that offer products we believe may interest you. If you prefer that we not exchange your name with third parties, or if you wish to clarify or modify your communication preferences, please visit us at www.ReaderService.com/consumerschoice or write to us at Reader Service Preference Service, P.O. Box 9062, Buffalo, NY 14240-9062. Include your complete name and address.

REQUEST YOUR FREE BOOKS!
2 FREE NOVELS PLUS 2 FREE GIFTS!

ROMANTIC suspense

Sparked by danger, fueled by passion

YES! Please send me 2 FREE Harlequin® Romantic Suspense novels and my 2 FREE gifts (gifts are worth about $10). After receiving them, if I don't wish to receive any more books, I can return the shipping statement marked "cancel." If I don't cancel, I will receive 4 brand-new novels every month and be billed just $4.74 per book in the U.S. or $5.49 per book in Canada. That's a savings of at least 12% off the cover price! It's quite a bargain! Shipping and handling is just 50¢ per book in the U.S. and 75¢ per book in Canada.* I understand that accepting the 2 free books and gifts places me under no obligation to buy anything. I can always return a shipment and cancel at any time. Even if I never buy another book, the two free books and gifts are mine to keep forever.

240/340 HDN GH3P

Name _____ (PLEASE PRINT) _____

Address _____ Apt. # _____

City _____ State/Prov. _____ Zip/Postal Code _____

Signature (if under 18, a parent or guardian must sign)

Mail to the **Reader Service:**

IN U.S.A.: P.O. Box 1867, Buffalo, NY 14240-1867
IN CANADA: P.O. Box 609, Fort Erie, Ontario L2A 5X3

Want to try two free books from another line?
Call 1-800-873-8635 or visit www.ReaderService.com.

* Terms and prices subject to change without notice. Prices do not include applicable taxes. Sales tax applicable in N.Y. Canadian residents will be charged applicable taxes. Offer not valid in Quebec. This offer is limited to one order per household. Not valid for current subscribers to Harlequin Romantic Suspense books. All orders subject to credit approval. Credit or debit balances in a customer's account(s) may be offset by any other outstanding balance owed by or to the customer. Please allow 4 to 6 weeks for delivery. Offer available while quantities last.

Your Privacy—The Reader Service is committed to protecting your privacy. Our Privacy Policy is available online at www.ReaderService.com or upon request from the Reader Service.

We make a portion of our mailing list available to reputable third parties that offer products we believe may interest you. If you prefer that we not exchange your name with third parties, or if you wish to clarify or modify your communication preferences, please visit us at www.ReaderService.com/consumerschoice or write to us at Reader Service Preference Service, P.O. Box 9062, Buffalo, NY 14240-9062. Include your complete name and address.

REQUEST YOUR FREE BOOKS!
2 FREE NOVELS PLUS 2 FREE GIFTS!

⬥ HARLEQUIN®

I N T R I G U E

BREATHTAKING ROMANTIC SUSPENSE

YES! Please send me 2 FREE Harlequin® Intrigue novels and my 2 FREE gifts (gifts are worth about $10). After receiving them, if I don't wish to receive any more books, I can return the shipping statement marked "cancel." If I don't cancel, I will receive 6 brand-new novels every month and be billed just $4.74 per book in the U.S. or $5.49 per book in Canada. That's a savings of at least 12% off the cover price! It's quite a bargain! Shipping and handling is just 50¢ per book in the U.S. and 75¢ per book in Canada.* I understand that accepting the 2 free books and gifts places me under no obligation to buy anything. I can always return a shipment and cancel at any time. Even if I never buy another book, the two free books and gifts are mine to keep forever.

182/382 HDN GH3D

Name _____ (PLEASE PRINT)

Address _____ Apt. #

City _____ State/Prov. _____ Zip/Postal Code

Signature (if under 18, a parent or guardian must sign)

Mail to the **Reader Service:**
IN U.S.A.: P.O. Box 1867, Buffalo, NY 14240-1867
IN CANADA: P.O. Box 609, Fort Erie, Ontario L2A 5X3

**Are you a subscriber to Harlequin® Intrigue books
and want to receive the larger-print edition?
Call 1-800-873-8635 or visit www.ReaderService.com.**

* Terms and prices subject to change without notice. Prices do not include applicable taxes. Sales tax applicable in N.Y. Canadian residents will be charged applicable taxes. Offer not valid in Quebec. This offer is limited to one order per household. Not valid for current subscribers to Harlequin Intrigue books. All orders subject to credit approval. Credit or debit balances in a customer's account(s) may be offset by any other outstanding balance owed by or to the customer. Please allow 4 to 6 weeks for delivery. Offer available while quantities last.

Your Privacy—The Reader Service is committed to protecting your privacy. Our Privacy Policy is available online at www.ReaderService.com or upon request from the Reader Service.

We make a portion of our mailing list available to reputable third parties that offer products we believe may interest you. If you prefer that we not exchange your name with third parties, or if you wish to clarify or modify your communication preferences, please visit us at www.ReaderService.com/consumerschoice or write to us at Reader Service Preference Service, P.O. Box 9062, Buffalo, NY 14240-9062. Include your complete name and address.

HI15